Savio

AN AGE GAP ARRANGED MARRIAGE DARK MAFIA
BILLIONAIRE ROMANCE

CALABRESI MAFIA
BOOK ONE

L.K. RYAN

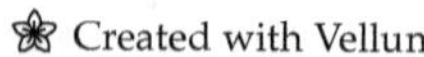 Created with Vellum

He hated me before I even walked through the door. Savio Calabresi was a force to be reckoned with when we first met. The don of the Calabresi family liked things his way and didn't want anyone to interrupt. Until I came along and shook up his world. Not only did my career cause a problem as a journalist, but knowing a secret that could hurt him and his family only left one thing for him to do. He forced me into an arranged marriage, or I compromised the safety of my family.

An arranged marriage, age gap, kidnapping dark mafia romance, Book 1 in an interconnecting stand-alone series, and guaranteed to have an HEA.

Disclaimer

Warning: There are a few scenes that may trigger. Be aware. Contains strong language and explicit sexual content and is only intended for mature readers. A dark mafia billionaire romance with an asshole alpha male, possessive, and aggressive. This story may contain unconventional situations, language, and sexual encounters that may offend some readers. This book is for mature readers (18+).

Calabresi Family

Elio Calabresi-Father, Retired Don
Adelina Calabresi-Mother
Savio Calabresi- Boss
Sante Calabresi-UnderBoss
Renato Calabresi-Enforcer

Acknowledgments

I want to dedicate this to my team that helps me behind the scenes, from my editors, test readers, graphic designers, and the list goes on. I truly appreciate each of you for keeping me on my toes.

Introduction

Are you signed up for my newsletter?

Join today and find out all the latest in new releases, contests, giveaways, sneak peeks and more.

www.authorlkryan.com

CHAPTER 1

Savio

I TWISTED the rosary in my hand, clenching my jaw in aggravation. Closing my eyes, I fought to control my blood pressure before I ended the display. As the oldest in the Calabresi Family, I ran a legit billion-dollar business on top of being a mob boss. My father, Elio Jr. Calabresi, is the son of Elio Calabresi Sr., a man I grew up watching as he built up the Five Families to what it was now. My grandfather was killed, and my father took his place when I was fifteen years old.

When I turned twenty-one, it was expected I would become the head of the Five Families, but I needed more education and time working alongside his team of hitters to make sure my decisions weren't made impulsively. I tended to kill first and ask questions second, but I'd calmed down as I got older. As my little brothers looked up to me, I wanted to set a better example, so they would feel like they had a choice; either the legit business of Calabresi's name or the crime part. Unbeknownst to me, they followed me into the mafia. Sante was the second oldest with a hot temper like me, but worse. Elio was third, and named after my father, his favorite. Then we had Renato, named after my dad's brother. And the baby of the group, Vincenzo; he was the surprise baby.

"My son hates that I'm writing a book." My father grinned, picking up the cup of tea. For a notorious drug gun runner, you wouldn't expect him to be sitting here at seventy-two, drinking tea so comfortably like he wasn't responsible for the deaths of hundreds of people.

"How much longer is this going to take?"

"Uh, probably twenty minutes." McKayla ruffled through the stack of papers in front of her.

I shifted and adjusted my dick, which jumped at the tone of her calm, sweet, soft-spoken voice.

McKayla Stanton, in my eyes, was the enemy, somebody I tried to stay away from because she represented what I hated. People like her thought they were saving the world by bringing to light all the bad things people did. As a writer and journalist for the Chicago Times, she was my sworn enemy, and we would never mix.

McKayla's plump, pouty lips pressed together, enhanced by the red lipstick against her ivory skin tone. Her wide, blue-gray doe eyes were deep as the ocean, and she had a round face with high cheekbones and and dimples. She appeared sweet and innocent, but she was sharp when challenged.

I was known as Savio "Beast" Calabresi, thirty-four years old, six-three, hazel eyes, shortcut black hair, athletically built, full nose, large hands, and an attitude for disrespect. So, I kept to myself often and barely spoke when we had our annual meetings. I allowed my brother Renato to conduct them in my absence as the underboss unless he needed my presence. Sante was the Enforcer, Elio was the Consigliere, and Vincenzo was the money guy who stayed on top of the finances.

I glanced down at my watch. "You have twenty more minutes."

McKayla looked up at me, then at my father. "My schedule was for an hour." Her right eyebrow dipped in a frown.

"Plans changed."

She glared at me, then peered at my father.

"Savio," Dad grunted and dropped his cup on the desk.

I leaned back on the couch with my hands in my lap and counted to ten in my head to keep my calm breathing down.

"Mr. Calabresi, can you tell me when you first killed someone?"

"Get out." I jumped up, stalked to the door, and motioned to my security.

"I have a right to ask these questions." She scrambled her papers together and rose out of the chair.

"Not anymore. We have a business meeting."

"He signed a contract," she argued, pointing at my father.

"Savio, I can handle my affairs." Father stood from his desk.

"We're running late for a meeting," I said to end the conversation.

McKayla rolled her eyes and gathered her purse and briefcase.

I hadn't paid attention to the pink silk blouse with the first two buttons open, highlighting her full breasts and form-fitting black suit jacket with her curvy hips, lush figure, and round ass.

I noticed the hard grimace on her face. I needed to get her out of his office before he could spill anything that would incriminate him or our family. My father loved entertaining people, and once he sensed you engaging, you couldn't break him away.

McKayla turned toward my father. "Mr. Calabresi, it was a pleasure meeting you today. Hopefully, we can continue this conversation."

"It would be my pleasure, McKayla. Do you need a ride home?"

"She's a big girl, Father," I interrupted before she could answer.

"I'm fine, Mr. Calabresi."

"Call me Elio. My father, God rest his soul, was Mr. Calabresi." He dazed off, staring at a picture of my grandparents sitting on his desk.

"You'll have to tell me more about them on my next visit," she said and reached out to grab the doorknob.

I pushed her hand away and held the door open. "I'll have my security walk you out."

"Savio, right?"

"Mr. Calabresi."

McKayla looked into my eyes for a moment, bit her bottom lip, shook her head, and left the office. I watched Enzo escort her out to the car, shut the door behind me, and turned back to my father with my left brow raised in annoyance.

"She's cute." He sat in his chair and picked up the phone.

"The book is cancelled."

"No."

"Are you crazy?"

"Watch your tongue!" He pointed his index finger toward me.

"The Five Families don't want this out."

He waved me off. "Nothing will hurt the family."

"How do you know that?"

"Savio, my life has been complicated, and I understand the lifestyle. Remember I made you the don."

"You never let me forget," I hissed, slamming my hand down on the desk.

The door opened. Renato walked in smiling and texting on his phone with Vincenzo following behind and plopped down on the couch.

"Renato, did you take care of the package?" I asked.

"Yeah."

"Savio, did you sign off on the new real estate plans?" Vincenzo questioned.

"Not yet."

"Shit!" Renato blurted out.

"What's the matter?" my father asked.

"The girl I saw last night told me that a member of the Colombo family was arrested."

"Where did you meet her?" I stood and slid my hands in my pockets.

"Doesn't matter," Renato replied, slipping his phone into his pocket.

"How did the interview go?" Vincenzo asked.

"We need to cancel it," I said, blowing out a breath.

"Your brother's scared I'm going to talk about the secrets of the mafia." Father chuckled.

"Do you hear yourself? If it weren't for me, you'd be dead right now."

"Savio," Renato muttered, cocking his head to the side.

I walked over to him in the back corner.

"The Five Families want to meet," Renato said.

"Fuck, I don't need this right now."

"We can't show weakness and not attend."

"He's causing more problems than our enemies," I mumbled.

"What are you saying?"

"Nothing." I started to walk off, but Renato grasped my arm. I looked down and back up to him.

"Savio, you're the boss of the family, and I follow as Enforcer, but I don't condone anything harming our father."

"I'm an asshole, but I would never harm our father."

He looked back at Vincenzo and our dad talking. "So, you think this writer is going to cause problems for us?"

I sighed, crossed my arms over my chest. "I don't know yet. She comes across innocent, but that could be an act."

"You're the best person at reading people," Renato pointed out.

"I wish our father would see that."

Renato sighed. "I'll talk with him."

"Thanks, but what about the Colombo people?"

"What are you two talking about over there?" Father called out.

"Business, Father." Renato winked, and Dad flipped him off.

"Where's Mother?" I asked.

"Shopping," he replied.

"Angel texted that Nevio was caught with a few items of ours." I informed.

"How did that happen?" Pop's probed.

"I'm working on finding that out." I answered.

"Did he speak with the police?" Renato asked.

"So far, she doesn't know." I shrugged.

"Find out." Pop's remarked.

"On it." Renato strolled over to our father, shook his hand, kissed the top of his head, and left.

"Savio, what's the problem?" Vincenzo wondered.

"Nothing for you to worry about. Handle the legit business."

"Calabresi business, legit or mafia, is my business."

"Not now, Vin."

"Savio."

"Father, you no longer make these decisions. I told you once I took over, Vincenzo would handle the legit part."

"I'm not a kid!" Vincenzo shouted, stormed out, and slammed the door.

My father chuckled. "You did the same thing when you were around eighteen."

I glared at him. "Maybe if you listened back then, I wouldn't be so damaged now."

"Why do you talk to me this way?"

"Why do you continue to push my buttons?"

A knock at his door interrupted him from answering. When my mother came inside, I smiled at her as she sauntered in with a bag in her hand. All her sons were tall at six feet or more, but she was a short, petite woman with long black curly hair.

"My favorite girl." I reached out, and she walked into my arms. I kissed her cheek.

"I'm the only woman who tolerates you," she joked.

"Mother."

"I heard the reporter girl was here." She went over to sit in my father's lap.

"Our first day of interviewing happened today," Father answered and leaned in to kiss her on the lips.

"How did it go?" she questioned.

"She's beautiful and smart," he replied.

"Really." Mom glanced up at me.

"I like her," Dad said.

"You like all women," I sighed.

"Savio, you sound upset," Mom said.

"You need to tell him this book idea would put a target on our backs," I told her.

"I trust your father, and you should too." She wrapped her arm around his shoulders, and he whispered in her ear.

I'd had enough of the cuddling bullshit and stormed out. I reached in my pocket to grab my cell phone and scrolled to Sante's number as the car door opened for me to slide inside. Enzo shut it, went to the driver's door, and started the car.

"Take me to my condo."

"Yes, sir," Enzo said.

"Mmmm… Sante," a woman moaned. I took the phone away from my ear.

"Shit!" Sante hung the phone up, and I was ready to torture all my brothers for pissing me off today.

Ring! Ring!

"Where are you?" I asked, not waiting for hello.

"Finishing up a meeting," Sante whispered on the phone.

"Come to the condo."

"Sante, baby, come here." I heard a woman's voice.

"I'm kind of in the middle of something."

"Put your dick on ice for a second and meet me now." I hung up the phone and tossed it on the seat next to me as Enzo drove through the streets of Chicago.

We were born here, but our roots came from Sicily. Our parents were an arranged marriage, but they wanted to be together. One of the conditions of growing up in Italy was continuing the tradition of having your oldest be arranged to marry in the family of the next mafia family at the top.

Gennaro Greco was still running his family's business, even though he was in his early seventies like my father. He tried many times to get me to date and marry his daughter Viviana. My parents even tried to convince me, but at thirty-four, I had no plans to marry her or anyone else. I liked the way my life was now. I had sex when I wanted and sent them on their way afterward. No need for conversation or ideas of dating when I only used them for pleasure.

The limo arrived at my condo, and I stepped out, not

waiting for Enzo to open the door. "Sante is coming. I'll call you if anything changes, but I'm fine."

"Yes, sir." Enzo started the car and drove off from the curb.

I headed inside my condo and passed the hostess up to my penthouse private elevator. Five minutes later, I slid the key inside the door and turned the lights on, removed my jacket, and picked up the whiskey bottle near the fireplace. I'd called the place home for the past five years, but I'd thought about selling and moving into a house. I'd never brought anyone over; only my parents and brothers knew of this place, for security reasons.

Bang! Bang!

I went to open the door, and Sante pushed me back and charged at me. I twisted to the side, and he fell on the couch.

I smirked. "Need to be a little faster."

"Fuck you!"

"Let me guess. She didn't suck your dick?"

"How did you know?"

"That's your signature move, Sante."

"I might like this one." He kicked his feet up on my table.

I chuckled and passed him a glass of whiskey. "You said that about the last three women." I smacked his feet down.

"What do you want, Savio?"

"Renato is handling the Colombo situation, but I need you to look into something else."

Sante frowned. "What happened to them?"

"Nevio was caught with some of your product."

"You think he'll talk?"

"If he's smart, he won't," I said ominously.

"What's the other problem?"

"Father."

He jumped up. "Is he all right?"

I waved him to sit back down and finished my drink. "This book is going to be a problem."

"We can get rid of any problem."

I shook my head. "Not this time."

"Who's behind it?"

"McKayla Stanton."

CHAPTER 2

McKayla

WITH MY COAT and backpack slung over my shoulder, I held onto my three notebooks and coffee and walked up the stairs to my office. The elevator was out, and the maintenance guy said it would take another two hours. I had a deadline and still needed to log my notes from my meeting with Elio Calabresi.

The exit door opened, and my coworker held it as I mouthed thank you with a pencil in my mouth. As soon as I left the estate of the Calabresi, I wondered if I would be allowed back to finish my work. At twenty-three, I was doing what I loved, and this was my big break. I fought all the veteran journalists to grab this story.

Going to my cubicle, I dropped everything on my desk, tossed the coffee in the trash, and plopped down in the chair, wiping the sweat from my brow.

"Tell me you have the night free." My coworker, Rena, leaned against the side of the desk and picked at her nails.

"Sorry, I have work to do."

"McKayla, you have to come with me to this club."

"Not tonight."

"You're becoming boring."

"Did you finish the story on the fire in Brooklyn?"

Rena rolled her eyes while popping the gum in her mouth. "I have the entire weekend."

"Joseph is going to put you on probation again." I looked over my shoulder at his closed office door.

Working at Chicago Times was a dream come true, and Joseph Wilson challenged me every chance he could. For him to allow me to run with this story was a privilege I wouldn't let fall through the cracks.

"Joseph will be fine. I need my friend to go out with me tonight." Rena grasped my hands and dropped to her knees.

"Are you begging now?"

"Yes, I'll even buy you lunch for an entire week."

I sighed. "What's happening tonight?"

"A new club is opening."

I removed my hands. "No thanks." I grabbed my backpack, removed my glasses, and turned on the computer.

"Whyyyy?"

Rena loved being the center of attention, something I hated. My career was more important, and I needed to make plans to see Mr. Calabresi again. "Rena, I have work. Besides, you'll leave with some guy, and I'll be stuck taking a cab home."

"You could leave with someone, if you tried a little flirting."

"Dating is on the back burner until I finish this story." I slid my sleeves up, pulling my notebook and recorder out.

"How was that today?"

"Fine." I pushed my glasses up on my face.

"That was a weird fine."

"How else do you say fine?"

She shrugged her shoulders and tapped on the desk. The loud commentary around the room stopped when someone turned the volume up on the TV broadcasting breaking news.

"We have Nevio Colombo released from custody," the reporter spoke, standing outside the courthouse.

"Lauren, can you tell us who was waiting for him?" the anchor questioned.

"From what I saw, he got into a limo that belonged to the Calabresi family."

I removed my glasses and focused on the screen.

"Thank you, Lauren. We will have more of this story when we return," the reporter said. The channel changed.

"McKayla, do you hear me?" Rena asked.

"Huh?"

"I said, I promise to not leave you. Just drinks." Rena held her pinky finger out, and I clasped our hands together. Rena grew up in a single-parent home with her mom and brother. I grew up in a two-parent household; both parents worked to provide me with an upbringing of love and structure.

"Drinks only."

She nodded. "I promise."

I went to sit back down when loud yelling started. I knew then the day would get crazier.

"McKayla! My office now," Joseph yelled.

Rena patted me on the back and walked back to her desk. "Good luck."

"Thanks for the support." I smiled, strolled into his office, and went to sit.

"No need to sit; you won't be here long."

"Sorry."

"How long have you been here?"

"Uhm, about twenty minutes." I glanced down, checking my watch.

"I'm talking about working here in general."

"Oh, um... I think a year and a half."

"So, you should know anything that happens at this paper I know about."

"I do."

"So, tell me why we didn't know anything about Nevio getting arrested?"

"I… I—"

"Save it. I gave you this story, but you're already screwing me over."

"I was on my way back from meeting with Elio Calabresi."

"You should have known about this."

"I can make some calls to find out."

"No need. Rory is on top of it."

"What do you mean?"

"I mean Rory will be working with you on anything Calabresi."

I bit my bottom lip and rubbed the back of my neck, getting heated at Rory latched onto my story. Everybody knew he was a leech and stole ideas, taking the credit. Just because I grew up in the suburbs didn't mean I was some naive girl who would let anyone walk all over her.

"I can handle the Nevio story. You can keep Rory where he's at."

Joseph stopped piling papers in front of him and glanced toward me. "What does it say on the door?"

"Editor In Chief."

"Which means I make the calls."

"Okay."

"Also, I need the story on my desk by tomorrow morning."

"But I—"

"You wanted to be in the big leagues. This is what happens." I nodded and turned to leave, but he called out, "Close the door."

I headed over to the break room and fixed myself a fresh

coffee. It was another going to be late night of research and work.

"There you are." Rory stood in the doorframe with his chest puffed out.

"Here I am."

"We need to meet to confirm the details."

"What details?" I pushed off from the counter and headed to my desk, with Rory following. An intern approached and dropped mail on my desk.

"Joseph wants me to get all the notes you have on the Calabresi," Rory said.

"No."

"That's not how this works."

I blew over the hot steaming coffee and sipped it again. "Rory, I'm not giving you my work."

"Take it up with Joseph." He treaded away as Rena popped back over to my desk.

"Ready."

"For what?"

"Drinks."

"Rena, I'm sorry. Joseph just piled me with work."

"McKayla, you promised." Rena snatched the mail out of my hand, tossed it on the desk, turned the computer off, and picked up my backpack. "Drinks, fun, and sexy men now."

"Ughhh." I grabbed my coat and pulled my hair up into a ponytail.

"No glasses." Rena held her hand out.

"You're pushing it."

"You need this just as much as me."

"The last thing I need is to deal with a new guy."

Rena pushed the exit door open, and we walked out of the building. "Maybe you and Rory will hook up." She nudged my arm.

"Not even if he's the last man on earth."

"Let's grab this cab." Rena held her hand out, and the cab stopped in front of us. "Drop us at Sanctuary," she told the cab driver.

I checked my watch and saw it was going on eleven p.m. "Don't you need to be dressed up to be at Sanctuary?"

"I know somebody who works there." Rena removed her jacket, unbuttoned her shirt a little, and plumped up her breasts.

"Who are you meeting?"

"No one," Rena replied, pulling out her lipstick and compact from her purse.

"I feel like you lied."

The plum lipstick on her tawny bronze skin meshed with her black silk blouse, red skirt, and heels. "I promise this will be only drinks, maybe a little conversation." She ran a hand through her hair, fluffing out her curls.

"Regretting this already."

———

The security guard smiled a wide grin at Rena and let us pass everyone who was standing in line. Sanctuary's an exclusive club frequented by celebrities and politicians. The flashing lights roamed the room. People were on the dance floor, grinding against each other.

Rena grabbed my arm and pulled me to the bar. She held her hand up to the bartender. "Two sex on the beach."

Rena swished her hips left and right as the R&B music played. She turned her back to the bar and wrapped her arm around my shoulder. "What do you think?"

I snapped my fingers, joining her in the dance routine. "So far, the place is cool, but remember I can't stay long."

"Don't worry, your precious work will still be on your desk tomorrow."

"Two sex on the beach." The bartender placed our drinks on the bar.

Rena reached in her cleavage and pulled out some money to pay. "Keep the change." She passed my drink, and we toasted to a fun night.

"This is good." I held the drink up in the air.

"Told you. Time to relax and enjoy ourselves."

I giggled and clinked our glasses together, following her down to the dance floor. The bass of the music bounced off the walls and thumped through the speakers. Each time the DJ called for people to clap their hands, they would gather in groups to sync the movements.

We stood near the stairs a few feet away from the dance floor as the crowd formed for the next Ariana Grande song. I scanned the room, and mostly everyone was dressed very upscale, except for the women who were showing the most skin. I looked down at my plain dress and felt a little over-dressed for the occasion, but there was no time to go home and change.

"Are you ready for another one?" Rena yelled in my ear, and I nodded.

She took the glass from my hand and walked back to the bar. I started to follow, and she held her hand up for me to save our place. While she went to get our drinks, I swayed my hips, but soon felt the presence of someone behind me. Then I felt his dick on my butt. I quickly turned around and looked up into the eyes of a sexy stranger.

"May I have this dance?" he asked.

"I'm waiting for someone."

"Are you here with your boyfriend?" he questioned, looking around the room.

I shook my head when Rena approached.

"Ohh, who is this, McKayla?" Rena licked her lips and gave me my drink.

"Marco," he replied and held his hand out toward me.

"McKayla."

"Do you mind if I dance with your friend?" he asked Rena.

"No, please go and have fun."

I started to protest when Rena snatched my drink away and pushed me into his arms. He pulled me in close to his chest and smiled. I glared at Rena. As he pulled me down to the dance floor, the song changed to a faster beat. After an hour of dancing, drinking, and laughing with Marco, I went to find Rena posted up with a guy near the back corner.

"Hey, I'm going to the bathroom."

"Okay, do you need me to go with you?"

"No, I'll be fine."

"This is my best friend McKayla. Gerald here is an investment banker." Rena tilted her head to the left, and I waved at him.

"Nice to meet you, Gerald."

"You too, McKayla."

"I'll be back."

"What happened to your date?" she asked.

"He's not my date."

"Really? You looked pretty cozy."

"It was just a dance."

She shrugged her shoulders. "I'll be here when you get back."

Someone bumped into me, and I yelled, "Watch where you're going."

He never looked back. He kept walking, and I ignored confronting him and went to the bathroom. The crowd was getting thick, and I knew it was getting late. I needed to wrap up the night even if Rena didn't want to leave. Joseph was itching to remove me from the story and give it to Rory if I messed up even one time.

While passing down the dark hallway, a couple stood

near the exit sign, making out. I felt like I was intruding on something private, so I covered my eyes and looked for the bathroom. I headed down another hallway and found the bathroom closer to the back with a line of women.

"Great."

The loud laughing and grumbles of people taking forever were heard throughout. I about to pee on myself, unable to hold it any longer. I made a dash for the nearest door with an exit sign. The last thing I wanted to do was pee outside, but I refused to wait any longer or use the men's bathroom. I pushed the door open and looked from left to right. It was empty. I jogged to the corner of the trash can, squatted, and relieved myself.

"No more drinking for me."

I shook off any remnants, checked my pocket for a napkin I'd held onto from earlier and cleaned myself up. I tossed it in the trash and headed back in when I heard voices coming from the other side of the building. I slowly stepped over to the back wall of the building and peeked around. Three or four men were standing over someone on the ground with a bloody face. My eyes rose in surprise when I saw a gun held in front of his face.

CHAPTER 3

Savio

RENATO CALLED me earlier when talking with Sante over the Five Families calling a meeting. At first, I wanted to decline and let him handle whatever business it was, but he told me it was about Nevio being compromised and putting our names into certain dealings. As the mob boss, I had to see what was happening before I made a final decision. I wasn't only dealing with my father, but our legit business was coming under scrutiny for money laundering.

I showered, changed my clothes, and told Sante to get with Vincenzo to see where the leaks were coming from with Calabresi Holdings. I jumped in the backseat of the limo Renato had waiting for me and went to Sanctuary. It was one of the businesses my family owned around Chicago and in a few other states like New York and Los Angeles. It was in the hottest part of town, and we wanted it to be a classy nightclub.

We made it down in record time, and I hopped out, not waiting for Enzo to open my door. My cell rang, and I answered, hearing loud noise in the background.

"Are you here yet?" Renato questioned.

"I just arrived."

"Come to the office."

I hung up, and the security guard opened the door, standing to the side for me to walk in. The bottle girls smiled and waved. I was here on a mission and ignored all the stares and admiration; the crowd even started calling my name.

I glanced around the room, saw the place was crowded for a Thursday night, and made a note to talk to Renato about more security. I headed down the long hallway, went to the janitor's closet, and tapped on the door. We had regular offices, and we had special offices our staff didn't know about for meetings away from prying eyes. The door opened, and a guard chucked his head at me. I went through another hallway and down a corridor to the private area toward Renato with three of our men and Nevio.

"Nevio."

"Savio, I never talked."

He sat in a chair across from Renato. The room was completely dark, with no windows.

"What happened?" I demanded.

"I'd just left a meeting with Maurizio."

"So, why did you have our product when the drop is handled by someone else?"

"Maurizio wanted me to oversee the drop because some of our men had other emergencies."

I watched his facial expression, which never wavered, not a hint of fear. That gave me pause; people knew if I had to be summoned, it meant you'd fucked up. So, for him to be so comfortable meant he didn't think he could be touched.

My eyes narrowed, and I dragged them down to his hands. "Where's your watch?"

He moved them from the table. "Ughh…"

"You don't remember. Cat got your tongue?" I laughed, and my men chuckled in response.

"I forgot to put it back on after showering earlier."

"Yeah, that's right after being held up at the police station," I said.

The room went quiet again. I glanced briefly at Renato. "What do you think, Renato?"

"I think Nevio wouldn't betray us to the police." Renato leaned back against the wall.

"Savio, we go way back," Nevio expressed.

"You're right. You can go." I pointed to the door.

Nevio looked surprised, then stood and strolled to the door. My guard stepped to the side and allowed him to leave.

"I know Savio Calabresi isn't giving favors." Renato pushed off the wall.

I slid my hands in my pockets, grabbed my black gloves, and placed them on. "Call Enzo to pull him to the side."

"Are you sure you want to do this?"

"It's been a while since I killed, and people think because I work at the Calabresi Holdings, I don't handle other business."

All the men followed me back to the front entrance and through the back exit to the corner of the dead-end alleyway. I saw Nevio on his knees with a bloody nose.

"Come on, Savio. You know I wouldn't hurt the families."

I gripped his chin and squeezed tight. "You lost the privilege to call me Savio. It's Boss to you." I punched him in the gut.

"Aghhh!"

I punched him again in the left side of his rib. "The moment you left without your watch, I knew something wasn't right. How much did they offer? Huh?"

"Nothing, I promise!"

I kicked him in the chest. Renato pulled a gun out and passed it to me. I clicked the safety off. "All Five Families have a watch. You not wearing yours lets me know the police promised you freedom if you gave names. My concern now is if Maurizio was in on this deception."

Blood dripped down Nevio's face and nose. "I didn't say anything."

"Good, because you'll be permanently silenced." I held the gun up to his face and pulled the trigger.

Pop! Pop!

"Oh my God!" a voice screamed.

I turned and saw a woman scramble backward and fall.

"Grab her!" I shouted to Renato and my men.

"Please! I didn't see anything."

The voice sounded familiar, and I looked over my shoulder as Renato brought her to me.

"What do you want to do with her?"

"Kill her."

Her eyes screamed in panic, with tears falling down her cheeks, begging to let her go. I could, but I didn't trust anyone.

"Take her to the car." I handed the gun back to Renato.

I bent to Nevio. Patting the top of his jacket, I flipped it over and found his wallet with a photo of him and a woman. I turned it around and saw a phone number on the back. I stood and walked to the limo, getting in as Renato sat across from McKayla with his gun trained on her.

"You can put the gun away. She won't scream."

He placed the gun back in his holster. McKayla wiped her cheek and scanned her eyes around the car.

"Where do you want to go?" Enzo asked.

"My condo."

Renato's eyes turned toward me in shock. "Savio."

I raised my hand to stop him from talking in front of her. "We'll talk later."

"Did... you kill..."

"Kill him. And now you're a witness. What do you think should happen now?"

Her eyes lowered, and she fidgeted with her hands. "I won't say anything."

"I don't trust you, which means I don't know you."

"But—"

"You think because my father likes you, I should let you go?"

Fifteen minutes later, we arrived back at my condo. Enzo parked the limo. opened the door, and pulled McKayla out.

"Renato, make sure everything is cleaned. We'll talk tomorrow," I instructed.

"You sure this is a good idea?" He pointed at McKayla, fighting to get out of Enzo's arms.

"No."

I left him in the limo, grabbed McKayla's arm, and headed inside.

"Please help!" McKayla screamed, fighting me.

"No one is going to help you," I whispered in her ear.

"You're a monster!"

"I own this building, and everyone working here is a part of the family. Your screams don't matter."

Her head swiveled to the security guard. The desk receptionist's head lowered, ignoring eye contact.

I pushed in the code for my penthouse. The doors opened, and I stepped in the elevator, pushed her in, and shut it.

"Rena's going to be looking for me."

I stood in the corner and observed her pacing back and forth. "Rena Clark, junior writer at Chicago Times. Tom and Missy Stanton at 3458 Naperville."

"How do you know—"

"You're not the only one who investigates their subjects."

She charged at me, and I grasped her wrists. I turned us, pushed her up against the wall, and raised her hands above her head.

"I hate you!"

"Good."

"Just kill me."

I grinned. "Don't tempt me."

When the elevator dinged, I released my hold on her and let the door open, motioning for her to step off. I locked it behind me. The lights popped on, and I set my alarm, removed my jacket, and went to my liquor bar for a quick drink. She stood in the same place, rubbed up and down her arms, and peered around the room.

"Once I don't show up for work, they'll come looking for me."

"You can have the room in the back, near the bathroom." I gulped the rest of the drink down and slammed it on the bar.

"I want to go home."

"When you decided to be nosy in my business, you gave up the right to go home or make any more decisions."

"Who are you?"

"Savio Calabresi, don of the Calabresi crime family." I extended my hand for her to walk toward the guestroom.

Before I could move, she raised her hand and smacked me across the face. "Fuck you."

"You wish."

My cell phone rang. I grabbed it out of my pocket and saw it was Renato calling. "Yeah."

"I put some men outside in case she tries to run," Renato spoke.

"McKayla doesn't seem like the type that would run.

But if she decides to, shoot on sight." I stared into her eyes, and ended the call.

———

Standing under the shower, I let the water flow down my back and head, working out the kinks with the extra steam. I tossed and turned in bed all night, constantly checking to make sure McKayla didn't leave. Renato texted that they found her friend back at Sanctuary, searching for her, and had the police show up at the club. He was able to pay off one of the guys on the force to give her a fake story that her friend probably went home with a guy.

"Help me!"

I heard loud screams and turned the water off. I placed a towel around my waist and went to find out what was going on. I noticed McKayla fighting Enzo to get released.

"She tried to run out," Enzo told me.

I ran a hand down my face, grabbed a hold of her waist, and tossed her over my shoulder.

"Let me go!" She hit my back.

I slapped her ass. "Shut up!"

I pushed the guest bedroom door open, and tossed her on the bed. I climbed on top of her, pushing her hands over her head.

"Please, Savio, I won't try to run. Just let me call my family."

"If you can be quiet for the next thirty minutes while I get dressed, I'll think about allowing you to call your family."

She nodded. "Can I go home?"

"Don't push it." I climbed off her, shut the door, and went to my bedroom.

Forty-five minutes later, my housekeeper had breakfast

on the table. I raised the newspaper, reading over it to see if anything popped up about Nevio.

"Hello, I'm Marilyn, the housekeeper for Mr. Calabresi," Marilyn introduced herself and poured juice in the glass for McKayla.

"Hello," McKayla replied, pushing the plate away from her.

"You should eat," I said.

"Not hungry."

"So, you plan on starving and think that will cause me to let you go?"

Marilyn glanced between the both of us.

"I'm not hungry," McKayla answered, but her stomach growled.

I picked up her plate, rose from the table, and gave it to Enzo. "Breakfast on me, Enzo."

"Thank you, sir."

"As for you, I'd advise to do as I say, or you'll find me unpleasant to be around."

Marilyn went back to the kitchen to clean up. I grabbed my coat and keys to leave.

McKayla jumped up to follow me. "You can't leave me here."

"I can do what I want."

"What about my job? Your father's expecting me today," she begged.

I walked up to her, grabbed hold of her hips, and dug my fingers in her sides with a hard glare. "You're fired."

She tried to smack me again.

I grasped her hand. "Not again, princess."

She yanked away from my hold. "You disgust me."

"Something I've heard many times in my life. Enzo, keep an eye on her."

CHAPTER 4
Savio

"WHY DID I hear about you kidnapping a woman?" Elio questioned in a boisterous voice.

"Wait, what happened?" Sante asked.

"Is she still there?" Renato inquired.

Elio frowned. "You know about this?"

"I barely got five hours of sleep. Hold off on the questions. Meet me at the house," I demanded and hung up the phone.

I zipped through traffic and made it to the gate of my parents' mansion in Highland Park forty minutes later. The guard opened the gates, and I pulled into the roundabout, parked my car, and jogged up the stairs. Growing up in a ten-bedroom, fifteen-bathroom, mansion with an indoor and outdoor pool and basketball court was normal. The number of times we had parties when our parents went out of the country played in my mind. I went to the kitchen to see my mother talking with the head staff manager, Elorna, an older woman who'd been with our family for over twenty years.

"Son, I wasn't expecting you back so soon." Mom

reached out for a hug. I bent down so she could wrap an arm around my neck and kissed the side of her cheek.

"I need to talk with your husband."

The front door slammed.

"Everything that happens needs to run through me!" Sante shouted.

"Take that up with him!" Renato shouted back and smacked Sante on the back of the head. Those two constantly fought. I knew it was a little jealousy on Sante's part because I was closer to Renato than him when it came to decisions of the mafia, but I spoke with Sante about more personal life issues.

"Boys, stop fighting and give me a kiss." Mom placed her hands on her hips.

All three of them grinned, walked up to her, and planted kisses on her cheek and forehead. She treated all of us the same, but we still fought to be her favorite. She'd never answer that question.

"What did you cook?" Renato released her and went to the stove.

"We're not here for that," I said.

Sante opened the fridge and took out a beer. Elio stood at the island, facing me with his arms crossed.

"Why are we here, then?" he questioned with that condescending tone.

"In the office. Where's Father?" I asked.

"He should be finished with his workout," Mom replied, grabbing a plate out of the cabinet for him.

"Let's go," I said to my brothers.

They dropped their arguing to come with me to the back office. I pushed the office door open and saw my father on the phone. He held his finger up, and I went to sit in the chair. Sante sat on the couch next to Elio, while Renato stood at the wall near the door. Renato, being a trained assassin and shooter, always needed to be near an exit, even in our family home. In case something broke out, he wanted to be able to know where all the doors were to get everyone out to safety.

"Damn it, Savio!" Father fussed and slammed the phone down.

"I assume it was Maurizio." I crossed my leg and sat back with my arm over the back of the chair.

"You sit back nonchalantly like what you've done can be forgiven."

I pushed my tongue against my teeth. "That was business."

"And kidnapping a woman?" he asked.

"She witnessed me."

"Who is she?" EJ called out.

"The journalist who's writing my story," Father informed me.

"Why didn't you kill her?" EJ asked.

"When do you question the boss?"

"Just seems like you're being sloppy," EJ said.

If Elio weren't my brother, I'd have my fist through his chest right now.

"Elio, no need to speak to your brother like that," Father said.

"Yeah, I forgot he and Renato can get away with anything," EJ mumbled under his breath.

"Silence!" I yelled, rising out of the chair.

Father whistled for us to focus on him. "Back to what you're going to do to fix this issue."

"Why did Maruizio call you?"

"Because he knows my stubborn son," Father answered and leaned back in the chair.

"I made a call as the don of this family, and the Five Families will understand."

"Savio, I was in charge for years with no major problems. I understood the politics," he explained. He stood and went to his cabinet of pictures. He held photos of us when we were younger with our grandparents.

"Maurizio must have something to hide for him to call you."

"Possibly, but we don't make enemies of the men in our circle."

"Renato agreed with my decision."

"But did you speak with Sante, your Consigliere?" His right brow hiked up.

"No, I found out afterward," Sante said.

"That's the problem. If they find a crack in our foundation, our enemies will grow, Savio," Father expressed with his fist clenched tight.

"I hear you and understand, Father."

"Nevio might have sold us out to have the Colombos take over, but Maurizio would be stupid to make a move on us," Father explained.

"Was he giving you a warning?"

"Maybe. If I were you, I'd look into the police station that he went to."

I hated this part of being in charge, having to get the opinions of other bosses in the Five Families when I made decisions that I felt were best. "I'll speak with Maurizio." I stood and prepared to leave.

"Bring McKayla over for dinner."

"No."

"Savio, I didn't ask you."

"Sometimes you have to let your pride go. I made a decision; she doesn't leave my condo."

The room grew silent at my statement, and his eyes grew darker.

"I've already had calls from some people who want to know where she is."

"She's alive."

"What do you think Viviana is going to say about this?"

"Viviana was in the past, nothing more or less."

"McKayla Stanton will be here for dinner tonight."

"If I don't?"

"Your position can always be replaced, Savio."

I pointed behind me.

"By whom? Sante, who's more focused on pussy, or Renato, who pops off in a split second if you look at him? Maybe your precious Elio, who loves to compete with me, thinking I want your attention."

"Fuck you, Savio!"

Renato laughed. Sante flipped me off, and EJ clenched his fists.

"Throwing a tantrum, son."

"I'm in charge of them, not you."

"According to the rules, if you don't marry Viviana, you're no longer going to be in charge."

I tensed at his words.

"What are you saying?"

"The deal is that once I retire, you would be the don, only if a marriage were to happen between you and the Greco family."

"You lied to me."

"I protected you."

"That's bullshit!"

He stood in front of me, nostrils flared. "The contingency is that you marry, otherwise the deal stands."

"All Five Families know about this?"

"Only Gennaro, Viviana, and I. To get his blessing when I retire, it was agreed."

"Shit. We don't have an agreement like that, right?" Sante asked.

"No, only Savio, since he's the oldest."

"I'm out of here." I stopped at the door.

"McKayla is not to be touched, Savio."

"I hear you."

———

I knocked back another shot of scotch at the bar in Sanctuary and turned my phone off after the conversation with my father. I planned to talk about the Nevio situation, but to find out they lied to me, and I didn't earn the position I thought I did, pissed me off more.

"Another one, Savio?" Lucky, the bartender, asked.

"Yeah."

He held the bottle over and poured the scotch to the top.

"I knew you'd be here." Sante slid up beside me. Renato came on the other side.

I tilted my head back and gulped the shot. It burned my chest, and I closed, then opened my eyes.

"I don't need babysitters."

"According to Elio Calabresi Jr., you do," Sante joked and slapped me on the shoulder.

I shrugged him off, and he held a hand up and backed away.

"How many shots have you had?" Renato pushed the glass away from me.

"Not enough."

Lucky approached us.

"One more," I said.

"He's cut off, Lucky," Sante said.

My lip screwed up in a scoff.

"Worry about your little dick not falling off." I pushed him away and slammed my glass down on the bar for another shot.

"And you worry about what wedding ring you're going to pick out for Viviana," Sante replied. I jumped up and punched him in the face. He spat the blood out, tightened his fist, and sent a punch back at me. Renato got between us with security.

"That's enough!" Renato shouted.

"Lucky you're my brother, or I'd have you hanging up, bleeding out like a pig." I picked up the napkin and wiped my lip.

"Get out of your feelings."

"We have bigger problems to talk about. We're family; shake hands and move on." Renato put his arms around both our shoulders. I hesitated for a second, then nodded and reached for his hand. I faked and punched him in the right jaw.

"Now, it's cool."

"Why do you have to be an asshole?" Renato helped Sante stand, and I grinned.

"Take after my father."

"Have you spoken to her at all today?" Sante grabbed the bottle of Ace of Spades from the back bar and popped it open.

"Who?"

"The McKayla girl."

"Shit." I reached into my pocket and took my cell out to call Enzo.

"You never checked in on her?"

"Was I supposed to?"

"You'll make a terrible husband," Sante said.

"I'm not getting an answer." I hung up and pulled money out to pay Lucky.

"We'll follow you," Renato said.

CHAPTER 5
McKayla

THE MOMENT HE LEFT, I bided my time and checked the clock to check when Marilyn would leave. Then I needed a way to get Enzo distracted. But he never fell for my suggestions to grab something for me to eat when Marilyn cooked more food for a party of ten. I prayed he wasn't hurt, but I had to do what was needed. I took a piece of statue, hit him over the head, and ran out of the penthouse as far as I could. I called Rena to pick me up.

So here I was, at her place, showered and sitting on her couch, drinking tea to help calm my nerves. I didn't have my phone, so I didn't know whether my parents or Joseph had called me today.

"Rewind everything that happened again," Rena said.

"Rena, it's too crazy even to repeat."

"I understand, but what you've been through sounds like a Lifetime movie."

I unlocked my legs on her couch, set my tea on the table, and wrapped the blanket tighter around me.

"After I finished dancing with that Marco guy, I went to the restroom."

"But went outside to pee."

I nodded.

"Yeah, and I heard some noise, so I went to look and stumbled on something I shouldn't have."

"The leader of the Calabresi killed a man in front of you."

Thinking back on that night was still too fresh, and I cried from the nightmares.

"What did you tell Joseph?"

"I told him you had a family emergency, but had Rory on the Calabresi story."

"Ugh… great."

"Yeah, I tried to tell him you would be back, but he didn't care."

Pop! Pop!

"Agh!" We both dropped to the floor and screamed. The door was kicked open, and I someone snatched me up.

"Help me! Agh!" I screamed. I opened my eyes in surprise to see Enzo standing with a gun in his hand, pointing at Rena. Another man who looked just like Savio stood next to him. Renato held me in his arms, and I saw the evilest look on Savio's face.

"Please, she had nothing to do with this. Don't hurt her."

Savio waved a finger at Enzo, and cocked it, ready to shoot Rena.

"No, wait! I won't run again. I promise."

"How can I trust that when you left once?" Savio questioned.

Renato let me go, and I ran to stand in front of Rena.

"She won't say anything, I promise. Just let her go."

"She's seen our faces."

"Savio."

"Renato, take her to the car," Savio said.

"No! If you hurt her, I swear I will."

He closed the space between us. "You what?" He raised my chin to look into my eyes.

"Whatever you think you're covering will be exposed. I'm not the only one working on your father's story."

"McKayla," Rena muttered.

"Shush…" I grabbed her hand.

"Are you saying more than one person knows about your book with my father?"

"Yes, and if something happens to her or me…"

"Then I'll kill them too."

"What? You don't even know who it is."

"I'll kill your parents, find your boss, and torture it out of him."

"You're insane."

"I've heard way worse. Take her to the car." Renato reached for me, but I slapped his hand away and wrapped my arms around Rena.

"No! If you kill her, you'll have to kill me too."

"Savio, maybe I have a suggestion?" the only guy with a short, black haircut and blue eyes asked.

"What, Sante?" Savio groaned.

"I'll take her friend to my place."

"What?" Rena and I said at the same time.

"You into kidnapping now?"

He motioned his hands out. "It hasn't worked out for you so far."

"Whatever, Sante. Take her and keep her out of the public eye until I decide what to do with her."

The guy Sante went to grab Rena, but she pushed him away and stood.

"Listen, Rena, just do what they say, and I'll call you."

"We can call the police, McKayla."

"How did that work out when you tried to find your friend here?"

"You must have paid them off, but I'm not scared of you," Rena answered.

"I don't need you to be scared of me," Savio argued, getting up in her face.

I placed my hand on his stomach to push him back. "Savio."

He looked at me, and something in his eyes seemed to click. He stepped back, and I dropped my hand.

"Grab what you need," Sante told us.

"How do we know you won't kill me when we're separated? It could be a trap," Rena demanded.

"You want to find out?" Savio remarked and walked out of the apartment.

Enzo grasped my elbow and forced me to follow Savio.

"He better not hurt her!" Rena shouted.

I clenched my jaw, seeing him sitting so casually in the limo like he didn't kidnap me twice in one week. Enzo nudged me to get inside, and I sat across from him and buckled the seatbelt, looking outside. It was getting dark, and I wanted to talk to my parents and check-in, but I hated the situation I would put them in with having to lie.

"Can I call my boss?"

The car pulled out into traffic. I saw Rena arguing back and forth with Sante and Renato, laughing at them.

"No."

"To be honest, this one-answer conversation is not helpful."

"I didn't ask for your thoughts."

I chuckled. "What does your girlfriend or wife think about this situation?" I couldn't fathom any woman dealing with a man who had no respect or regard for her feelings.

"That's none of your concern."

"So, someone likes this attitude on you."

He stopped texting and peered over at me. I felt a little self-conscious because Rena only had shorts and a shirt for me to change into, and I never went back to my apartment to change. I thought he'd find me there first.

"Our time together can go one of two ways."

"Which are?"

"Do as I say or find yourself on my bad side."

"Those options aren't surprising."

"Good, because I wasn't trying to surprise you, McKayla. I'm direct with everything I say."

———

The curtains were pushed back, and the sun shined down on my face. I groaned, not wanting to be woken.

"Mr. Calabresi wants you down for breakfast."

I pushed the cover back. "Marilyn, right? Tell Mr. Calabresi I'm not hungry."

"He's not going to like that answer."

"He might be able to kidnap me, but he can't force me to eat with him."

"I know it's difficult being in your situation."

"Can you get me out of here? I have some money saved up."

"What's taking so long?" Enzo stood in the doorframe.

"Tell your boss I'm not hungry."

"You can tell him yourself when you come downstairs." He started to approach the bed.

I jumped up and went behind Marilyn. "Don't touch me!"

"Enzo, it's fine. Tell Mr. Calabresi she's coming."

He shook his head and walked out.

"Come on, I started a bath for you. Please do as he wants," Marilyn told me.

I sighed and sat on the edge of the bed. "How long am I expected to be here?"

"As long as he wants you here."

"I have a life, friends, and family."

"Whatever you did must be important enough for him to keep you here."

"I..." I caught myself before I explained the sordid details.

Jumping up, I walked into the bathroom. I saw clothes on the marble counter with my correct size—underwear and bra set, a black blouse, and jeans. I looked at myself in the mirror and saw bags under my eyes. I opened the cabinet and felt a little better that he had a few skincare products, but I wondered what woman left them there.

"Shake it off," I told myself, feeling weird at thinking of another woman and him together. He was the biggest jerk and asshole I'd ever met.

I picked up the brush, combed through my curls, and wrapped my hair to get ready to wash it since I'd gone almost a week. An hour later, I came out of the bedroom and walked into the living room to see Savio sitting and reading the newspaper like the first day I woke up here.

"You enjoy the shower?"

I cleared my throat. "Thank you, I did." I placed the napkin on my lap, poured orange juice into my cup, and took a bite of toast.

"I have a few meetings today."

"Okay."

"You're going with me."

"What? I don't want to be anywhere near you killing people."

"I leave the killing to the other people."

"Could have fooled me."

"That was a special situation."

"You only kill in special situations?" I cut into the pancake, poured syrup on top, and scoffed it down.

"You have a little syrup on the bottom of your chin."

I grabbed the napkin to wipe it off. "Did he steal money from you?"

"Who?"

"The guy you killed."

"I don't talk about my business at the table."

"Why do I have to go with you today?"

"Because you can't be trusted to be alone."

"That was a mistake, and you said we would start over fresh."

"We are starting over, and the consequence of your mistake is coming along with me for the day."

"Can I talk to my parents, at least?"

"You can if you behave."

"I'm not a child."

"How old are you?" He closed the newspaper and placed it on the table.

"Twenty-three."

"Are you a virgin?"

I choked on my drink.

"What?"

"I need to know if a guy is lingering and looking for you."

"That's none of your business. If you don't answer personal questions, neither will I."

"I'm not a virgin."

"How old are you?"

"Thirty-four."

"You look twenty-five."

"Good genes. Now answer the question."

"There's no guy in my life at the moment."

"Perfect, one less person to kill."

He rose from his seat, and stalked over to the door and grab his jacket.

"Are you dating anyone? I saw women's skincare and shampoo in the bathroom."

"Nothing for you to worry about."

I rose out of the seat and went to confront him. "Be honest. How long do you plan on keeping me hostage?"

"Until I figure out a plan to keep you from talking that doesn't involve me putting a bullet in your head."

"The last thing I want to do is talk now that my best friend is involved."

"Grab your shoes, and we can go to your place for a few things."

"Why?"

"Because you made it a point to talk about the female skincare products and shampoo in the guest bathroom."

"I wasn't saying it like I was jealous."

"My mother bought it for guests. If you're going to be here for a while, it might as well be comfortable."

"I want to go to my job."

"No."

"Why not?"

"I'm letting you call your parents and go to your home. And I let your friend live."

"I kept my mouth shut!"

"After running away!" he yelled.

I started to tear up. "I need to grab my shoes."

I started to walk off, and he tried to reach for my hand. I pushed him away, grabbed my shoes, put my hair in a ponytail, and wiped my eyes free of tears.

You won't let him break you.

CHAPTER 6

McKayla

THE CAR RIDE to my apartment was quiet, and I preferred it because my thoughts ran nonstop. I wasn't trying to get on Savio's bad side, but he made it hard to talk and reach common ground. All I wanted to do was go back to my everyday life. I'd been thrust into a new world that didn't make sense to me.

We finally stopped in front of my apartment, and I reached to open the door.

"Never open a door when you are with me." Savio glared at me.

I pulled my hand back in surrender. "Sorry."

"Enzo will go with you upstairs. You have twenty minutes to get as much as you can."

"What's the rush?"

"Now, McKayla, we talked about you asking personal questions."

"Right, sorry. It's the journalist in me."

"Try not to pack a lot of things. I can have my assistant shop for you."

"Okay."

"One more thing."

"Yeah."

"If you try to run when you get out of this car, your friend will be dead before you even make it to a phone booth," he threatened.

A knot lodged in my throat. "I understand."

He sat back in his seat and I continued to text. It was Saturday around ten a.m. A part of me wondered what business he had to handle, while another part of me didn't care because my investing in his life caused me more problems than I needed.

Forty minutes later, I came back, and Enzo placed three large bags in the trunk of his car. I got in the backseat and sat next to him.

"What was your time limit?"

"Huh?"

"If you huh, then you heard my question."

"I was given twenty minutes."

"It's been forty minutes, and I'm late for a meeting."

"I apologize, but I needed some personal things."

"Like what?"

"My work notes and private items."

"I suggest you think hard if you want to speak with your parents today."

My head turned fast at his comment.

"What does that mean?"

"It means those additional twenty minutes may delay you contacting your parents indefinitely."

"You bastard!" I reached over and smack him, but he caught my hand and pushed it behind my back, tightening his hand around my waist and pulling me into his chest.

"I say what I mean and mean what I say."

I took in his masculine cologne and full lips. I opened my mouth to speak when the car stopped suddenly.

He pushed me away. "Behave." I started to get out, and he shut the door again. "You stay in the car."

"But you said I was going to a meeting with you."

"Going to them and attending are two different things. Think about your latest fuckup while you sit in the car with Enzo."

I gritted my teeth and crossed my arms over my chest like a child being scolded. "Asshole," I mumbled under my breath.

I slapped my hands at the window while he talked to some men outside the high-rise building. *He thinks he's one step ahead and in control, but I have a few things up my sleeve.* I reached into my bookbag, pulled out the tape recorder I'd hidden, and hit rewind.

"If you try to run when you get out of this car, your friend will be dead before you even make it to a phone booth."

I set the recorder on the correct timestamp, put it back in its place, and waited for him to finish up whatever he was doing.

I tapped on the window partition, and Enzo rolled it down. "I want to apologize for hitting you the other day."

His eyes narrowed in anger.

"You have to understand. I've never been in a situation like this before."

"Mr. Calabresi doesn't want you talking to us."

"Can I at least use the restroom?"

He shook his head. "No."

"I promise I won't run. Besides, he has men outside the limo and probably inside."

He looked thoughtful. "No."

"Enzo. It's Enzo, right?"

"Yes."

"Do you have a wife or sister? Would you want them suffering like this?" I tried to play on his feelings.

"You can't persuade me."

I blew out a breath. "What happens if I tell him I peed

on his seats because you wouldn't let me use the restroom?"

"You try anything, and I'll kill you and suffer whatever consequences."

"I promise, just the restroom."

Enzo texted and waited a few moments. It chimed with an incoming text. He held it up for me to see the response.

Savio: *She runs, kill her.*

"You have five minutes." Enzo came around to the passenger side and escorted me in.

I scanned the lobby, which was full of people talking on phones and security guards laughing. The place smelled of money and felt larger than life. Sparkling, tall glass windows shined through as people went on as if nothing were wrong with a high-profile mobster who walked through the doors. Then I saw the sign hanging on the wall.

"Calabresi Holdings."

"This way." Enzo dragged me down the lobby hallway and pushed the bathroom door open.

"I can take it from here." The women didn't seem surprised at him checking the stalls.

He must do this often.

"Five minutes."

"I understand."

Enzo left the bathroom, and I ran to the window to try to push it up.

"What are you doing?" a girl asked, wearing a black dress and heels with a high bun on top of her head.

"Listen to me. I need your help." I grabbed her shoulder.

She pushed me back. "Who are you?"

"My name is McKayla, and I'm being kidnapped," I whispered.

She laughed, turned on the faucet, and washed her

hands. "Who kidnapped you?"

"Savio Calabresi."

She didn't seem surprised, and she looked back at the door. "Take a little advice and don't rock the boat or make him upset."

"Did you hear me?"

She tossed the paper towels in the trash. "Mr. Calabresi doesn't do things unless they harm his family."

"Which part of the mafia are you?"

"I work at Calabresi Holdings, and I advise you not to speak about something like that," she replied, waving her hand around.

"Wow, you're protecting him. Are you sleeping with him or something?"

"Savio isn't my type."

A banging at the door startled me, and I forgot I needed to use the restroom. I went to the furthest stall and pulled my pants down to relieve myself. A few minutes later, I came out and washed my hands. She was no longer here, and I checked over my face, wiped the tears away, and checked my hair.

"I need to check on Rena."

My lip curved up, and I figured out a way to get Enzo distracted so I could see Rena. I saw Enzo standing opposite the door and threw him a harsh glare. "Enzo, my stomach hurts, and I need a doctor." I held my stomach, blinking my eyes.

"What's wrong with you?" he questioned.

"I don't know, but I need a doctor, please."

"We need to wait on the boss."

"I can't wait. I feel like I have to throw up." I held a hand over my mouth.

"Let me text him."

"No, it's going to take too long!" I shouted, and a few people looked at me.

"Let me call him." Enzo reached for his phone, and I panicked, smacking it down on the ground. I took off, running to the stairs.

"Stop!" Enzo yelled and pushed some people in front of me. He went to the exit doors and ran down the stairs. I was lucky we were on the main lobby floor as I pushed the exit door to the alley and saw no one in the back. I took off down the street as cars passed. I looked back and saw Enzo and two other men running behind me.

"Please, let me get away from them." I almost tripped but caught myself when I ran into a door opening.

"Watch out!" a guy yelled.

I ran into a local bar and hid behind the wall.

"Can I help you?" the hostess asked.

"I need a phone." I bent over, trying to catch my breath.

"Are you in trouble?"

"Please, I need to use the phone. I'll pay you." I checked my pockets. I'd left my wallet back in the limo. "Shit."

"Calm down and tell me what's wrong," she said.

"Some men are after me."

"Why?"

"I don't have time to explain. I need to use the phone."

"Okay, you can use the phone at the bar."

"Thank you." I walked to the bar, looking over my shoulder to ensure no one was coming. The phone was placed on the counter, and I dialed Rena's cell.

"I'm busy, so leave a message," Rena's voice message repeated for the third time.

"What if he killed her already?"

"Anything to drink?" the bartender asked.

"No, but who owns this place?"

"I do."

I froze in place and dropped my head at the sound of his voice. He took the phone out of my hand and calmly placed it on the base.

CHAPTER 7

Savio

WHEN ENZO TEXTED that McKayla needed to use the restroom, I knew she'd try to run again. But to be this bold and end up at another owned by my family was amusing . Her heart seemed to drop with fear etched through her eyes, and I felt a moment of guilt at what I would do as punishment. Then I thought of what she put my men through, running around the city to find her.

"Take her to the car," I told Enzo.

"Wait! Savio, you can't do this," she pleaded and struggled against Enzo.

I grabbed her arm and pushed her against the wall. Her eyes ballooned wide in shock. "Shut the fuck up. You lost the right to plead your case."

"No! If I'm going to die, I won't make it easy for you."

"Bitch!" I bent double in pain and almost released my hold as she kicked me on the balls.

"I'm calling the police on everyone here," McKayla shouted.

"Take her to the car. Now!" I demanded.

"Get your hands off me!" McKayla spat.

My guards grabbed her arms and legs as she squirmed in their hold and carried her to the car.

I stood with a hard glare and slowly walked out of the bar behind them. They put her inside the limo, and she leaped across the seat and tried to scratch my eyes out as I got in next to. her.

"Sit the fuck back."

"Call me a bitch again and see what happens." She slapped me across the face.

"You think that little slap is going to stop me from killing your parents?"

"Don't you dare threaten me."

I sighed in regret for getting this far in a situation with this woman. I had enough problems with Viviana calling my office when I was in a meeting and wanting to meet up. Then my father was still adamant about McKayla coming over to finish the book, on top of Maurizio causing problems.

"Enzo, take us to the Calabresi home."

Enzo pulled out in traffic, and we both stayed quiet as the limo headed to the freeway.

I pulled out my phone to make a call.

"Yeah." I heard Sante's voice.

"How is she?"

"Driving me crazy," Sante replied.

I chuckled and felt the same way. "Put her on the phone for a second." I turned the speaker on and held it out.

"Hello," Rena said.

"Rena! Are you okay?" McKayla questioned.

"McKayla! Yeah, I'm fine. Are you okay?" Rena asked.

We both made eye contact, and she tried to reach for the phone. I yanked it back.

"Speaker only."

"I'm okay, Rena. Have you been at work?"

"No, Sante refuses to let me go to work," Rena replied.

"Because you tried to kill me!" Sante shouted.

"It was an accident!" Rena screamed back.

"Sante! What happened?" I took the phone off speaker.

I heard rustling in the back, and Sante got back on the phone. "She's crazy, and I'm ready to put a bullet in her head."

"You're good, right?"

"Yeah," Sante muttered.

"Enzo's taking us to our parents' house. She tried to run again."

"Can we end this now?" Sante asked.

"Not yet."

"You like her, don't you?"

"This isn't high school, asshole." Deep down, this woman was testing me at every turn, and her challenging me was aggravating and sexy at the same time. I'd been with women for one thing only, and that was sex. Somehow, she'd made me want to be around her more and more with no thought of wanting sex from her.

He chuckled on the other line, and I hung up on him.

"Savio."

I put my phone in my pocket and looked up at her.

"I understand I made a mistake when I stumbled on the Nevio situation."

"Stumbled on."

"If you're going to kill me, can I at least have one last request?"

"No."

"Why not?"

"Did you not have my men running down the street in broad daylight?"

She licked her lips and blew out a breath. "What do I have to do to get you to trust me?"

Thinking over her statement, I had a nagging feeling

this could be the best decision I ever made or the worst, but it would solve all my problems.

"Marry me."

She burst into laughter. "Really, what can I do?"

"Marry me."

She stopped laughing and stared at me. "You're serious."

I nodded.

"I can't marry you."

"Not for love. I need to cut a problem before it starts and solve your problem."

"What's my problem?"

"Your family and friends not dying."

"Savio, there's no way I can marry someone like you."

"Someone rich?"

"I don't care about money."

"What do you care about?"

"I mean, you're a mob boss, and I'm a journalist. Our lives are totally different."

"Again, this isn't about love. We both need to solve a problem."

The car finally arrived at the gate, and Enzo pulled in the round next to Renato's car.

"Can I think about it? I mean, your girlfriend might not agree to this."

"Let me make the decision for us both. We're getting married." The car stopped, and I pushed the door open and stepped out.

"Savio!"

I jogged up the stairs as Renato opened the door holding a plate of food in his hands. I pushed him aside.

"Are you listening to me?" McKayla asked as she ran up the stairs behind me.

"Glad I made it on time for the show," Renato said.

"Where's Father?" I slid my hands into my trench coat.

"In the kitchen with Mom."

I still felt sore from her kicking me, so I slowed my steps.

"Renato," McKayla called his name.

"Miss Santon," Renato answered.

"Can you please talk to your brother and tell him to kill me?" she blurted.

He choked on his food. I grasped her wrist and pulled her in the kitchen with me.

"Savio, my baby's here, and he has a guest." Mom cheerfully came around the island and held her hands out for a hug. She stepped back and smiled at McKayla and me. "Hello, I'm Savio's mother, Adelina."

McKayla pinched my wrist and jerked her hand away. "I'm McKayla. It's nice to finally meet you."

"My husband is very smitten with you, McKayla," Mom teased and wrapped her arm around my dad.

"McKayla, I hear my son has been keeping you busy," Dad said.

She bit her bottom lip. "Mr. Calabresi."

"Are you staying for dinner?" Mom asked.

"No."

"Yes."

We both answered at the same time.

They looked at us both as Renato walked into the kitchen.

"Is everything okay, McKayla? My son can be a bit over-bearing at times," Mom said.

"Mom."

She chastised me in Italian.

"He's making me marry him!" McKayla blurted out.

Mom gasped. "Savio, what is she talking about?"

"I need to talk with Father for a minute."

"You can talk to us both," Mom replied. "This is about Viviana, isn't it?"

"Who's Viviana?" McKayla asked.

"Me." Viviana walked into the room wearing the shortest dress, showing off the cleavage she knew would taunt me and cause an argument.

The person I was trying to avoid all day and the past week had made herself known. I needed to get McKayla on my side before Viviana sabotaged things.

CHAPTER 8

McKayla

I PEERED from the beautiful woman who came in the kitchen to Savio, noting his glare, I was jealous he wasn't paying attention to me any longer. I couldn't explain why I was pissed, but I didn't want him to know.

"Adelina, so nice to see you again." Viviana reached out for a hug, but the smile didn't reach Adelina's eyes like it did when I'd stepped into the room.

"Mr. Calabresi. You're still as handsome," Viviana said.

"Who invited you in, Viviana?" Savio asked.

"I'm family, Savio."

"McKayla, let's go to my office to speak." Mr. Calabresi placed his hand on my shoulder and escorted me to his office.

I looked over my shoulder at Viviana and Savio arguing.

"Come have a seat."

"Thank you."

"I know you're probably confused and have a lot of questions."

"Is it obvious?"

"Let me try to explain."

"Please."

"Savio is the don of the family, and he doesn't like that I'm doing an interview and letting them write the story of my life."

"I got a hint of that the other day."

"In our family, we have arranged marriages; my wife and I were one."

"You weren't scared?"

"Never. She's been my best friend for many years. Savio is the eldest, and once I agreed to let him take over, I had to make a deal with some associates."

"The other families."

"Yes, and Viviana is the daughter of one of them."

"So, why doesn't he marry her?"

"He's against marriage in general. He's never wanted to do things expected of him."

"Rule breaker."

"He's hardheaded, but smart. What he's done for the family has brought us into a new way of doing things when it comes to our legit business."

"What about the mafia business?"

"He's called *the beast* for a reason."

"The beast."

"Renato kills for fun, but Savio kills with a plan."

"Oh."

"You witnessing a murder put you in the sights of every boss and family in the business."

"So, I'm a target?"

"Yes, not just for Savio, but for others."

"Can't you do something to stop them?"

"I have some power, but not much." He chuckled.

"Mr. Calabresi, I can't marry your son."

"Normally, I would agree. My son is a little impulsive in his decisions."

My brows furrowed. "Can I make a call?"

"Sure."

"Just like that. What if I call the police?"

He stood "You can call the police, but they won't do anything."

I grabbed the phone to call my parents.

"Stanton," Dad answered.

"Dad."

"McKayla…" he whispered.

"Yeah, it's me."

"Where have you been? Your boss called and told us you disappeared."

"Um… I need to talk to you."

"What's wrong? Are you in danger?"

"I…I…"

"Tell him you're getting married," Savio growled behind me.

"Who is that? And what is he talking about?"

"I'm fine."

"So, where have you been?"

I glanced up at Savio and squirmed in my seat.

"Answer him," Savio responded.

"I was kidnapped by the mob boss Savio Calabresi," I answered, staring right at Savio.

"What?" Dad shouted.

Savio laughed and took the phone out of my hand. "Mr. Stanton."

"Who the hell is this, and where is my daughter?"

"McKayla and I are getting married. She's been secretly dating me and was afraid to tell you."

My entire body felt hot, and I tried to reach for the phone, but Savio turned his back to me.

"I want to speak to my daughter right now."

"She's a little preoccupied, but I'll have her call you later," Savio replied and ended the call.

"What is your problem?"

"You." Savio picked me up, placed me on his father's desk, and stood between my legs.

"Your girlfriend is outside the door. I suggest you move."

"Are you jealous, McKayla?" he questioned.

I scoffed. "I despise you, and everything you're about." I tried to push him away.

He grabbed my wrists, placed them on the desk, and closed the space between us. Our lips almost touched.

"Either you move, or I'll kick you in your balls again."

"Try it again and see what happens."

"You don't scare me."

"Some people might find this innocence cute, but I'm getting exasperated at the belief I need you to be scared of me."

"Savio, we're not done talking," Viviana interrupted, pushing the office door open.

I tried to move out of Savio's hold, but he wouldn't allow it.

"Go home, Viviana," he said, not removing his eyes from me.

"Who is she?" Viviana asked.

"My wife," Savio answered, and my eyes rose in shock.

"What about us? My father is going to hear about this." Viviana charged into the room.

"Tell Gennaro he'll get a payment," Savio said.

"Viviana, right?" I asked.

"McKayla," Savio grumbled, reaching up and grasping my chin.

I moved my head out of his hold. "Hi, I'm McKayla. Savio—"

Before I could finish, he placed his hand on the back of my head and pressed his lips to mine. I hated myself for feeling something through the kiss. I tried not to moan, but his tongue sucked me in.

"Savio!" Viviana screamed, waking me from a trance.

I pushed Savio away and jumped off the desk.

"McKayla."

"No, take care of your girlfriend."

I tried to get out of the office, but he picked me up and tossed me over his shoulder again. He stalked out of the office with Viviana behind his back in shock.

"Where are you taking me?" I demanded.

"Shut up."

He walked

to the elevator, pushed the button, and stepped in to keep Viviana out. He placed me on my feet, grabbed both sides of my face, and captured my lips again.

"Savio," I moaned. I wrapped my arms around his neck and fell into his chest.

The elevator stopped, and he pulled back, peering into my eyes. "Go freshen up for dinner."

"Huh?"

"We're staying for dinner."

"Savio, we need to talk about what happened."

"We will. Later."

He walked out and pointed to the bathroom at the end of the hall.

———

A week later, I was still at Savio's penthouse, not at the office like I wanted, but at least he allowed me to continue working with his father. I was exhausted from going back and forth, and when Rory tried to get in touch, that made it even worse. Savio acted cool and calm, but the minute a guy tried to talk to me or come near me, he was all possessive, and back to the asshole I hated.

"So, you have five sons. Savio, Renato, Sante, EJ, and Vincenzo," I repeated to Mr. Calabresi.

Savio's father had come to have lunch with me and go over more questions for the book. I decided to keep some extra-sensitive information out of the book in respect to Savio's mother. Mr. Calabresi grew up in Sicily as a young boy and was expected to do what his legacy established for him as a mob boss. At first, he fought against being in the lifestyle and wanted to be an artist. He showed me some of the artwork he'd made for his wife, and I asked him if he still painted, but he said no.

"Mr. Calabresi, you're turning seventy-three, correct?"

He smoked the cigar he'd snuck out of the house. It was cute the way Adelina wasn't scared of him like everybody else in the world. If you read the papers and searched the internet, Elio Calabresi was the devil reincarnated. I could answer that and say he'd been replaced by his son, Savio.

"I still look thirty-five, though." He laughed.

I chuckled. "I've seen Renato and Sante. What about Vincenzo and Elio? Are they in the family business?"

He opened his mouth to answer when he looked up, and I turned to the patio door. Savio came out with Enzo behind him. I grabbed my smoothie off the table and took a sip.

"Son, how are you today?"

Savio bent down and hugged his father. "Good. Finished taking care of some things."

Savio never took his eyes off me as he answered his father. Even though we lived together, we'd barely crossed each other's paths since the day of the kiss at his parents' house. Based on my conversations with his father, Savio had always been cold and distant, even when he was younger. He explained that Viviana had been around the family for years, but Savio never took her seriously. My being here caused friction within the Five Families. Gennaro had called for a meeting this month, and Savio was sending Sante in his place.

"You speak with your brother EJ?" his father asked.

"Yeah, he told me about going to New York."

"Will that be a problem?"

Savio was hesitant to answer, and I didn't understand why, so I closed my book and stood.

"Leaving so soon?" Mr. Calabresi asked.

"Just to grab a refill from the kitchen." I picked up the smoothie and turned toward the patio door. As I stepped into the kitchen, Marilyn was wrapping up a plate of sandwiches.

"You're done for the day?" I said, opened the fridge, and grabbed the container that held my premade smoothie. When I stopped fighting Savio on living here, I wanted some of my favorite foods and juicing items stocked up. He ate healthily, but was a coffee drinker. I liked tea and juice in the morning.

"Yes, Miss. Stanton."

"Please, call me McKayla."

"McKayla."

"Great, do you have a family and kids to get back to?"

"Marilyn, can you excuse McKayla and me for a second?" Savio walked into the kitchen.

I rolled my eyes, poured the rest of my drink, and took a sip, pushing my hair to the side.

"Of course, Mr. Calabresi."

Marilyn walked out of the room, and Enzo stood at the door on watch. We'd gotten along a little better since my two attempts at escaping. Savio leaned against the door-frame and scanned me up and down.

"How was your meeting?" I asked.

"It was long as usual."

"Who was it with?"

He smirked at my question.

"I don't care, just asking."

I pushed off the counter and started to walk past him,

but he stuck his hand out and blocked me from leaving. He grabbed the drink out of my hand and took a sip. "This is gross."

"It's healthy."

"To whom?"

"It's a green kale smoothie."

"It's disgusting."

"What do you want, Savio? I haven't tried to escape, and I've played nice."

"We need to discuss marriage."

I rolled my eyes and ignored him for the rest of the day.

———

The next day.

Back in my apartment, my usual routine was eating breakfast, drinking tea or a smoothie, then turning on yoga videos and setting my intentions for the day before I started working on a story.

Like right now, I was sitting in the living room of Savio's condo, bent over and counting to ten before letting my mind and body connect to let go of the stress that had come into my life recently. I cracked my neck, took slow breaths, and laced my hands forward.

"You ever do yoga?"

Marilyn came in from the kitchen and refilled my strawberry smoothie that sat on the table. "A few years ago, but not lately."

I stood up straight and crossed my feet in front of the other. "You're never too old to do yoga."

"I'll add that to my list of things I need to do before I die."

I took a sip of the smoothie. The door slammed, and our heads whipped in that direction. I rolled my eyes as Savio walked in nonchalantly.

"Morning, Savio, would you like some breakfast?" Marilyn asked.

I put the smoothie back and put my back to him as he talked with Marilyn.

"What are you doing?" Savio walked in front of the TV.

"What does it look like?" I stretched my arm out and aligned it with my leg.

His head dipped low.

"Can you move? I'm trying to watch something."

"My men told me you tried to contact someone in Italy about my father."

"It was research."

Savio stepped around the table on my left, bent down, and pressed his hand on my lower back. "Do you like fucking with me?"

My breath hitched when his hand moved around to my stomach.

"I hear taking slow breaths helps with yoga."

"I'm not fucking with you."

"Then why are you making calls to people about my family?"

I turned my head toward him. "Sorry. I thought that since I'm a journalist, it's a part of the role."

His upper lip turned up in a smile.

"Are you coming back from work?" I grabbed the towel and wiped the sweat off my face.

"None of your business."

"I didn't get much out of the research in Italy."

"Make this the last time I have to deal with you over-stepping."

I dropped the towel on the floor and continued with my stretches. "Marilyn, can you make a salad for lunch today?" I called out, and she nodded.

"So, you're ignoring me."

"I refuse to let you tell me how to do my job."

"If your job compromises me, then yes, I will."

"You might control your family and friends, but not me."

Marilyn brought a cup of coffee to him. He sat in the chair, watching me and drinking his coffee.

"What are you doing?"

"Same as you, my job."

He pulled out his phone and made a call on speaker. "Vincenzo," he answered.

"Did you get the waterfront pricing?"

I reached for the remote and turned up the volume. "Bastard," I mumbled.

Savio grabbed the remote and turned the volume down.

"It was around a hundred thousand," Vincenzo informed him.

"Asshole, I'm trying to work out."

"Not my problem." He winked at me.

CHAPTER 9
Savio

I TRIED to talk myself out of doing this and telling Gennaro he could go fuck himself and his daughter, but if I wanted to show I was no longer *the beast,* I needed to pay him a visit. Viviana was nothing to me, and I'd been clear about my intentions never to marry her.

McKayla was my way out. The only thing I couldn't explain was how that kiss changed me from wanting to kill her to feeling obligated to protect her. I was still against her doing the piece on my father, but we compromised and it would no longer bring up issues with our family, so she continued her work. I talked with her boss a few days ago, and we agreed I wouldn't kill him if he dropped the article on Nevio.

Flashback.

I stalked through the office with my men behind me and forced the door open. I caught Joseph and some woman kissing.

"Who the fuck—"

Going around his desk, I jacked him up by his shirt and pushed him against the wall.

"Agh!" the woman screamed, and Enzo took her out of the room.

"I'm sorry! Please, don't kill me," Joseph begged.

"Listen to me and listen clearly."

"Okay… okay…" he stuttered.

"You know who I am?" He nodded, and I squeezed his neck. "Answer me!"

"Yeah…" he rambled on.

I narrowed my eyes at him. "Anything having to do with the Calabreses will be destroyed. Do I make myself clear?"

"Yes."

"Yes, what?"

"Yes, sir?"

"If I find anything about my family in this newspaper, they'll find your body floating in Lake Michigan."

"I promise, it won't happen."

I released him and helped to straighten his shirt.

"Mr. Joseph, I called security," a guy wearing brown slacks, a white shirt, and a blazer with a short buzz cut spoke from the door.

Enzo strolled over, and I motioned for him to stop. "No need for an audience. Mr. Joseph and I cleared up a misunderstanding."

"You might scare other people, but you don't scare me." His voice trembled with doubt.

I studied him for an extra moment, then smiled. "What's your name?"

"All that matters is that I know your name," he replied.

"Rory, leave it alone." Joseph fixed himself up.

"Rory. Well, Mr. Rory, I'll leave you and Joseph."

"What did you do to McKayla?" he questioned.

I tensed at her name. "McKayla is no longer your concern."

"And Rena."

"Well, you might need to call my brother, Sante, about that situation."

"Mr. Calabresi, is everything all right?" the security guard asked.

I grinned as Rory and Joseph looked perplexed. "Everything is great, Gerald. How are the kids?"

"They're great, sir. Thank you again for the recommendation of the school," he answered.

"My pleasure. Anything I can do to help."

"Wait, are you going to arrest him for trespassing?" Rory remarked.

"Why? He owns the company," Gerald responded.

Their mouths dropped in shock.

I shook my head. "Joseph, remember what I said. And Rory, you're fired. Gerald, escort him out."

Present.

Savio

"When I get married, it will be for love and only one time," McKayla declared.

"You have no choice."

"I thought we were getting to a better place?" She moved a piece of loose hair behind her ear.

She'd washed her hair the night before and my place smelled like strawberries. She didn't know I was here when she was asleep, and I looked in on her in the room.

"We are in a better place."

"So, just marry Viviana."

"You owe me."

"I—"

"I don't want to hear your excuses. This is the deal we agreed on."

"An arranged marriage and kidnapping is not a deal I agreed to!" She pushed my hand away, stomped out of the kitchen, and tried to go back out on the patio with my father.

I grabbed her around the waist and went upstairs to my bedroom with her screaming to put her down.

"Let me go!"

"Shut up!"

Slap!

I smacked her on the ass, and she squirmed and wiggled to get down. McKayla was short but thick in all the right places. The second I pulled her into a kiss at my parents' home, I was ready to fuck her on his desk with Viviana watching.

"Put me down!"

"Savio! I'm leaving," Father called out.

Enzo would make sure he got to his car fine. I pushed my bedroom door open and dropped her on her feet, shutting the door behind me. I leaned against it to keep her from leaving.

McKayla paced in front of me, and I noticed the small freckles on her nose. Her chest heaved up and down. She was getting riled up to fight back.

"Mr. Calabresi!" she yelled.

"He's gone."

She clicked her tongue and looked around my room. "This is your bedroom." She motioned her hand around.

"We can keep things the same. You have your room, and I stay in mine."

"I'm not marrying you."

"It's no longer an option."

"What do you mean?"

"Gennaro wants you dead."

"But I didn't do anything."

"You know too much."

"I thought you're some type of big badass mob boss."

McKayla didn't know that Gennaro had basically declared war if we didn't kill her and was convincing the other heads at the table. I tried to spare her feelings, but I wasn't into babysitting and handling the comments from my family about why I had her kept alone in the penthouse.

"Your parents are coming to dinner tonight."

"How… Wait, what's the catch?"

"No catch. I wanted to apologize to your father and meet them since we're going to be in-laws."

"This a trick?"

"No trick."

She reached out and picked up a photo of me when I was younger playing soccer. She looked like she belonged in the room; trying to fight that feeling was a losing battle.

"How does this work exactly?

"What work?"

"Marriage, you, and this world."

"I've never been married."

"So, you're testing it out on me." She grabbed another photo of me and my brother and tossed it at my head. I moved out of the way before it hit me, and it fell against the wall.

"Are you crazy?" I ran to grab her.

She jumped on top of my bed and ran out of my grasp. "Asshole!"

She went to the door and tried to open it, but it was locked. I licked my lips, slowly approaching her, and removed my jacket.

"Don't come any closer."

I rolled up my sleeves. "Or what?"

She lifted her right brow, then glanced down at my dick. "Come and find out."

"McKayla, I swear to God if you knee me again, I'm going to spank you."

McKayla flipped me off and looked around the room for something else to toss at me.

I made it to the door and placed my hands on both sides of her face.

"Can I at least have a date?" she asked.

"A what?"

"Date."

"I don't date."

"What do you do with your women?"

"I fuck." I shrugged my shoulders, not sweetening the answer for her.

"You're a prick."

"What do you use in your hair?"

"Don't change the subject."

"This isn't a fairy tale, McKayla. I never said this would be love."

"I want a date, and then we can talk about marriage."

"The marriage is happening whether we go on this date or not."

She pushed against my chest, but I didn't move. "How long do we have to be married?"

"At least a year."

"A year!"

"Gennaro's a boss. He needs to be convinced, and Viviana is a part of that convincing."

She turned her head. "This is about your girlfriend."

I grabbed her chin, causing her to look back at me. "She's not my girlfriend."

"What other secrets are you hiding?"

"None," I lied, not telling her about me buying the newspaper she worked at.

Once she finished with the story, I would kill it and make her think her boss was behind everything. Keeping Joseph on worked out in my favor. He knew he was on borrowed time if he double crossed me.

McKayla was strong-willed, and her hard glare seemed to look through my soul. She knew I was lying. I cleared my throat and moved away from the door, unlocking it to allow her to walk out.

"I need to shower and prepare for my parents to come over."

"That's fine. I have a few items coming for you try on."

"Can Rena come to dinner too?"

"No."

She stopped, and I bumped into her back. She almost fell, but I grabbed her around the waist to stop her.

"I want a double date tomorrow night with Rena."

"Sante can barely stay in the same room with her."

"Oh, I know the feeling." She snatched away from me and stomped down the stairs.

"Be ready for dinner in two hours. I have a few phone calls I need to make."

She ignored me and slammed her bedroom door.

I groaned and walked down the hall to my office. I locked the door and called Sante first.

"She didn't kill you yet?" Sante laughed over the phone.

"Fuck you."

"I can tell you're stressed."

"Man, I don't think I can go along with this marriage."

"What's the alternative?"

"We vote the Greco family out."

"That's calling for war."

"Why won't she just walk away?"

"Who?"

"Viviana."

"It's hard to tell, since your love life has exploded overnight." He laughed.

"Where's Rena?"

"Hopefully in hell," he mumbled.

"So, your guest is driving you just as crazy."

"You have no idea, and you owe me big time."

"What has she done?"

"Where do I start? The crazy bitch shot me, then almost set my house on fire."

Right as I was getting ready to comment, a knock came at my door. "Let me call you back." I walked around to unlock the door and saw McKayla's gaze lighten up.

"They arrived with some dresses."

"Anything else?"

"Is the dinner going to be formal or—"

"Pick out whatever you want. You own all of them."

"What do you mean?"

"I bought all of them for you."

"But how do you know my size?"

"I had Rena help pick them out."

"Am I supposed to pay you back for them? I already have to pay you back in marriage."

"Just pick something out. Not everything is a fight."

I stepped back and slammed the door in her face.

"Bastard!"

"I know!"

I smirked at her comment and went back to work, so I could be free for her parents' visit. They didn't seem like the type to be good with their daughter marrying a man they'd never met. I hoped it wouldn't come down to me putting a bullet in her father's head. I knew I was a bastard. But the Calabresi family always came first above anything else, right or wrong. That was the rule of our family.

CHAPTER 10

Savio

THE DAY WAS GETTING AWAY from me, and my eye was twitching while I watched Maurizio arrogantly light his cigarette and stare at me. I'd been gone all day from one meeting after another with Vincenzo to scope out new ventures we could bring into the fold of the Calabresi. To get a text from Sante that Maurizio wanted a sit down to discuss Nevio was the last thing I needed.

He blew smoke out of his nose. "You understand why this is concerning, don't you, Savio?"

I clasped my hands in my lap and scanned the round table. We were in the basement of the bar near our building. "Explain it to me again?"

"You want to vote Greco out and pay me off for killing my man," Maurizio repeated.

"What Greco and I have has nothing to do with this situation." I knew the gleam in his eyes would show that he was itching to call Greco and let him know my plans.

"Nevio was family."

"Your family tried to get my family's name on the books. What was he doing with our product?"

"Did you ask him?"

Maurizio thought he could challenge me because he was a little older. "His last breath was spent begging."

"Son of a bitch!" Maurizio jumped up from his seat and tried to charge at me, but my guards pushed him back.

"Maurizio, we conduct business as gentlemen." Tommaso cleared his throat.

His eyes darted at Tommaso, then Alize, the other bosses in the Five Families. "He thinks I care about his tainted money. I have to bury my sister's son." Maurizio spat on the floor, pushed the guard back, and sat.

I chucked my chin to Sante, and he lifted the bag of money and placed it on the table. "I'm prepared to pay you five hundred thousand."

Alize grabbed the bag and took it over to Maurizio. "The girl?"

"She won't be a problem."

"Why?"

"She's my fiancée."

"Why not kill her?"

"Because you don't question me."

"Greco wants you to marry Viviana, and you think this will counteract that," Tommaso stated.

"Greco has no choice but to accept my fiancée." I rose from my chair.

"We're not done," Maurizio spat, came around the table, and stood a few feet away.

"Nevio will be avenged," Maurizio said.

"If Nevio was doing anything that put our names on the police radar, then he put himself in the grave. Remember, you don't exist with the Calabresi family." I held my palm out for a shake, and he glared, so I slid my hands in my pocket, turned, and left the basement with Sante and my other guards.

We climbed on the elevator, and Sante pushed the

button for the main floor. "You're leaving them down there by themselves."

"There's a camera and audio. They wouldn't be stupid enough to try anything. Plus, our men are guarding."

The doors chimed and opened, and I stepped off, walked out through the main floor, and paused when I saw Viviana pointing her finger aggressively at the hostess.

"Is that Viviana?" Sante stepped in front of me.

"Move, Sante."

"We're in public. Enough heat is on us."

"She's following us around now." I moved around him to grip her arm and took her back to the office as she tried to pull away.

"Savio, let me go." Viviana reached up to smack me across the face.

I caught her hand and pushed it down.

"Savio," Sante called out.

"Sante, tell him if he doesn't let me go right now, my father will have something to say about this."

I opened the office door and pushed her inside. She almost tripped.

I stood at the door as she rubbed her wrist and glared back at me. "Drop the act, Viviana."

She swished over to me and reached out to touch my cheek. "Are you scared your feelings will show?" Viviana slid her palm down my chest toward my length.

I caught her and twisted our bodies with her against the door. "Keep your filthy hands off me."

Viviana smirked and blew me a kiss. "Does McKayla make you feel like I do?"

"Let me make it clear for you and your father."

"He'd probably love to know that Tommaso, Alize, and Maurizio's cars are parked out front."

I laughed at her thinking her little threats could do anything. "Tell him. I don't give a shit. We're not together, and never were. You were just a slut who took my dick down her throat." I backed up off her.

"The only way you stay the boss is by marrying me, so tell your little girlfriend to pick out her room. Because your wife is here," Viviana explained while smiling.

"Funny enough, my fiancée already picked out the decorations for our condo," I lied, not letting on that McKayla and I were still arguing.

Knock! Knock!

"Savio, it's time to go," Sante yelled through the door.

I reached around her to open the door and held it wide for her to leave. "Make sure she gets out of my place of business and all the other Calabresi buildings."

"I won't be sent away like some cheap whore."

"How many times have we fucked, Viviana?"

"You know I love you!" she spat.

"You're nothing to me. Leave before I forget who your father is and let the beast out."

———

"What are we doing?" Sante asked as he held up the weight bag while I worked through some anger and frustration.

Boxing was my form of working out. With everyone trying to take away what was rightfully mine and disrespect my decision, I needed to relax and work out some thoughts, while picturing Greco and Viviana's faces.

I stopped to catch my breath. Sante threw the towel to me, and I wiped the sweat off, then picked up the bottled water in the workout room. Vincenzo came through the door.

"Keep an eye on Greco. If he makes one wrong move, he's dead." I looked over at Vincenzo's stone face.

"I'd love to know why my brother's face is being brought up in a possible murder."

"What are you talking about?" Sante questioned.

"You're not the only one who has friends in certain places."

"Quit with the riddles and speak."

"Someone says you're possibly connected to the death of Nevio Colombo because of a drug deal gone bad."

"Who told you that?"

Ring! Ring!

Sante's phone rang, and he answered with it on speaker. "What's up, Renato?"

"We might have a problem."

"Location?" I asked.

"At Sanctuary." The call ended, and I looked at Sante, then back at Vincenzo.

"No."

"I'm riding with you."

"You have enough heat on you."

"I agree with Sante. You can't go around killing people as the CEO of a billion- dollar business."

"Give me five minutes to change."

———

The night breeze prickled cool against my skin as I marched into Sanctuary and looked around for Renato, but he wasn't to be found.

"Probably in the office." Vincenzo wasn't supposed to be around activities that dealt with the mafia side, and he knew that was my only condition as the baby brother of the family.

As the next in line of Calabresi Holdings, we didn't need any photos or video of him coming from a situation that would look criminal. I left through the employee entrance, down the hall to the fake door, and went through the guard.

I came upon Renato holding a gun to someone's head. "Who is this?"

"He's Nevio and Maurizio's people."

"What's your name?" I questioned him.

"Fuck you." He was tied to the chair with bruises around his eye and mouth.

"I asked one simple question. Why do people have to make it so hard?"

"We found him trying to look around here," Renato explained.

"Who sent you?"

"I don't answer to you."

I punched him in his stomach and gripped his shirt. "Who the fuck sent you!"

He grinned with one eye closed.

"Give me the knife."

"Savio, let Renato handle this," Sante said.

"Give me the knife!" I shouted, and Renato pulled it off the table of toys we liked to use when we tortured people.

"Normally, I'd leave the fun to my brother, but today has been shitty, so I need something to make me feel better."

"I'll meet you in hell before I talk!"

"Hell is too good for me." I stabbed him in the kneecap, and he screamed in pain.

"Argghhhh!"

"Keep screaming; it reminds me of opera. Have you ever been?" I asked my brothers, and they shook their heads.

"Very soothing and calming."

I slashed his left arm.

"Pleassseee… someone help!" His blood ran down both sides of his body. He was having trouble controlling his breathing.

"I bet you wish you'd given me a name, right?" I leaned toward his ear.

"I'll tell you anything I know," he begged.

"Too late. I like this way better." I grabbed the gun from the table and shot him between the eyes.

"Was that Savio or Beast?" Renato asked.

I passed him the gun, wiped my hands off with the towel from the table, and walked out to go home.

"Doesn't matter. He'll never know. Get this cleaned up."

Vincenzo followed me while Sante and Renato worked on cleaning up my mess. "You seemed like a different person."

"That's a part of the game, brother. You need to be to survive." I reminisced on the words our father instilled in me at an early age, same that his father explained to him. Once you're in, no going back. It was just a matter of coming up above water with your family by your side.

CHAPTER 11

McKayla

TWO DAYS LATER, the weekend seemed to come by fast, bringing on more anxiety that the wedding to Savio was really happening.

I came out of the guest room and thought about speaking with Savio about our living situation after the wedding. *Would I have to sleep with him? What about my apartment?*

Dressed in a halter top and shorts, I went to the kitchen and saw Marilyn talking with Enzo. "Hi Marilyn. Enzo, is Savio already gone?"

Marilyn smiled at me. "Good morning, McKayla. Did you have a good night's sleep?"

"I did." I picked up a piece of toast and some bacon.

"Savio went to the office," Enzo replied and grabbed the glass of orange juice sitting across from me.

"He works every day?"

"The boss is important."

"Did he tell you I'm going shopping today?"

He nodded and reached in his pocket to pull out a cell phone and pushed it across the table.

"What's this for?"

"You're allowed to have a phone again—only to make calls to your family and friend Rena. It's tracked, so I would suggest not making any false movements to the police."

"Is this a joke?"

"Beast doesn't joke."

"Thanks."

"Savio is coming around," Marilyn expressed, sitting with her mug of coffee.

"Are you married, Marilyn? Have kids? What do they think of your job?"

"You have a lot of questions for someone who's under surveillance," Enzo remarked.

"I'm a journalist." I shrugged.

Marilyn chuckled. "It's okay, Enzo. I don't mind. No, I'm not married."

"Children?" I mixed the oatmeal and fruit together and lifted it to my mouth.

"I have one daughter. I'm grateful for the opportunity to provide her with a wonderful life."

"That's wonderful."

"Do you want kids?" Marilyn asked.

Enzo cleared his throat and glanced at Marilyn. She cowered from probing more.

"Breakfast was great. I'm going to head out." I rose, removed the napkin, and gulped down the rest of the drink. "Enzo, let me grab my purse, and I'll be ready."

"You don't need that. Savio has it covered." Enzo walked to the living room table and picked up an envelope.

"What's this?"

He handed it to me. "Open it and see."

I eyed him for a few seconds, then flipped the seal open. "A credit card."

"He wants to make sure his future wife is covered."

"I don't need his money."

"The way it works is that everything goes through Calabresi funds, and this black card is monitored."

"Ridiculous." I dropped it in my purse and turned to leave with him trailing behind him.

———

"McKayla, where have you been? Your father and I are worried," Mom shouted through the phone.

"Mom, let me speak."

"Is she pissed?" Rena mouthed the words slowly in the seat next to me, while Enzo drove to the mall.

I rubbed my forehead from the headache coming on.

"What's going on? We've called you at work. Your neighbors said you haven't been home for days."

"I'm getting married!" I blurted out.

"What?"

"It's a little complicated."

"McKayla Stanton, you better explain what the hell is happening."

"His name is Savio Calabresi."

"The mobster they've talked about in the papers?"

"Something like that, but he's a businessman."

"McKayla," she sighed.

"I just arrived at the mall. He invited you to his place for dinner tomorrow night."

"There is no way you're marrying somebody we've never met."

Enzo pulled into a parking space, turned the car off, and jumped out to open the door for Rena and me.

"I want you to come to his place for dinner."

"Are you crazy? We do not associate with those types of people."

"I need to go."

"You better not hang this phone up."

"Mom, I have to go. I'm heading in the mall." I made some unintelligible noise to end the call before she went into World War III.

I couldn't explain over the phone about the circumstances with Savio and me. Bad enough he was tracking and recording my calls, my parents already had a possible target on their backs with me mixing up with Savio.

"What did she say?" Rena removed a piece of gum from her purse.

"She's pissed, and I don't blame her."

"Maybe you should tell them the truth."

Enzo held the door open to the mall. We walked to the escalator and pointed to the Neiman Marcus store. I put the cell in my purse, crossed my arms, and listened to Rena ramble on.

"Bad enough I know what's going on, I can't let them know."

"How far are you with the article and book?"

I had all my notes and wrote everything up. Matter of me fine tuning and meeting with Mr. Calabresi one more time before sending it to the editors. "I need to finalize one more thing."

She stepped off the escalator and pointed to a red dress in the front window of the store. "What's this date about?"

"We don't know each other, and I want to make sure we have an understanding of what we're going to tell my parents."

"You're not marrying for love. So, you can't fake it in front of your parents."

"I know, and the last date I've had was months ago. Work has consumed me. So, they'll know something is off about me."

"Have you spoken with him about the wedding night?"

That topic was something I was still worried about. Since the kiss in his office, I'd noticed him in a different light when we were just the two of us. I couldn't say the kiss was bad; in fact, it was out of this world and left me wanting to taste his lips again. I was more embarrassed that I wanted to kiss him again.

"We kissed." I turned, picked up another dress from the rack, and held it up under my chin. It was a gold and black shoulder knee dress.

"Tell me everything."

"It was in his office, but some girl busted in the room and said she was his girlfriend."

"Who is she?"

"Someone named Viviana."

Enzo coughed, and I glanced at him. "Enzo, I know you work for Savio and are protective of him."

"I'll never betray the family."

"I understand, but who is Viviana?"

"No one you have to worry about." Enzo continued to watch people come in and out of the store.

"If that's his girlfriend, I have a right to know."

"Enzo, you can answer. It's not like Savio is here." Rena grabbed two leather skirts and shoved them in my face.

"Savio can answer your questions better than I can," Enzo said.

"Great, I'll talk with my future fiancé." I put on a smile and sauntered to the dressing room.

Ten minutes later, I came out wearing a leather skirt and white silk crop top and stood in the mirror.

Rena clapped her hands together and squealed. "I love it for you."

"I think I'm showing too much skin."

"A little skin can work in your favor."

"Are you saying to seduce him?"

"It can't hurt to get him under your thumb; every man can be brought down to his knees for the right woman."

I turned to the left, then right to see how short the skirt really was. "I'll take this one."

"Good, now let me grab something, and we can go for lunch."

I checked the time and noticed it was getting late. "I still need to do some work, then prepare for our date tonight. Do you mind if we grab something quick?"

"There's a gleam in your eyes. Are you excited for tonight?" She shoulder bumped me.

"What? Of course not. This is business. Life and death for me."

"The Calabresi family."

"Savio isn't the only crazy brother."

"Let's not bring up anyone else. The less headache I get the better."

I chuckled and looped my arm in hers. We paid for our items and left to grab lunch.

———

The next evening arrived sooner than I thought. I was nervous with not knowing how Savio would treat me when it was the two of us alone in a romantic setting, but he probably thought it would be more of a business meeting. I wouldn't be surprised if he had lawyers come for me to sign papers to make sure I got an allowance if I acted like a good little girl.

The car stopped in front of the restaurant. It was going on eight p.m. We kind of matched, which I brought up, and he just grunted in acknowledgement. Enzo drove us in a limo and tried to ask what the occasion was, but one thing I learned about Savio, you didn't question him unless you were ready for the answer, even if that answer hurt your feelings.

"I've never been here before." I looked around at the

front of the restaurant, saw a valet holding doors open for the women to get out.

"Life of Italy has been around for years." Savio stepped out of the car, came around to the passenger door, and extended his hand to help me out. His eyes lingered on my legs and scanned up my thighs to my face.

"What? Do I have something in my teeth?"

"Nothing." He shook off his thought. "Enzo, you and the team can grab a table inside or wait in the car," Savio told his men.

He had at least five bodyguards with us, which only brought on more eyeballs.

"Maybe we should have done something at your condo."

Savio stopped walking, peered at me, and bit his bottom lip. "Are you embarrassed to be seen with me?"

"No. I just think the amount—"

Savio held his hand up to stop me from talking.

"Do we need this much protection?"

"Hello, Mr. Calabresi. Your table is ready," the hostess chimed in when we arrived at the entrance of the restaurant.

"Thank you." Savio released my hand and placed his palm on my lower back, giving me the go ahead to follow the hostess.

"Here you two are, and your drinks will be out soon," the hostess told us and laid the menus down.

Savio pulled my chair out.

"Thank you."

The hostess walked away, and Savio clasped his hands together. "Let's get the rules out of the way."

"Rules."

"Si," he replied.

I closed the menu, adjusted in the seat, and placed my arms on the table, leaning forward.

"One, there will be no questioning my business and how I handle myself in public."

"But—"

"Two, you and I both know who I am, and you unfortunately got mixed up in a bad situation."

"Can I speak?"

"Three, for this evening to go well, we need to understand rules one and two."

"Anything else?"

"I see I'm going to have to teach you to behave."

"I believe you have me mixed up with your girlfriend, Viviana," I muttered and tried to rise from the chair.

He grasped my wrist, and our eyes held a long stare off. "Sit."

"What assurances do I have in all of this?"

CHAPTER 12

Savio

"YOU GET TO LIVE."

"I might take my chances with the police, or even better, the Columbian people."

I released my hold on her wrist and watched her not get two feet away when my men stood and blocked her from leaving. Was I enjoying her torment? No. Did I get off on forcing women to be in my space, or even marriage? Hell, no. But she would see this arrangement benefitted both of us in the long run. I got to stay in my position as boss, and we were covered for Nevio's murder. We'd had my men set up that McKayla and I were together on the night of his murder if the police questioned me. The two biggest problems, Maurizio and Gennaro, would be handled soon if they weren't aligned with the solutions I'd provided. Avoiding bringing my father in was my idea, even though Sante and the rest of my brothers wanted him to be aware.

"You staying?"

She rolled her eyes at my remark, and I wanted to laugh, but she looked stunning. Becoming enamored with her beauty would only make my decisions harder.

"Hello, Mr. Calabresi. I have your usual scotch, and for

the lady, red wine." Carolyn, the waitress at Life of Italy, placed my glass down, then filled McKayla's wine glass. Carolyn was an older Italian woman who catered to me whenever I came here for dinner.

"Thank you," McKayla answered.

"You're welcome, dear. Are we having your usual, sir?" Carolyn replied.

"Please, two of each," I said.

"How many times have you come here?" McKayla inquired, leaning back in her chair.

"I order from here most nights when Marilyn's off," I answered truthfully.

"Great, two linguine with fresh tomato, prosciutto salad, and beef braciola." Carolyn wrote down and took the menus away.

"I have some rules of my own," McKayla blurted out.

"Really? Let's hear them."

"I'm keeping my apartment."

"No."

"I will continue to work."

"No."

"We will sleep in separate beds, and there's a time limit on this marriage."

"No, and extra no on the time limit."

McKayla grabbed her purse, tossed her napkin down, and went to stand again. "Kill me."

"McKayla." I rubbed my chin.

As she turned red in the face, her nostrils flared, her lip poked out, and her chest heaved up. "No, kill me. Get it over with and spare my parents. You psycho!"

Some of the other guests stopped to stare at us. I hated when attention was on me. I rose from my seat, waved my men off, and dragged her by the hand to the bathroom for privacy.

"He's going to kill me!" she cried out.

I pushed the women's bathroom door open and walked over to check if each stall was empty, then locked it from the inside. "What are my rules?"

She rolled her eyes and crossed her arms, which pushed her breasts upwards. "I don't have time for this."

"McKayla, I will call my men to go to your parents' house. Before they even find the bodies, they'll announce you as the sole heir of the fifty-thousand-dollar insurance policy."

She gasped in shock.

"I know everything, love. So again, what are my rules?" I stalked toward her, boxed her against the counter, and placed both hands on either side of her body.

"There will be no questioning your business."

"And?"

"I know who you are and unfortunately, I got mixed up in a bad situation." She peered into my eyes, and a lone tear fell down her cheek.

For a split second, I wanted to feel sorry for her but showing any weakness would allow her to think she ran things. "I don't need to force any woman to sleep with me;. You'll do that on your own."

"So, what are you saying?"

"I'm not an unreasonable asshole when it comes to certain negotiations."

"Does that mean…?"

"You can keep your apartment but continue to stay with me full time. You can work from home."

"But…"

"I can revise my answers."

"Sorry, go ahead."

"The marriage timeframe is non-negotiable, and like I said, when it comes to sex, I already know your little pussy is screaming for me. No need to pretend."

"You're full of yourself." She tried to push me away, and I didn't move.

I grinned and leaned over to whisper in her ear, "Am I, or are you wet right now at the sound of my voice? When you purchased this skirt that barely covers your ass, were you hoping I would smack, grip, and hold onto it when I made you come?"

"I... I think our food is ready."

"The swell of your breasts and pouty lips are wondering when I'll bless them with my tongue. Are you ready for me to do that, McKayla?" I pressed my hard on against her.

She opened her legs for me, and I trailed a kiss on her cheek, down to her chin. "Tell me, McKayla, have you been fucked so hard you've passed out at twenty-three?"

"No..." She brushed her lips across mine.

I kept my lips a few inches from her hers to allow her to take the lead this one time. "Do you want to kiss me, McKayla?"

She nodded.

"Take control and kiss me, princess."

McKayla reached her arms out, pulled me in, and smashed her lips to mine. I gripped her by the hips and picked her up to sit on the counter.

"Mmmmmmmmm..." she moaned into the kiss.

I rubbed a hand on her exposed thigh, moved up her chest, gripped her around the neck, and bit her bottom lip. Her perfume engulfed me. I growled, wanting to rip off her clothes and fuck her in the bathroom.

I pulled back, rubbing my palm down her cheek. "We understand each other?"

"Yes."

"Good. We should eat, and then we'll go to the court-house this coming week."

"What about my parents?"

I helped her down to stand. "We can have dinner with

them after the wedding."

She met my gaze with hesitation. "Don't we need to sign something?"

"I know everything from your parents' address to your blood type. I'm not worried about you taking any money from me."

I helped her sit down again when Carolyn placed our food down.

"What do you like to do for fun?" McKayla moaned when she ate the linguine, and a small bit of sauce lingered on her bottom lip.

"Sex and make money."

She dropped her fork and laughed, covering her mouth. "You're joking, right?"

"I don't joke, McKayla."

"So, a thirty-four-year-old man likes to have sex and make money for fun. Do I have that right?"

"Yeah." I gulped the rest of the scotch.

"Do you go to Italy often?" She changed the subject, reached her fork over to my plate, and took a piece of linguine.

"We have the same food."

"I'm sorry. This is good, and you didn't look to be eating."

"I want to watch you eat."

"Can you be honest with me?"

"Always honest, only to what is needed to be answered."

"Why not marry Viviana and end this confusion?"

"Viviana was one of many women I fucked. I don't sugarcoat anything."

"I know."

"She wanted more, but she has no substance. I'm not interested in having an enemy in my family."

"But she knows about your world of the mafia better

than I."

"That's what I don't want."

"Why? Wouldn't that be easier than threatening me and my family?"

I smirked at her getting bossy with me. "Viviana is only good for sucking dick. Gennaro thinks he could run the Five Families if I married his daughter. In Italy, we have arranged marriages, but I've never been the type."

"But you're willing to marry me?"

How could I tell her I was more nervous about taking her as a wife than she would be with me as a husband? I hated feelings, having to compromise and think of another person besides myself. "This is a business arrangement."

"Are your brothers like you?"

"Sante and Elio are, but Renato shoots first, and Vincenzo, we keep away from this family business."

"He's the youngest one, right?"

"How is your meal? Do you need anything else?" Carolyn questioned.

"We'll take it to go and the check."

"Sounds good, sir."

"It's still early."

"You know we're not on a real date, right?"

Carolyn ignored the hard stare on McKayla's face. When she got upset, it made my dick hard, and I wanted to do more shit to piss her off.

"I know exactly what this is, Mr. Calabresi."

"Good, I have some work I need to finish."

"I need to meet with your father to go over a few more items before I finish my article."

"I'll get Enzo to take you to him after the wedding."

"Do your parents agree with this fake marriage?"

I placed money down, took her hand, and walked us out of the restaurant to an awaiting limo. "They understand what I need to do."

She crossed her legs, her left meaty thigh exposed, and I licked my lips, thinking of her taste. The pull between us was palpable, and I knew she wanted me. Our agreement would only cause confusion if we took it there.

Maybe I need to get a woman on the side, I chortled to myself.

"What?"

"Huh."

"Why are you laughing?"

"Nothing."

"Tell me. If we're going to be a couple, I want to know what you're thinking."

"I was thinking if I should have a side chick for sex. That way you won't have to worry about sex with me."

She scoffed and turned away from me. I reached for her shoulder to turn her around, and she smacked my hand away.

"Look at me."

"No need to explain."

"I wasn't going to explain myself to you."

"Enzo, can you take me to my apartment please?" She knocked on the partition.

Enzo rolled it down. "Sir."

"I want to go to my apartment."

"He only answers to me."

"Of course he does."

"You're jealous."

"I think your ego has grown too high, that you believe every woman wants you."

"I don't need every woman to want me."

"Then?"

"Look at me."

Enzo rolled the partition up.

I gripped her left thigh. "Open your legs."

"What?"

"Open your legs."

"No."

"What are you afraid of?"

"Nothing."

"Turn toward me and open your legs." My voice dropped low, and I could see in her eyes that she was curious what I was about to do. Only this time, I'd let her have the reins. When I did get her in my bed, it would be her choice. I liked to dominate and have my woman submissive.

"I want you to understand something."

"Savio..."

"Would you like to touch yourself?"

She seemed embarrassed, peered at the partition, and then out the window.

"Did I make you jealous and turn you on?"

McKayla bit her nail. "I... I." She cleared her throat.

"I can smell your scent, princess. Your nectar probably has your panties soaked, dripping wet, and ready for my tongue to tease, kiss, and suck the ache away."

The car pulled up to the building.

"I'm fine, actually."

"Do you mind if I check?"

"Yes, I do mind."

I smiled at her playing hard to get.

"So, I can go and get my dick sucked then, because you have me hard as a rock, baby." I gripped my dick, and her eyes rose wide in surprise. She licked her lips. "Would you like to suck my dick instead, McKayla?"

"You're an ass." She pushed the door open.

I watched her pull on her skirt to adjust herself as Enzo followed her to the door. I fisted my dick and thought of something else to calm him down, so I could walk in the condo and prepare for the workday tomorrow and meeting her parents. Ten minutes later, I shut the door behind us.

She stomped toward her bedroom, and I went to my bar and grabbed another drink to ease my thoughts.

"You sure about her, boss?" Enzo inquired.

I stared at the empty hallway. "If I plan on making the move against Gennaro and Maurizio, I need her under my thumb."

"So only business. You're not feeling her in real life."

"Do I want to fuck her? Yeah, she's a beautiful woman. Do I love her? No."

"Savio Calabresi getting married will cause some problems."

"Viviana won't be a problem."

"Her father."

"Bingo."

"We're ready for him."

I nodded at him and headed over to my office to finish looking over some documents before going to bed. I walked to her door and heard the shower running.

"Soaking wet, princess."

————

Monday morning sprang around, and I sat in my office scanning over the documents Vincenzo asked me to verify before I agreed to us buying up a few mall strips around Chicago. Calabresi Holdings ran a global business from investing, real estate, retail, entertainment, and land that we purchased to cover our mafia business with warehouses and offices to hold conversations.

My office sat on the top floor that my mother decorated modern and clean with a cream carpet, grey stainless-steel chairs, a couch, and old Italian paintings from Sicily.

Knock! Knock!

"Yeah."

"What do you think?" Vincenzo opened the door, then

shut it behind him.

"How much land is it?"

"At least four different areas, about fifteen thousand square feet."

"What do you want to do with it if you move forward?"

"Break them down and rebuild."

"How long will it take to rebuild? We have other things we need to make priority."

"The construction part can be estimated for you."

I leaned back in the chair, with my hands behind my head, and looked him up and down. "Keep me updated, but you're handling things well."

"A reason I'm the president."

"You could be better if you stop running behind pussy so much."

"Says the guy who kidnapped a girl to marry him." He rolled his eyes.

"At least I have control over my women."

"According to whom, Viviana or McKayla?"

"If you focused just as much on my love life like you do this business, I wouldn't need to follow up on your mistakes."

"I make things happen."

"No, you make rookie mistakes—partying all night and missing meetings. I get the calls from staff and other business partners."

"You're just like Dad."

Ring! Ring!

"I need to take this."

"If you're lucky, this arrangement won't backfire on you." He shook his head in annoyance, and I wanted to let him know this was about him taking on responsibility and not throwing the opportunity away by constantly partying all hours of the night and missing family gatherings. Ring! Ring!

CHAPTER 13

Savio

"YOU THINK SETTING up a vote to get me out would work?"

"Gennaro, is that you?"

"You son of a bitch!"

"I don't have time to listen to you cry."

"Either you come down to your lobby, or I'll let off some shots."

I rose from my seat, looked out of the window, and saw a few limos downstairs.

"Got your attention now." The phone call ended.

I marched to my desk, grabbed my gun, checked the chamber, and texted Enzo to make sure he was downstairs.

Me: *Gennaro is here.*

Enzo: *He has about five men.*

Me: *I'm coming now.*

Enzo: *Should we empty the lobby?*

I pushed the elevator button and waited for it to open.

"Mr. Calabresi, is everything all right?" my secretary asked.

"I'm fine."

"Someone named McKayla is asking if she could come up."

"Fuck!"

"Sir."

I didn't know she would come here. We had breakfast this morning with causal conversation. If Gennaro saw her, more problems would arise. "Tell her to stay put and find Enzo."

"Yes, sir."

Vincenzo came out of his office and noticed me jump on the elevator. "What's the rush?"

"Gennaro's here."

"Right now?" He blocked the elevator door from closing.

"Vincenzo, I don't have time to talk."

"Coming with you."

"Don't have tell to argue with you but stay behind me."

The doors opened, and I stalked out and scanned the reception area. I saw Gennaro in a stare off with Enzo and my men. McKayla stood with a couple, and I could more than guess they were her parents.

"What are you doing here?" I stepped in front of Enzo.

"Who's the sexy girl who's staring you down in the back of the head?"

"None of your business."

"Savio," McKayla called my name.

"That's her." He started to move around me toward McKayla.

"If you want to walk out of here with both legs, you won't take another step."

"This the bitch you moved on with over my daughter?"

"Enzo, make sure Gennaro finds his way out."

Enzo went to grab his arm, and he pushed him away. "Get your filthy hands off me."

"Make a scene, Gennaro, I dare you."

"This won't be over because of a fake whore!" he shouted.

I punched him in the face.

"Aghhhh!" McKayla screamed.

I heard scuffling and yelling, both Greco and my men started fighting. I went to grip him by the shirt when he pulled out a gun.

"Fuck you, Savio."

"Pull the trigger."

His breathing increased.

"Do it. Show me how much of a man you are."

"You disrespect me and my family."

"Get out of my building."

Gennaro's eyes moved toward McKayla, and he turned the gun toward her. "Maybe I'll save everyone by taking out the problem. I think Maurizio would like to know what you've been up to."

"Your only lifeline is the other families, and they've already voted you out."

"I'm a made man and elder."

"You're nothing to me but an old man waiting to pasture."

Gennaro dropped the gun, put it in his holster, and walked away with my men following him.

I explained to Enzo to make sure they left and to double check all sides of the building. Vincenzo stood with McKayla and her parents near the building security guards.

"What are you doing up here, McKayla?"

"Your eye looks like it's swelling." She reached to touch my face, but I moved out of her hold. She looked embarrassed, but I didn't have a minute to comfort her with everything that just went on.

"Is this the man you're planning to marry?" her dad said.

"Dad, Mom, this is Savio."

"I'll let you handle this. Call me later," Vincenzo told me.

"He's a thug, McKayla. You're not marrying him," her mom spat.

Her mouth opened, then closed.

"With all due respect, Mr. and Mrs. Stanton, McKayla is a grown woman."

Her father stepped in my face. "I'm her father. If you think we're okay with our daughter getting mixed up with you, you're delusional."

"McKayla knows me better than anyone, and I can protect her."

"Are you pregnant, McKayla? Is that why you're in a rush?" McKayla's mom held both of her hands.

"I told you on the phone that it's complicated, but I trust Savio."

"You don't even know him."

"I know enough, and over time, we've gotten to know each other very well," McKayla explained.

"Over our dead bodies. If you have any sense, you'll run and stay away from him."

"McKayla, if you go through with this, understand you're no longer a part of our family," her father remarked. He reached for his wife's hand, and they left.

———

Several hours later, I finished checking in with my staff to make sure Gennaro didn't cause any more damage. I met with a few people from Vincenzo's team for the construction company set for the mall strip and talked with Tommaso about the casting vote for Gennaro.

I slid my key in the condo door and saw McKayla sitting on the couch, wrapped in a blanket, and watching an old black-and-white movie.

I tossed the keys on the night table, removed my jacket, and sat on the opposite end of the couch. "What's your favorite color?"

"What?" she asked.

"What's your favorite color?"

"Pink, why?"

"What's your favorite snack you could eat anytime of the day?"

"I don't know, chocolate probably."

"Do you come from oral or penetration?"

Her mouth dropped open. "Are you trying to get to know me?"

"I know you felt some type of way, with your parents wanting to disown you."

"I tried calling them all day after they left."

"You want me to have Enzo bring them over?"

"Please no. You've done enough damage."

"You know why they call me the beast?"

"No, but I see you're going to tell me anyway."

"Your attitude can get adjusted, princess."

McKayla rolled her eyes. Something about her defying my orders ticked me off and turned me on at the same time. I reached for the remote out of her hand and turned the movie off.

"Why'd you turn it off?"

I reached over and snatched her up to lay flat on the couch under me. She automatically opened her legs to allow me control.

"I can feel the heat between your legs."

"I don't know who you think I am."

"You're my bitch."

McKayla's face turned sour, and she extended a hand to smack me. I caught it and pushed it over her head, causing her shirt to rise and show off her little shorts and thin t-shirt.

"Move before I scream."

"I think you like to be under me. You have a dominant and submissive side about you."

She turned her head and I nuzzled my face in her neck. I licked down her neck, and she moaned that sexiest noise.

"Savio…"

"What do you want, McKayla?" I sucked on the back of her ear, lingering back down her cheek. I tweaked her nipple and watched her eyes strain to stay closed. "You want me to stop?"

"Fuck."

"You want me to stop McKayla? Just tell me to stop." I gripped her chin. "Look at me."

"I… I… can't."

"Would you like me to stop pleasing you?" I rubbed her bottom lip, stuck my finger inside, and watched her slowly suck my index finger, staring back at me. "Good girl. You like that?"

She nodded. I wanted to eat her pussy and hear her cries. Whenever I was with a woman, it was always about my pleasure, but something in this woman called out the beast in me. I eased my finger out and sucked her tongue in my mouth. Releasing her arms, she wrapped them around my neck, pulled me into her chest, and we humped each other like teenagers.

"I want you to fuck me."

"Where do you want me to start, princess?"

"I want you eat my pussy."

"I'll do more than that."

I moved off her and lifted her up in my arms, bridal style.

"Where are we going?"

"Your room."

"What about your room?"

"Yours is closer."

The process of calculating how long I could last while eating her pussy and before my dick could taste her was waning thin. When I got to her bedroom and placed her on the bed, she removed the t-shirt and shorts—she wasn't wearing underwear.

"Have you been naked under these clothes all night?"

"Yes." She tried to unbuckle my pants.

"Did my men see you?"

"Savio."

"I asked a question, McKayla." I smacked her on the ass.

"No." She rubbed the sting away.

"Let me rub the sting away."

"How are you going to do that?"

"With my tongue."

I removed my shirt and shoes, then unbuckled and slid my pants down to the floor, leaving my boxers on. I placed both hands on her face and bent down to suck on her bottom lip, curling my tongue with hers.

"Savio…" she moaned into my mouth.

My hands rubbed her shoulders, down her back to grip her ass, closing the space between us. Her full melon breasts aroused my dick to grow harder. "I'm going to have so much fun fucking you."

"Prove it."

I dared her with my eyes at the challenge. "You want the beast to come out?"

"I want to know what it feels like when you let your guard down."

"McKayla."

She covered my mouth with her palm. "No love, just arrangement."

I felt a tightening in the chest to be selfish and not let her see how she was affecting me. Already, I had her at my home. I wanted her to be liked by my brothers, the most important people in my life.

"As long as we have an understanding."

I nudged her on her back and hovered over her chest, trailing kisses down her stomach without touching her breasts. I nibbled, sucked, and bit slowly. She gripped the sheets, raising her hands on the back of my head.

CHAPTER 14

McKayla

"SSSS… AHHH!" I felt the first touch of his wet long tongue, and I was embarrassed that I'd never experienced this type of pleasure before from a man. I shouldn't like this so much; he'd told me plenty of times how possessive he was, so having sex would possibly make me just as crazy over him.

I cupped the back of his head, and my body tensed from his tongue teasing my bud. The sheets were plastered in no time with my nectar.

"Wha… What… Ughhh… God!"

He stuck his tongue in my asshole, and I all about trembled in his hold. My head moved left to right as sweat dripped down my chest. My breathing was elevated.

"Just off my tongue, I got you like this."

"Savio… please."

"Hmmm, you want my dick, baby?" He crawled up my body.

I was ready to pass out when I felt the head of his dick at my entrance.

"I need an answer, McKayla." He licked my neck,

moved to my breasts, sucking and rolling my nipple in his fingers.

"I want your dick, please."

We made eye contact. He winked at me and moved off the bed to grab a condom from his wallet. "Once I slide in, you're no longer McKayla Stanton."

He grabbed my ankles, moved me to the edge of the bed, and pushed my legs back to my head. "McKayla Calabresi is born."

He pushed inside, and I pushed his stomach to ease him up some.

"Fuck! Savio, you're too big."

Savio spread my legs wider, pushed my right leg over his shoulder to straighten me in ways I'd never thought of before. To know my twenty-three-year-old self could feel such intense pleasure was an out of body experience.

"Shit, you're leaking all over my dick, baby."

His hips slowed down; he was making love to me now. His hands smoothly roamed over my legs, down to my stomach. Savio hovered over me and gazed into my eyes. Should I question him? Was this him showing vulnerability with me?

"Yes… I'm about to come." I lifted off the bed and met his thrusts.

"Not yet." He slid out and fisted his length. "Turn over."

I struggled to turn, and he helped to put me in a position he liked and pushed back in, gripping both sides of my hips.

"Ughhh… Fuck, come for me, McKayla."

"Ahhh!" I screamed and fell flat on the bed as he continued to pump in and out, breathing heavy in my ear. His gruff voice, sweat, and heavy body made me feel protected and secure. Something I shouldn't be thinking about.

"Shit! Baby, I'm coming. Don't move."

A few seconds later, he pulled out, removed the condom, and came on my ass. He bent down, kissed me on the cheek, and started to pick up his clothes.

"Where are you going?" I hated how I sounded with him.

"To shower and bed."

"Yeah, sorry."

"What? You want me to stay with you?"

"No, I was crazy for thinking that." I rose out of bed, grabbed the shirt off the floor, and wiped his seed off me. I then turned to stroll to the bathroom when he stopped me.

"We have an agreement."

"I know that. You don't have to keep reminding me."

"Black."

"What?"

"Black is my favorite color," Savio said and headed out of my room.

I shook my head, perplexed by his different moods. One minute, he hated me; then the next, he was spilling his secrets.

———

My eyes fluttered open, and I felt a heaviness weighing me down. I looked at my chest and saw a thick muscular arm attached to a mob boss who fucked me so good last night, I wanted to forget the arrangement and everything he put me through.

"Don't make it a big deal," I heard him mumble.

"What are you talking about?"

His eyes popped open, and he tightened his hold around me, rolling me onto his chest.

"This, us, me sleeping in the bed with you."

"I wasn't thinking anything."

"Good."

"Can I get up now?"

"Yeah, make sure you pick your best dress today."

"Why?"

"We're going to the courthouse."

"Oh."

"It happens today." He released me, swung the blanket back, and stretched, revealing a large tattoo on his back of the Calabresi name with his brothers' names underneath.

"What time do we need to be there?"

"We need to get there early, because I have work to do."

"On your wedding day?"

I stepped in the closet, went through the rack of dresses, and pulled out an off-white lace and silk dress. The front would cover me, and the back was open. I picked heels to match and underwear and sauntered to the bathroom.

"Not a real wedding."

For a split second, my stomach dropped at his words, and a tear started to fall. I caught myself, slammed the door to his back, and threw the dress and shoes on the counter, cursing him out in private. "He wants a wife; he's going to get a wife."

The car ride to the courthouse was dry and dead. Savio was staring a hole in my head, and I focused on my phone and texted back and forth with Rena, ignoring his stare.

Rena: *You had sex with him?*

Me: *Unfortunately.*

Rena: *Was he good?*

Me: *I won't lie. It was mind blowing, but he's an asshole.*

Rena: *Maybe he'll relax once things calm down with this mafia beef.*

Me: *I really don't care.*

"Who are you talking to?"

"No one."

Rena: *How big is he?*

Me: *I'm not answering that.*

Rena: *Size of a hammer.*

I chuckled, about to reply, when Savio ripped the phone out of my hand.

"Hey! Give me my phone back!"

"McKayla, another rule of mine is not to ignore me."

"Whatever."

Savio scrolled over my conversation and smiled and handed it back to me.

"Happy now?"

"I can see my hammer might need to help you with your attitude."

"Please, I wouldn't want that thing near me ever again."

The car stopped at the courthouse, and he looked around the area, like someone was following him.

"Is something wrong?"

"No, why do you ask?"

"You're looking around like someone is watching you."

"No one is crazy enough to follow me."

He reached for my hand. I automatically clasped our palms together and followed to the front entrance.

"Nervous?"

"No."

"You ever get nervous about anything, Savio?"

"Not really."

"Let me guess, you're always in control."

"Bingo."

He stopped in front of the clerk's office, and my hand gripped his tighter. I closed my eyes and counted to five to get ready to step into a new world. When I walked out of here, I would be a married woman, to a man who was hated around the world and supposedly putting myself in danger. I regret every day going out that night with Rena.

CHAPTER 15
Savio

"CONGRATS!" I raised my champagne glass in the air and took a sip with my brothers, parents, McKayla, and Rena in the condo after we got back from getting a quickie marriage. McKayla looked a little sad while talking to Rena, and I knew it was from her parents not answering her calls.

"Any regrets?" Renato came from the kitchen with a bottle of whiskey and offered me a shot, which I took after sipping champagne.

"Weirdly no."

"What about her folks?"

"What are you two talking about?" EJ yanked the bottle out of Renato's hand.

"Any word on Tommaso and Alize siding with us?"

"From what Sante is saying, they're not leaning toward your favor."

"Maurizio is pissing me off."

"He took the money but still wants to cause problems."

"How so?" I asked.

Renato peered at Elio, both avoiding my eye contact.

"What do you know, Renato?"

"He's moving some product without approval."

"I think he's stealing our product."

"He thinks I'm not going to do anything because I killed Nevio."

"He's pretending to care about Nevio's murder," Renato replied.

"One of the reasons I tell you to stop going off without consulting us," Elio explained.

"Boys, no work talk at a celebration." Adelina hooked her arm in mine.

"Mom, you know your oldest son can't stop thinking of work."

"I'm still mad you didn't do a big wedding." She poked her lip out.

"We can do something down the line."

"I hope so, but McKayla doesn't seem very happy."

"She's still taking it all in. Her parents weren't onboard with her marrying me."

"Do you blame them?" She peered at me.

"That's true. You know I'm the sexiest one out of your boys," Renato joked.

"I love all my boys the same. Go talk to her, Savio."

"I will."

Mom went to talk with Marilyn and my father and stared at McKayla's back in thought.

"Keep an eye on Maurizio and his plans. Greco needs to be voted out asap."

"Do you want to get Father involved?"

"No, we can handle everything." I put the whiskey glass down and sauntered to McKayla's back.

"Can I speak with my bride for a moment?"

"Sure. McKayla, call me so we can do lunch on Savio's dime." Rena reached to hug McKayla and picked up her purse and coat to leave.

"My men will drive you home," I called out.

"I'm a big girl. I can get home safely," Rena responded.

"I got her." Sante came from the kitchen, holding a phone in his hand.

"Like I said, I can handle getting home fine," Rena quipped.

"And like I said, you're our responsibility, especially after drinking," Sante argued.

"Savio, tell your brother I don't answer to him," Rena spat.

"Rena, let Sante take you home for me, dear," Adelina pleaded.

Rena relaxed her shoulders and smiled in Mom's direction. "For you, Mrs. Calabresi."

He tried to grab her hand, and she smacked him away, storming out the door.

"Remind you of someone?" Father asked.

"No, should it?"

"Congrats, Son. I know this decision was fast, but I see you already maturing," Father told me, holding my mother's coat up and helping her to gather her things.

"I want you both to come over for dinner soon," Adelina said.

I bent down to hug her and pressed a kiss on her forehead. "Tell McKayla to set something up."

McKayla rolled her eyes, then stomped off to her bedroom. Everyone stopped in surprise that I didn't run after her or get angry.

"Make sure she knows I'm here for her too, Son." Mom held her palm against my chin.

———

The next afternoon.

"He's a fucking liar." I pushed the cell phone call log to Renato.

"What happened?"

"All this time, he's been playing me for a fool."

"How?"

"He has a few contacts within the police."

I told McKayla I wouldn't do anything to her family, but to see these call logs of her father trying to get the police involved wouldn't be ignored.

"You want me to handle him?"

I slumped in my seat. "No."

"You think McKayla will stop talking to you?"

"I can't make her father disappear without causing alarm."

"Says who?"Renato threw the papers back on my desk.

"The entire fallout is giving me a headache."

"Where is she anyway?"

"Shopping with Rena."

"We can have our people tap his calls."

"Do it."

"Her mom?"

I pushed up from the chair and sat forward.

"From what I've learned, she is easily persuaded."

"Most women are."

"McKayla's not most women."

"But your life would be so much easier if she was."

The door opened, and Senior walked in with a glare.

"What?"

"Why am I hearing from your mother about your in-laws?"

"Who told you that?"

"Apparently, McKayla and your mother talk."

"Shit."

"Let things play out, Savio," Senior said.

"And let him put our business on everyone's radar?"

"If you wouldn't have been so rash, this wouldn't be happening," he shouted.

"Spare me the lecture."

"Savio, chill out." Renato shot me a look.

"Take care of what I said."

"What orders?" Senior probed.

"If you hurt her parents, it only will push her away."

"Funny coming from you."

"You speak in this manner as though I'm a stranger."

"Believe me, I know who you are, Father."

"Ugh, here we go." Renato snorted.

"What?"

"No, Renato. He has to learn." Senior pointed at me and turned to leave.

Ring!

"McKayla," I answered the phone.

"Are you still at work?"

"Yeah."

"I was thinking we could do dinner together."

"I can't. I work late."

"Oh."

"Sorry."

"No worries, I'll see if Rena or Marilyn can join me."

"McKayla?"

"Yeah."

"Have you heard from your parents?"

"No, why?"

"Nothing."

"Okay."

"I'll be late, so don't wait up."

"Yeah."

"What did she say?"

"She wanted to have dinner."

"Maybe you should."

"Focus on what I need."

"You're a bigger asshole than me." Renato flipped me off, snatched up the papers, and walked out of my office.

"I get that a lot."

———

Three days later.

"Hey! You can't go back there," the nurse or whatever they call them yelled behind my back.

McKayla was in a somber mood for the past few days, and I tried to take her out for dinner to cheer her up, but deep down, it was her parents who could only make things right. So doing what I did best, I made my presence known at her father's medical practice and stormed through the hallway to his office door.

"What the hell!" her father yelled.

"Mr. Ronan Stanton."

"Get the hell out of my office." Ronan jumped out of his seat and walked into Enzo's chest.

"Take a seat, sir." I sat in his office chair and waited for him to join. "I don't repeat myself, sir."

"Get out of my office before I call the police." Ronan picked up the phone and waited for me to stop him.

"No."

"You might have brainwashed my daughter, but you don't scare me."

I kicked my feet up on his desk. "Make sure you ask for Detective Byron Landers."

His nose scrunched up.

"Take a seat."

Ronan was around the same age as my father, no taller than five seven or eight with a thin build and a small gut hanging over his pants.

"Here's what's going to happen."

Ronan sat in the chair and pushed his glasses up.

"You're going to reach out to McKayla and make amends."

"She disobeyed me and her mother."

"She did, but there's a reason for that. I can't go into detail."

"Is she pregnant?"

"No."

"Did you threaten to hurt her?"

"Not me, but someone else."

"McKayla has never been into trouble, so I'm having a hard time digesting this."

"You can take all the time you need to digest, but when McKayla calls, you answer."

"I know about your family."

"Then you know we take all threats seriously. Don't be an enemy, Mr. Stanton."

"Don't hurt my daughter."

"My wife is safe in my hands."

I stood, came around his desk, and strolled to the door. "I'm taking her out of the country. When we get back, I hope to see her in a better mood."

I shut the door. My men followed me out of the building to the car. I took my cell out of my pocket when I slipped my seatbelt on. "Sante, I want the jet ready for Italy."

"What's going on in Italy?"

"I'm taking McKayla to get away."

"Savio, now isn't the time for a vacation when we have two enemies to worry about."

"That's why you and Elio are in place to handle those situations."

"Not that easy."

"What are you saying?"

"This entire McKayla situation has only added more stress on the workers."

"Tell them we'll add an extra five thousand as a bonus for extra protection."

"Money can't solve everything. Our people are worried."

"Are they worried or you?"

"Savio, save the threats."

"Let me know if you're capable of handling this position."

"Maybe taking a trip will help clear your mind."

"I met with her father, and he's not thrilled with me."

"Did you threaten to kill him?"

"Only time will tell if it works."

"So, you're really starting to feel something for this girl."

"She's a pawn in a bigger play; that's it and nothing more."

I ended the call and shoved the phone in my coat pocket when Enzo arrived at my condo. It was still early in the afternoon. I'd give Marilyn the week off with pay while I was gone.

CHAPTER 16

McKayla

THE SAME DAY.

Knock!

I stood in the kitchen washing the dishes while listening to mellow jazz to get my mind off my parents.

"What are you doing?"

I looked over my shoulder at Savio and shrugged. "Washing dishes."

"Why?" He stepped in the kitchen and stood beside me at the counter.

"Cleaning helps me think."

"I pay Marilyn to clean."

"I gave her the day off."

"You shouldn't have done that."

"Only one day."

"Nothing from your parents?"

"No."

"It's not like they can really cut you out of their lives."

"Do you ever regret anything you've done?"

"Like what?"

"I don't know. Killing, kidnapping, or torture."

"Who says I do those things?"

I dropped the sponge in the sink. "Savio, be honest. You're a mobster."

"I'm a businessman."

"Who gets what he wants by hurting people."

"If that were true, you wouldn't be here."

"I guess you're right."

"Always right."

"Never one to shy away from your ego being enlarged."

"Something tells me your parents will come around soon."

"If they don't?"

"Life has a way of making things happen."

"If that were true, I wouldn't be in this situation."

"Why not go out with Rena?"

"I thought you hated when I went out?"

"I do, but you're not helping yourself being stuck in here thinking about your parents."

"Giving them time."

"Time is something I don't have patience for."

"Is this the businessman or the mob don?"

"Both."

"You admit to being the largest cartel in North America."

"I admit to being the owner of the biggest family-owned business"

"I'll try your way."

"Which is?"

"Making things happen."

———

Later that night, the door opened, and I ended the call. "Hi."

"What are you doing here, McKayla?"

"Mom, I want to talk."

"Your father isn't home."

"Let me explain."

"You're married to a killer."

"Can we talk about this inside?"

"No, leave now." She stepped back and shut the door in my face.

I wiped the tears and headed back to the car.

Savio grasped my hand. "Give them time."

"Easy for you to say."

The car backed out of the driveway and turned left toward the stop sign.

"What can I do?"

"Nothing."

We reached home and parked the car. I jumped out, ran inside, stripped out of my clothes, and slid under the covers.

I felt a hand brush against my face. I groggily moaned and turned over to see Savio sitting on the bed.

"You hungry?"

"Not really."

"Rena called."

"Okay."

"I think you should get out of bed."

"I like the bed."

He snorted.

"My parents have always been there."

"I understand."

"They hate me so much."

I sat up against the headboard, and the comforter fell below my breasts.

"Eventually, they will come around."

Savio caressed my cheek.

"I should call Rena."

"Yeah."

"Okay."

He moved the cover back and helped me out of bed. "Give it a few days and then contact her again."

"Giving them another day will probably have them trying to disown me." I chuckled.

Same night.

I sipped the wine while listening to Rena complain about the latest issues she'd been having with some guy she met at the store.

I looked around at the couples in love and wondered if I would ever experience such a love. Our waitress came and filled our glasses with wine.

"Sorry, my babbling is annoying you."

"Not your fault."

"You wanted a night away from thinking about your parents."

"Savio said to give it time."

"He's right."

We sat in a local restaurant owed by Savio.

"Weird to hear you agree with him."

"I know."

I blew out a breath.

"Lost my appetite.

"Try calling your dad."

"He's working."

"Then let me distract you with my love life." She grinned, started on the latest dating issues.

"Anything new?"

She smiled wiggled her brows.

"Tell me about them."

"Nothing crazy, but a few dates around town."

"I'm glad." I bit my bottom lip.

Rena placed her hand on top of mine. "Hey, things will work out with your folks."

"I hope so."

My world has completed erupted into chaos.

CHAPTER 17

Savio

DAYS LATER.

As our bulletproof car drove through the early morning streets of Italy, McKayla stared at the buildings ahead and behind us.

After I got home and surprised her with the trip, she fell asleep on the plane. When she asked if I really was taking a trip or doing business to cover it up, I felt like lying. I was on a trip for her. It didn't feel good to be ignored and given one-word answers lazily for the past few days. The distance between us was aggravating. Since I had a taste of her, I wanted to take her again, but given the circumstances, she would probably fight me.

The gate opened to our family home as the sun rose,.

I heard a small gasp from her lips in surprise. "This is your home?"

"My family's estate."

"You grew up here?"

"Off and on for the summers and family holidays."

"It's really beautiful."

"My grandparents passed it down to my father and mother."

"Why are you sharing this with me?"

"I have business to take care of out here, and leaving you alone is not an option."

"I stopped running, Savio," she fussed.

The car pulled up in front of the door, and the staff came out to greet us.

"Mr. and Mrs. Calabresi, welcome home," the house manager, Angelina, said.

"Thank you, Angelina. This is my wife, McKayla."

"Hi, nice to meet you," McKayla said.

"You're gorgeous. Mr. Calabresi is a lucky man," Angelina replied and smiled.

"Thank you."

"Come, I'll show you your room. All of the staff is here for your pleasure." Angelina motioned for McKayla and me to come.

"How many square feet is this place?" McKayla's eyes gazed around the front entryway. There were two winding staircases on opposite ends with paintings and artwork, along with statues, displayed around the room. "It looks like a castle."

"Calabresi have held this home in their family for generations," Angelina said.

"I'm surprised people don't get lost."

"Angelina is going to show you to our room. You can freshen up, and then I'll give you a tour, or you can sleep if you're tired."

"Okay."

"Is there anything special, sir, you'd like for breakfast?"

"No, the usual would be fine."

McKayla looked back at me and softly smiled, and I watched her head upstairs to the room Angelina set for us.

———

After breakfast, I took her on a ride on the back of the motorcycle that my mother hated we bought. When I presented the first activity, she pushed the helmet back toward my chest, and I chuckled as she complained about me doing this on purpose to kill her without anyone knowing.

"Hold on to me tight."

"Where are you taking me?"

"Sit tight and shut up."

"Yes, Mr. Calabresi," she teased and slid her arms around my waist.

I started the motorcycle, charged it up, and zoomed out of the front long driveway of the home.

"Aghhh! Slow down."

I laughed and slowed a little at a minimum speed. "You're being overdramatic."

"That's not funny, Savio."

I'd taken her through the local streets of Palermo so she could see what I grew up around and my lifestyle of food and fun from the locals. Enzo was in the car behind us as protection. Even though we were here in our family's country, our enemies were everywhere.

I parked in front of a shop, turned the bike off, and let her get off first. I helped remove her helmet.

"It's beautiful out here."

"We can walk from here."

"I didn't bring my purse."

"Don't insult me, McKayla."

"You're going to leave your bike here?"

"We won't be long. This is a wine market we can check out."

"I love wine."

"Maybe you can find something you like here." I pushed the door open, and old-fashioned Italian music played in the background.

"Mr. Calabresi, you're all set for your visit."

"Thank you, Marco."

McKayla looped her hand in mine, and we walked through the back of the room toward the wine dispensary. They closed for the day to give us a private tour.

"The marble paintings are breathtaking." She rubbed her hand across the stones of the wall.

"Here you go." I handed her a glass of red wine.

"You're not drinking?"

"Driving."

"What are we doing after this?"

"A museum, then we have dinner."

"What's the occasion?"

"Just enjoy the break."

"Can we get in the pool at your house?"

"If that's what you want to do."

McKayla leaned against my shoulder. The tour guide described how the wine company was established in 1945. It was a family-owned company, one that my family invested in, but I wouldn't tell her that part as not to make her feel like this was a setup of some kind.

———

"I hate you!" she screeched when I dunked her in the water and kept her in my hold before letting her go.

She was lounging outside by the pool, wearing a tiny, red thong bikini. She had never showed me what she bought when she went shopping with Rena, but I planned on burning this up when I got home.

Yesterday, we had a long day at the winery, museum, and dinner. So today was mostly chilling inside and getting to know each other better.

"I can add my wife to the list of my enemies now."

"Do you know how long it takes to get my hair back to normal?"

My head cocked at her comment. "Normal?"

"Naturally, my hair is curly."

"What's wrong with that?"

She swam around me. "Takes a long time to get hair straight."

"Why not wear it curly?"

"Because in my business, people won't take me seriously if I look like a nineteen-year-old college student instead of a journalist."

She'd only worn it straight, in a bun, or a ponytail around me. I could understand wanting to be seen in the right manner. "Try wearing your curls naturally."

She swam over to the corner edge of the pool and kicked her feet up. "Men. You have no clue how much work it takes for a woman to look good."

I swam over to her. My men turned their backs and headed to the front entrance of the back door, giving us privacy. I placed both hands on either side of her, closing the distance, and stared into her eyes. "My favorite time of the year is the holidays."

"Why are you telling me this?"

I dropped my hand around her waist, moved it to her ass, and gripped her left cheek. "We should get to know each other better."

"But you said this wasn't love. Right?" McKayla licked her bottom lip.

I darted my eyes down to her chest, slid her bikini top to the side, and noticed her erect nipple. I gritted my teeth, eased my hand around her breasts, and darted my tongue on her sweet pebble. Automatically, her legs wrapped around my waist. Her head fell back, and chest pushed forward for me to take her other breast. I grabbed her legs from around my waist and dropped underwater, holding my breath for a few seconds and swiping my tongue across her.

"Oh, shit!"

I popped up, stuck my finger in her canal, and watched her pretty face drown from my touch. She scrambled to hold onto my shoulders as I pleased her, kissing her neck across her shoulders.

"Can I come? Please, Savio."

"Let's take this to our bedroom."

I lifted her, helped her redress, and grabbed the towel. We walked through the house and took the elevator upstairs to our bedroom.

"The shower."

I smacked her on the ass. She jumped in my arms and passionately kissed me on the lips. I walked us back to the bathroom and locked the door, still holding her in my arms. I released her on her feet, ripped off her bathing suit, and turned on the water. After checking the temperature, I let her step in first and dropped my shorts. My dick sprang up, ready for its home.

"That was my favorite bikini."

"Showed too much skin."

"Ouch!"

I bit her on the shoulder. "Turn around, hands on the wall."

"What are you going to do?"

"Fuck you."

"We had sex last night, and you're still horny?"

"You'll learn about my appetite for sex."

"Are there rules for that too?"

"Rule one is never go to sleep in clothes." I shoved my tongue down her throat.

"Mhmmmmm…"

Her moans made me want to keep that beautiful sound constantly coming out of her whenever we were alone. There was a look her in eyes the first time we had sex, one of hunger, wanting to be dominated and pleased from her heads to her toes.

CHAPTER 18

Savio

"FUCK!" My hard girth pressed at her entrance, and I had to stop myself from moving any further.

"Savio, please… fuck me."

The pleading in her voice stirred my groin. I wrapped my hand tight around her hair and pounded her at a fast pace, giving her what she wanted.

"McKayla… You've made the worst mistake, baby."

"What?"

"You walked into my life."

I picked up the pace as she cried out, trying to hold up on the bathroom wall. I didn't want to come just yet. I jerked out of her and turned her around. Sitting on the edge of the seat in the bathroom, she slid down on my throbbing member. My head dropped down to her chest. She then rotated her hips and fucked me instead of me fucking her.

She bounced on top of me once, then twice, slowed down, and rolled her hips. Her groans filled my heart with such a sweet ache when she whined and threw her head back. I cupped the back of her neck and captured her growl with a hard kiss. My fingertips angled around her throat as our mouths wrapped together in our sexual need. Hearing the unsteadiness of my voice and my balls ready to release, I wasn't ready for this to be over. Running my hands over her breasts, with our hearts pounding, our eyes didn't break contact, and I plunged even deeper.

"What the fuck are you doing?"

"Don't tell me you can't handle me on top," she challenged.

I growled and groped both her ass cheeks, fucking her from the bottom and meeting her thrusts. Our eyes focused on each other, trying to see who would break first. I moved a hand up her neck, holding her in place and easing in and out. She grazed her hand down my chest, and I held onto her tight as the fight for control engulfed us.

———

We were lying in bed hours later after the shower. McKayla had washed her hair and dried it off. Her curls were full and covered her face. She lay on my chest, and I'd planned for us to go out to dinner, but she was slowly going to sleep.

"McKayla."

"Huh."

"We need to get up. We have dinner reservations."

"I want to stay here and sleep."

"Not tonight, princess. I have plans for dinner."

McKayla looked up at me, perplexed. "We didn't use a condom."

"What?"

"In the bathroom. We didn't use a condom." She removed her arms from around my waist, jumped up out of bed, and ran to her bag. "I'm not ready for a baby." McKayla took her birth control out and left to go to the bathroom for a glass of water.

"You feel better?"

"Why are you not freaking out?"

"I never came inside you."

"That doesn't matter, but that brings up a question of children."

"I don't want any." I grabbed my robe, treaded to the closet, and picked out a suit for tonight.

"You mean right now?"

"No, ever."

"But what about what I want?"

"McKayla. Let's go to dinner; nothing else matters."

"I'm not hungry. Have dinner by yourself."

She tried to walk off, and I grasped her elbow. "Stop with the spoiled brat attitude and get dressed."

"When are we leaving?"

"In ten minutes, the car is outside waiting."

"I need to do something to my hair."

"Your hair is fine." I let her go, and she stalked to the bathroom and slammed the door.

Forty minutes later, we were sitting alone out on the top of a hill overlooking the city, with a waitstaff I personally had cater our meals. McKayla was still pissed from the comment I made about not wanting any kids, but I wasn't planning on changing my mind or letting her go.

"What were you like as a little boy?"

"It wouldn't surprise you if I said I was bossy. I took after both my father and mother."

"Your father seems sweet though."

"He's older now and changed over time, but Elio Calabresi Jr. was a killer back in the day."

"Did it ever bother you when you killed someone?"

"No."

"What about the families?"

"The type of business I run, McKayla, you can't have friends."

The waiter brought out our stuffed shells and calamari first.

"Thank you," McKayla said.

"Tell me about your childhood."

"I grew up in the typical American family—two-parent household with loving parents."

"They seem strict."

"They were, but they still let me have a little wiggle room."

"Is that why you're always running now?"

"You never really gave me a good reason to stay."

I paused at her comment, nodded, and grabbed the napkin to eat. "For this to work, we must have honesty."

"I agree, but I told you I wouldn't go to the police."

"It's not just the police."

"Well, besides your other mafia enemies."

"Colombo is after me because of Nevio's death."

"I heard police reports talk about drugs."

"He had our product, which makes me believe he tried to set us up or sell our products behind my back."

"But death shouldn't have been the answer." McKayla grabbed her wine and took a gulp.

"In this business, it has to end in death."

"So why didn't you kill me?"

I paused at her question in thought. "Because you did me a favor when you interrupted Gennaro's plan."

"Oh, now we're getting somewhere."

"I'm not telling you anymore."

"No, you opened the door. Please walk through it, husband." McKayla batted her eyelashes.

I froze at her flirting with me. The light across her face made her look so innocent and sweet. Maybe I was corrupting her and didn't even know how far I was taking things. "Viviana is Gennaro's daughter."

"I remember that."

"She and I used to mess around."

"She's beautiful."

"She's just as corrupt as her father."

"Hard to agree when I'm sitting here with you."

"Different, I know when to let go. Gennaro was forcing my hand and trying to get our families to join forces."

"Wouldn't that put you in a better position?"

"No, because I have an idea that he was planning on killing me once I married his daughter. Only way I was to continue being in charge as Don was to marry."

"Through an arranged marriage."

"Yes."

"Are they both still making decisions in the Five Families?"

"I've talked enough; let's change the subject."

"Fine, when are we going back home?"

"Day after tomorrow."

"This was a short trip."

"I have a charity event and business back home."

"Thank you for inviting me."

"You don't have to thank me."

"When did you lose your virginity?"

I spat my wine out at her question. "McKayla."

She laughed. "What? I was nineteen. Come on, changing the subject, remember."

"I'd rather not say."

"What? Big bad Savio is tongue tied."

"Fifteen," I mumbled.

"Excuse me?"

"I was fifteen."

"Did your parents know?"

"No, only my brothers."

"Who was she?"

"A whore."

This time she spat her drink out and choked. "What did you say?"

"She was a girl I was seeing, and we slept together. Then she cheated."

"Did she break your heart?"

"I don't have a heart."

The rest of the meal of mussels and fettuccine came out, and we continued talking and learning about each other for the rest of the night. We finished off the evening in bed, with her legs wrapped around me, screaming my name.

CHAPTER 19
Savio

TWO WEEKS later

Back home from Italy, I was preoccupied with work while McKayla was still interviewing my father. I'd been summoned by the other heads of the Five Families about me trying to oust Gennaro and get the Maurizio situation swept under the rug. Because things were escalating, I hired more guys to trail McKayla and my family.

The car pulled up to a warehouse that Vincenzo had purchased for us to do business, and I headed in to make sure our product and money were accounted for before I had the sit down.

"What is it looking like?" I asked Elio and Renato.

"The money is here, but our men had trouble in the Colombo area."

"What kind of trouble?"

"His men shot at us," one of our soldiers called out.

"What's your name?"

"Agosto," he replied.

"Did they say anything to you?"

"Just that we aren't going to be paying for much longer," Agosto repeated the words.

I picked up the stack of money from the duffel bag and held it to my nose, then up to the light.

"You're quiet. That's not a good thing," Renato blurted out.

"Colombos are playing with me."

"What are you thinking?"

"This is the same bag I tried to give money to Maurizio a few weeks back."

"You're shitting me." Renato looked through the bag and saw our logo on the inside stitch.

"I want eyes on him when we get to this meeting."

"We have our people on Gennaro. We have to pick and choose our battle, Savio," EJ explained.

"Why don't we just kill his ass?" Renato said.

"Because he's technically a made man. I have enough surrounding me right now."

"Are you going to the meeting?"

"Yeah, I'm already five minutes late."

"I'm riding with you." Renato slid two guns in holsters.

"No, I need you to make sure these guns get shipped out properly and the money counted.

"I don't like this, Savio," Renato said.

"Me neither, but we can't show weakness to our enemies."

"I need to go with you and make sure you stay in your seat."

"Do whatever makes you happy, brother."

We all piled into our cars and pulled out of the warehouse, toward Tommaso's place of business. My trigger finger was ready to release, but another dead body would only put the police on my radar.

Fifteen minutes later, we arrived. I got out of the car, and Elio walked in beside me. Tommaso looked stressed, and Alize was drinking already, which meant something happened or was going to happen.

"Gentlemen." I took a seat next to Elio at the far end.

"Savio, thank you for coming."

"Glad I could accommodate."

"Tell him!" Gennaro shouted.

"Gennaro, I must ask you to behave, or you'll be escorted out," Tommaso said.

"I'm not some fucking child you can dismiss!" Gennaro yelled.

"Could have fooled me."

Gennaro cut his eyes at me. "That bitch of yours has you thinking you're better than us."

"Tommaso, why was this meeting called?"

"Gennaro brought up our last meeting without him and tried to remove him from court."

"It's what's best."

"For whom?" Gennaro shouted.

"Before I continue talking, he's going to have to take a seat or find my fist down his throat." I pointed at Gennaro.

"He has a valid point, Savio."

"Alize, you don't want to do this."

"I understand the situation, but we have a tradition for a reason."

"I'm married and not getting divorced. So, either he can take the money or get out like Colombo."

"You son of a bitch!" Genaro jumped over the table and tried to lunge at me.

I shoved him back, took my gun out, and pointed at this head. "I have three seconds of patience with you and your whore of a daughter."

He tried to charge again, and I shot close to his foot.

"Savio!" everyone screamed in surprise.

We weren't supposed to bring guns in the meetings, let alone shoot at another made boss. As the don over everyone, I didn't give a fuck about rules. My actions spoke for themselves.

"He needs to be stripped and voted out," Gennaro complained.

"I agree with Gennaro. All he's done since he's been the don is cause chaos," Maurizio complained.

"Coming from the guy who's working with the police."

All eyes glanced at Maurizio.

"He's lying." Maurizio waved me off.

"Tell us why Nevio had our product when he was pulled over."

Maurizio tried to charge around Gennaro and get at me. Elio pulled his gun out, took it off the safety, and pushed on the back of his head.

"I'm my brother's keeper. Take one step and let me prove it to you," EJ remarked.

"We all need to put the guns down and talk this through," Tommaso demanded.

"Fuck him." Gennaro jerked out of their hold and stormed out of the room.

"That money he paid you, Maurizio, should count toward a good faith." Tommaso stepped between Maurizio.

He smirked and raised his hands in surrender. Something about his cocky demeanor pissed me off. I had a feeling he was up to something.

"It's going to cost more than five hundred thousand." Maurizio shifted and walked out of the room.

Ring! Ring!

"I'm in a meeting."

"Before you freak out, she's all right."

"Who?"

"McKayla."

I ended the call, gripped the handle of the gun in my hand, and clenched my teeth. Thinking who would be foolish enough to walk a thin line of touching anything that belonged to me.

"What's wrong?" Elio asked.

"We need to go."

———

I pushed the door of the hospital room open, ignoring the nurse's orders as my men put our people in place and checked security in the back and front.

"What room is McKayla Calabresi in?"

"Sir, you can't just walk in here and demand anything."

"Either you give me her room number, or I will find a room for you because you'll be lying right next to hers!"

"Savio!" Sante called out.

I jogged over to him and followed him down the hall to the last room in the back corner. I stopped at the door and calmed my breathing before she saw me go into beast mode.

"She's banged up, but mostly shaken," Sante explained.

"Who did this?"

"I have our people looking into it now."

"I want names, or you don't sleep for the next forty-eight hours."

"I gotcha, Sav."

The sound of the monitor beeping and light tears caused my chest to burn in agony. For someone who didn't willingly come to me by choice, over time I'd learned to see all her faults and what made her special.

"Get out," McKayla said.

"Savio, where have you been?" Adelina questioned, holding McKayla's hand.

"McKayla."

"No, I want you to leave." Her monitor started beeping fast as I approached her bed.

A nurse burst through the door. "Sir, I'm going to have to ask you to leave."

"She's my wife."

"I don't want him in here," McKayla begged, and my jaw twitched.

"Savio." Adelina came around the hospital bed and pulled me to the door.

"I'm not leaving."

"Just for tonight, Son."

"She's not thinking clearly."

"I understand, Savio, but she's been through something traumatic."

"And I can help."

"Not when you're the cause of the trauma, Son."

"Fuck!"

"Hey! You need to leave, or I'm calling the police." The nurse pointed in my face.

"He's going to leave," Adelina said.

"McKayla."

She turned her back to me, and the door opened again. Rena walked in with food and a somber look on her face.

"This isn't over," I said and stormed out of the room. Sante directed our men to stand guard. "What did she say?" I asked.

"That she and Rena were driving back from work and out of nowhere, someone shot at them."

"Son a bitch. Who? Gennaro?"

"Could be or Maurizio."

"Maurizio wouldn't be this sloppy."

"I agree with you on that."

"Any police?"

"Since it was on a busy street, yeah, our men were questioned."

"Anybody talk?"

"No, of course not."

"All right, keep me updated."

"Where are you going?"

"Getting back to McKayla."

"Savio, her words to you were to stay away."

"She's confused."

"Go home. I'll stay up here and report back."

"I can't just leave her here."

"You really care about her."

"She's under my protection, Sante."

"There are deeper reasons than your willingness to acknowledge."

I dismissed his comment. "No one goes in her room without you approving."

"I know."

"The second she asks for me…"

"I'll call you."

"Keep Renato updated and text me if she needs anything."

"Go find out who did this."

"They want the beast to come out."

"Are you going to the dinner for the families?"

"I have to. If not, they'll know something is wrong."

"McKayla won't be up for it probably."

"We'll decide when the time comes."

"Just remember she's your wife."

"I've tried to forget and can't get her out of my head."

CHAPTER 20

McKayla

A FEW HOURS prior to the hospital.

"What's the latest on the government oversight report?" Joseph inquired from Gabby.

We had a staff meeting early, and Savio would still only let me go to work in the office in small doses. Other than that, I had to work from home. I had a meeting scheduled with his father to finish going over everything we had planned for the article and book. Even the cover was coming together in what he envisioned.

"I have everything ready for press. I wasn't getting anywhere with the oversight board," Gabby spoke.

"Try Linda on the third-floor human resources," Joseph said.

"How can she help?"

"She owes us a favor," Joseph explained.

Gabby smiled in delight and printed her name.

"Rena, what's going on with the reports on entertainment and celebrity?"

"I have the fashion column finished from the latest award show," Rena replied.

"Did you get comments?"

"Yes, and some stylists asked to be quoted."

"No time for that."

"It can't hurt, Joseph," Rena responded.

All eyes turned to Joseph. "McKayla, what's going on with you and Rory?"

"Um, well."

"She hasn't worked with me, sir," Rory blurted out.

Joseph's eyes darted toward me.

"That's because my piece is almost done."

"How much?" Joseph questioned.

"Two more questions, and then it's being written up for you."

"I specifically asked you to work with Rory." Joseph dropped his pen and notepad on the table and leaned back in his chair.

"Joseph, everyone knows Rory would never get anywhere near the Calabresi family."

"Yeah, because you're sleeping with the leader."

A few people murmured in a hushed tone when Rory muttered under his breath.

As I cleared my throat, I rested upright in the chair and glared at him.

"My personal life has nothing to do with my job," I lied. It wouldn't make it easier if I explained the reasons for Savio and me getting married. I didn't care for him, but I didn't want to get him hurt because of my actions.

"Time is slipping away, so I need everything on my desk immediately," Joseph demanded.

"But Joseph—"

He cut me off. "Either you have it on my desk or turn everything over to Rory."

"I understand."

"All right. Meeting adjourned. Go find the story; don't let it find you."

Everybody stood. Rena came into eyesight, rubbing my

arm. "Joseph's trying to throw his weight around; don't let him get to you." She bumped my hip and wrapped her arms around me in comfort.

"Ugh… Maybe I should give up the story."

"What! No! You've come too far."

As I walked to my desk, I tossed my notebooks on top. Rory walked out of the conference room, talking shit when a few people pointed at me.

"How about I treat you to lunch? Forget about him and Joseph," Rena offered.

"I'm going to head home for the day."

"Lunch first, then you can go home."

"Enzo can bring you back up here."

Rena stepped over to her desk and picked up her jacket and keys as I packed up to leave. "Is Enzo single?"

"I'm in enough drama. Please don't go there."

Her head swung back in laughter.

I pushed the front entrance door open and stepped off the curb to get in the waiting SUV that Savio demanded I ride around in when he wasn't with me.

"Have you talked to your parents?"

"Not since I've been back from Italy. I plan on calling one more time today." I buckled my seatbelt and closed the door.

"I know your parents love you. They'll come around."

The car pulled into traffic, and we chatted about my trip with Savio when suddenly, a loud pop was heard.

"What was that?"

Bang!

"Agh!"

The car swerved left and right.

"Hold on!" The passenger window rolled down, and they started shooting.

"Shit! They're shooting at us!" Rena screamed.

"Oh, my God!"

"Get down!" my bodyguard shouted.

Pop! Pop!

I closed my eyes, and the first thing that flashed before them was Savio and I in Italy. Then I prayed my family would be okay. I know I'd disappointed them, but I hoped this wouldn't cause more heartache and distance.

———

Present time.

I tried to sit up in the hospital bed, but I was too sore to even lift my arm. Adelina and Rena were chatting when the nurse came back in to check my vitals.

"How are you feeling?" she asked.

"Sore, sleepy." I tried to reach for the cup of water.

"Let me get that for you," Adelina said.

I was grateful she came when everything happened. Savio stormed in like a rampage, demanding to see me. I'd never been in this type of position. The sounds of the tires screeching, the windows blowing out. Then I woke up with a bandage on my head, and my arm and ribs were attached to monitors.

"Are you hungry, dear?" the nurse asked.

"Yeah."

"I'll grab you something. This hospital food is drab." Rena stood, stretched her arms, and strolled over to hug me.

"Adelina, you don't have to stay."

"I promised Savio."

I rolled my eyes at hearing his name brought up.

"I can see in your eyes, you're angry with him," Adelina said.

"My life was simple before him."

"Your life is different, I understand." Adelina covered my palm.

"I want a divorce."

Rena and Adelina locked eyes.

"Get some food in your stomach and rest." Rena tapped my leg and walked out.

"Did my parents come by?" I questioned.

"Yes, earlier when you were brought in." Adelina poured more water in my cup.

"I'll call them tomorrow."

The cell phone on top of the desk in the corner of the room vibrated.

"It's probably Savio," Adelina said.

"Can you turn it off?"

"He probably wants to know if you're doing okay."

"I just need space."

"Well, get some rest."

———

After eating, I dozed off and woke up bright and early to more yelling the next day.

"Sir, you are blocked from entering her room."

"Either you move out of my way, or you'll find your family gone in the blink of a phone call."

"What's going on here?" I heard Adelina ask.

"He's on a list to not be around, Mrs. Calabresi," the nurse explained.

"You hit the nail. Mrs. Calabresi. My *wife*. Now get the fuck out my way," Savio growled.

Sante held him back, and the nurse held her hand up in shock and walked back around the desk.

"Savio!" I shouted, trying to get out of the bed.

"McKayla, sit down. It's okay." Adelina walked in and dropped a bag of food on the counter, then helped me get back in bed.

"McKayla, listen to me." Savio tried to talk to me, but I blew him off.

"McKayla, just listen please," Adelina pleaded.

I looked from Adelina to Savio and sighed. "Fine, talk."

"Whoever did this to you will pay."

"You did this to me."

Clenching his jaw, he tried to hide his anger.

"When can I leave?"

"The doctor said you can come home today," Savio answered.

"I'm going to my apartment."

"No."

"Yes."

"Okay, you two. Stop it. This isn't helping," Adelina barked.

`We exchanged glares.

"I can take care of myself."

`Savio bent down, cupped my chin, and pecked my lips. "I'll have the car brought around."

CHAPTER 21

Savio

Tonight was the night the Five Families and other mafia associates came dressed in ball gowns to show off who was the best and throw money around. At the end of the event, the money went to a charity that we all agreed upon at the beginning of the year. Some people would call us hypocrites because we dealt with drugs, guns, and murder.

McKayla seemed to be in a better mood since the accident. She wasn't ignoring me as she normally would. But the tension was still high, and I tried to give her a little more space without crowding her.

"How much did the dress cost?"

"A thousand dollars."

"Rena must have picked it out."

"Is that a problem?"

She wore a tight-fitting black gown with a split on the side. Her breasts spilled out, looking succulent and ready for me to devour.

"Savio. Nice to see you this evening," Alize approached and cut me off before I could answer.

"Alize."

"Is this your wife?"

McKayla reached out to shake hands.

Alize grinned and kissed the back of her hand. "You're extremely gorgeous, Mrs. Calabresi."

"Alize, if you want to keep your hand, I suggest you release hers."

"He's so possessive. What's your name?" McKayla smiled back at Alize.

I sensed the shift in her mood, and she was going to make the beast come out with her flirting.

"I'm Alize Brambilla, one of the mob bosses."

"Do you throw this event every year?" McKayla's reporter instincts were coming out.

"We do," Alize replied.

"There's a lot of people here. Where's your wife."

"She's powdering her nose."

"She's a lucky woman," McKayla quipped and sipped on her champagne glass.

I grabbed McKayla's hand, pulled her close to my side, and whispered in her ear, "I wouldn't get too comfortable trying to piss me off."

"I would never try to piss you off, dear," McKayla gritted through her teeth.

"Let's dance." I turned her into my chest, lowered my hands to her back, and pushed her into my groin. I heard her moan lowly. "You feel that?"

"No."

"Not the right answer."

She tried to shove me away, but I pressed a kiss on the side of her neck.

"Well, isn't this cute?" The voice of Viviana caught my attention, and I saw her standing with her friends.

"What are you doing here, Viviana?"

I moved McKayla behind me, and she pushed my hand away.

"Oh, looks like trouble in paradise," Viviana joked.

"Savio, you're making the biggest mistake of your life. Viviana is way better looking," her friend said.

"Yeah, Viviana understands our world," the blonde said.

"She can have him," McKayla mumbled and tried to walk off. I yanked her back.

"Obviously, she's not tough enough to handle you." Viviana blew a kiss at me.

"I should be asking where you were when my wife was in the hospital."

Viviana giggled, tossing her hair back.

"Making plans for us." Viviana tried to touch my chest.

McKayla listened to me go off about Viviana's bullshit. Her friends tried to move in closer. McKayla grabbed my arm.

"McKayla, hold on."

"She's threatened by me," Viviana said.

"Who?"

"Your little tramp," Viviana spat.

"It's fine," McKayla said.

I nodded for the guards to move in closer. "What do you want, Viviana?"

"You think because he allows you at his home, you're winning," Viviana fussed, pointing her finger at McKayla.

"Okay," McKayla answered.

"After your little affair, what did you think would happen?" Viviana's friend questioned.

"I'm not sure what you're asking," McKayla replied.

"He might fuck you, but he's thinking of me," Viviana growled.

"Well, if he wanted you—"

I raised my hand to cut McKayla off.

"I want Savio back," Viviana responded.

"If he wanted you, he'd be with you, right?"

The scowl on her face increased.

"Or I could kill you," I said.

"So, you'd kill me because of her." Viviana gasped.

"Business."

"No, you're not fully aware of your emotional state, and I'm guessing Savio specifically stated he'd never be with you."

"Trying to use your journalist ways on me?"

"You can go."

"I'll leave when I'm ready."

She started to walk up to us.

"My guard will kill you the moment you touch her."

"Fuck you and that guard." Viviana sassed.

"She's behind the crash?" McKayla wondered.

"Either her or her father."

"I don't need to kill her to know I'm better for you than her," Viviana commented.

McKayla threw her drink at Viviana.

"Bitch!" Viviana lunged at McKayla.

My men blocked her and shoved her back.

"This isn't over," Viviana's girlfriend spat.

"Escort them out."

"What? We paid just like everyone else," Viviana complained.

"The charity sends their thank yous."

"Does your wife know we had sex a few weeks ago?" Viviana shouted.

The crowd stopped talking and glanced at the commotion.

"The last time I slept with you was over a year ago, and you still couldn't suck dick."

"Bastard!" Viviana tried to charge at me.

McKayla walked off, and I went to follow her before she tried to leave.

"Boss," my guard called out.

"Keep the music playing. Make sure they're kicked out." I motioned to Viviana and her cackle of friends.

"I need to use the bathroom," McKayla complained when I marched in with her.

"Hey, this is the woman's bathroom," a girl screeched.

"Get out."

"But—"

McKayla rubbed her temples, and I waited for the woman to wash her hands and leave.

"You're such a jerk." McKayla turned to look at herself in the mirror.

I walked up behind her and stared at us in the mirror. "I don't like you flirting with other men to make me jealous."

"Since when do you care?"

I placed both hands on her hips, pressed up on her ass, and watched her bottom lip tremble. "What makes you think I don't care?"

"When is this going to be over?" She opened her eyes and looked at me.

"Never."

I reached around, extended my hand around her neck, and pulled her back up to my chest. The other hand went down to her naked thigh, and I slid my finger over her thong.

"Savio… not here."

Slowly, I teased her pussy lips and glided my finger across her as I nibbled on her bottom lip.

"Oh…"

"What was that?"

"I… I… think we should… wait."

"Do you want me to fuck you?"

The bathroom door opened, and I turned my head. "Get the fuck out!"

"Sorry!" A woman quickly ran back out.

I shoved her forward and raised her dress up around her waist.

"Hold onto the counter."

She spread her legs automatically.

Smack!

"Aghhhh!"

Smack!

"Shit!"

I dropped to one knee, sucked on her pussy, then rubbed the sting in her left cheek that I spanked.

"Ahhh… God!" she cried out when I slid my tongue in her asshole.

"She's wet, warm, ready for me," I taunted, stood back, and unbuckled my pants.

"Wait, lock the door."

She was right. I didn't want anyone seeing her sweet ass. This belonged to only me. I marched to the door, looked out, and saw my men talking amongst themselves. "Watch this door."

They nodded in response, and I locked it, then got back to pleasing McKayla.

"Hurry up," she pleaded.

"I give the orders." My pants dropped to the floor.

I wrapped a hand around her neck and thrust into her fast. Her head fell back. I sucked on her neck, then her lips. I pumped hard and fast, losing all my control as the beast was awakened.

"Yesss… Baby." Her back arched even more and my girth drowned in her juices.

"Don't you dare touch yourself," I demanded when I saw her try to ease herself with her hand.

"Make me come."

"You will when I say so." I circled my hips, playing with her clit.

"Right there."

"Fuck! She has a grip on me, baby."

"Come in me," she told me.

The flood gates opened. I filled her up with my seed. I didn't hesitate, and that was a problem. I was always firm about not having sex without a condom.

"Arghhh… Savio."

We both came, and I eased out, picked up my pants. She cleaned herself up, then handed me a wet paper towel. We were still in shock over what we'd just done.

———

The next day, I had a meeting with Sante, Elio, and Renato to go over the car crash evidence. I'd left McKayla at home, asleep in bed.

"I heard Viviana showed up," Renato probed.

"She did, with her pack of clowns."

"That was probably to throw you off."

"What do you mean?"

"I find it interesting that a few days after your wife ends up in a shootout, Viviana pops up," Sante said.

I nodded, rubbing my chin in thought. "See where she was that day."

"I already know. She was out shopping," Renato replied.

"Gennaro is behind it, I know."

"At this point, it could be all of them," EJ blurted out.

"You don't like the way I conduct my business?"

"As your brother, I will always have your back, but this has gotten messy."

"You're right."

"Let her go."

"So, Maurizio and Gennaro can kill her. Then I'm put back with a target on my back."

"Our family is too strong to be pushed out," EJ remarked.

"That's because I made it that way."

"Savio, you're playing a dangerous game and almost got that girl killed, plus our men."

"A little danger can be exciting."

"What's going on with her parents?" Sante shoved a stack of photos in my direction.

"What's this?"

"The drugs and guns went out through Colombo areas with another shootout."

"He thinks we're bluffing."

"We need to pay him," Sante said.

"I gave him half a million."

"It's out of respect, Savio," EJ told me.

"What do you think, Renato?"

Renato cleaned his guns, watching all three of us. "Kill them."

"We've done enough of that. Why even bring Renato in this?" EJ asked.

"Because, little brother, I'm the best at what I do." Renato smirked, kissing his gun.

"Trigger happy," Sante joked.

"Keep an eye on them, Renato."

"Did you tell McKayla about dinner with the family?" Sante questioned.

"I've been too wrapped up in other things to even remember."

"It's coming up."

"She wants her parents there," Sante said.

My left brow lifted in surprise. "Tell her no."

"No one disobeys Adelina Calabresi."

"I wish she'd find a hobby."

"Like you with kidnapping and marrying innocent women?"

"Fuck you."

"The dinner shouldn't be that bad."

"Is Rena coming?" EJ directed his eyes at Sante.

"How would I know?" Sante responded.

"Just asked a question," EJ said.

"Any more news about the Nevio case?"

"We've been able to suppress any mention of you, but you need to still lay low," Sante said.

"The car crash and shootout could have blown everything up," EJ told.

"We have contacts on the force," Renato reminded me.

"Yeah, for extreme emergencies, not your brother fucking up because of a girl," EJ complained.

"Elio," I groaned.

"Either you want me to give to you real or not. I'm not your flunkies," EJ said.

"If Maurizio's men make another move, shut them down." I stood, buttoning my jacket.

"Savio." Sante rose and stood in front of me.

"I'm done being nice."

CHAPTER 22

McKayla

"I CAN SEE if he wants to have dinner." I pushed my file folders in my backpack, logged out of the computer, and headed out of the library.

"Excuse me," a voice called out.

I turned, and a tall man in a suit held a book in his hand.

"I think you dropped this."

I glanced at the book in his hand, then gazed up at the smile on his face. "That's not my book."

"Who is that?" Rena questioned on the other line of the phone.

"You caught me. I was thinking of how I could come talk to you."

"Talk to me?" I pointed at myself.

"I saw you in there and wanted to approach you, but you seemed in work mode."

"McKayla!" Rena yelled and brought me back to the conversation.

"Sorry, Rena." My phone got snatched out of my hand and ended the call.

"She's unavailable." Savio stepped in front of me.

"Um, sorry. I didn't know," the guy said.

"Now you do." Savio stared him down.

The guy looked behind Savio at me. Savio growled.

"I should go." He headed to leave.

"Take the other exit," Savio stated.

"Savio!"

"You out here flirting in my men's face."

"What?"

"I have work to do. We need to get going."

"Give me my phone back."

He held it out, and I reached to take it back. He snatched it away. It started to ring, and I knew it was Rena.

"Keep playing games."

"I'm not playing games."

Savio passed the phone back to me.

"Where are you coming from?"

"Eh-Eh."

I followed him down the stairs to the town car. "What does that mean?"

"You're asking too many questions."

"I'm just asking about your day."

"Normal day like you, McKayla."

Ring!

"Rena's going to kill me." I climbed into the car.

"She'll be fine."

"Did Marilyn cook?" I changed the subject.

"I don't know."

"Do your other girlfriends make you jealous?" I gazed into his smoldering, deep-blue eyes.

"If I had girlfriends, they'd behave better than you."

"How so?"

The car drove into traffic.

Ring!

"You should answer her."

I caught his grin and smiled back.

Later that evening as I finished work, Savio demanded I

come with him to a restaurant that was holding a dinner for a few men associated with the mob.

"Gentlemen, I want to thank you all for coming." Savio held his glass up for a toast.

Supposedly, this was a business dinner, and wives and girlfriends had to show up, so he made me dress up and stick around a bunch of killers.

"To the Calabreses!" A younger man clapped his hands.

"Carmine." Savio held his hand out for a shake.

"I wondered when you would bring us all together."

I drank the champagne and smiled.

"Where have you been keeping this one, Savio?"

Carmine smirked at me. Savio didn't try to hide his glare.

"McKayla," I said.

"McKayla. Beautiful name for a beautiful woman," Carmine responded.

"Thank you."

"Would you excuse me, Carmine? I need to talk to McKayla."

"Of course." Carmine walked backward, turned, and headed to a group of men.

Savio wiped his lips. "You having fun?"

"Mmm… huh."

"Carmine works for one of the other Five Families."

"Why am I here?"

"I needed a date."

"I thought you didn't date."

"Change of plans."

"Is this some kind of mob family get together?" I asked.

Savio looked at the men talking to each other. "Business."

"Some of the wives have ignored me."

"Well, do you blame them?" Savio asked.

"Rena said it would be perfect for tonight."

"I like the dress."

I ran a hand down the silky red short dress that crossed in the front with a low cut in the back. "Surprised you noticed with the way these women are gawking at you."

"Let's dance." Savio closed the space between us, placed his hand around my waist, and slid his other hand to my waist.

"You smell good." I extended my arm around his neck.

Savio lingered his fingers across my arm. "Are you flirting with me, McKayla?"

Renato approached us. "You two look like you're about to fuck each other."

"Shut up, Renato," we both answered at the same time.

The next day.

I was home listening to music while typing on the computer and eating spicy chicken and rice that Marilyn made. I was relaxed in only my shorts and half t-shirt with my curls out, busting through the notes I had left to go over with Mr. Calabresi.

The front door shut, and Savio stalked in holding a briefcase, looking like a Greek god in a grey double-breasted suit. "Get dressed."

"What?' I dropped the fork on the plate.

"We're going to dinner."

"With whom?"

"Our families."

"What? When?" I jumped out of the chair and followed him upstairs to his bedroom.

"Tonight."

He removed his jacket, went to the walk-in closet, and shuffled through some dresses. I had a few items in his closet, but not by choice. Whenever I tried to sleep in my bedroom,

I'd find myself waking up in his arms in his bedroom. So, I stopped fighting on trying to keep independence. Even when I was mad, he'd still only give me an arm's length of space.

"I'm not in the family dinner type of mood, Savio."

"Well, either you can stay here and have my mother send out a team to drag you over, or you can get dressed and pretend to be happy."

"When did this dinner come about?"

"It doesn't matter." He dropped a few dresses on the bed.

I stood my ground near the entrance of the door with my hands on my hips. "Can I get a smidgen of honestly from you?"

"McKayla, this wasn't my idea."

"I'm just getting back good with my parents. I don't know if this dinner will work."

"Good thing I was able to make that happen."

"Cocky much?"

"Just my nature, princess." He smacked me on the ass.

"How long do I have?"

"Thirty minutes."

"Thirty minutes! Savio, I need more time."

"You're wasting time." He grabbed a pair of black slacks and a white shirt.

"Fucking crazy," I muttered, heading to the bathroom to get dressed.

Thirty minutes later, we piled in the car and headed over to his family home. I thought about how my parents would react to sitting down with a crime family. I put on simple makeup of lip-gloss and blush.

"Rena should be here."

"How did you make that happen?"

"Thank my mom."

"Please try to keep the details of our arrangement to

yourself." I checked my hair in the mirror as the car stopped in front of the gate.

"I need to tell you something," Savio said.

"What?"

The gate opened, and the car rode up to a stack of cars parked.

"It can wait." Savio pushed the door open.

I scooted over, and he helped me out of the car. I checked my dress was decent and not revealing. I went with a long, wool, black shirt dress and ankle boots with my hair down in curls.

"Mr. Calabresi, welcome again. Everyone is in the dining room talking," the butler told us, holding the door open.

"Hello, thank you." I greeted with a smile.

Savio put his hand on my lower back and escorted me to the dining room. We heard conversation and a little arguing. I prayed it wasn't my parents.

"Leave me alone," Rena snapped at Sante.

"What's going on here?" Savio questioned.

"Your friend is playing a dangerous game," Sante said.

"Rena."

"He's a bigger jerk than you, Savio. Acting like I can't talk to my friend Renato," Rena flirted and winked at Renato.

"Sante, leave her alone," Adelina commanded.

"Tell that to Renato," Sante fussed.

Rena giggled, switched over to me, and clasped her hand in mine.

"Rena, what are you doing?"

She walked me out of the dining room to the hallway. "Nothing, just having a little fun."

"Where are my parents?"

"With Mr. Calabresi."

"Wait, in his office?"

"Yeah, don't worry."

"How can you say don't worry?" I started to march to his office.

Rena jumped in front of me. "Relax, have a cocktail. I love your hair like this." Rena ran her hand through my hair.

I drank her martini. "I need something harder."

"You never wear your hair out."

"Savio mentioned me wearing my hair different."

"Hmmm."

"What does that mean?" I jerked my head back.

"Nothing, I just find it interesting."

"Don't think anything more than what it is please."

"I like his brothers, except Sante."

"I wonder why."

"McKayla!" Savio called my name.

"Yes."

"We're about to eat," Savio said.

"Okay, I'm coming."

"McKayla." I heard my dad's voice. "I want to talk to you alone," he said and looked over at Savio.

I was curious about that stare but would question Savio later. "Okay."

"You can use my office, McKayla," Mr. Calabresi offered.

"Thank you, Mr. Calabresi."

"Call me if you need me." Rena hugged me, then took the glass out of my hands.

I followed my father and mother back into Mr. Calabresi's office.

"How are you?" Missy looked like she wanted to be anywhere but here.

"I'm good."

"Do they know who's behind your accident?" Dad asked.

"I have no clue." I stood near the door, and they sat on the couch.

"We'll never agree to this marriage."

"I know."

"Do you love him?" Mom asked.

"It's something I can't explain."

"He came to my office," Dad told me.

"When?"

"A while back, and basically threatened me," Dad explained.

I grew hot and flushed. Savio promised he wouldn't threaten anyone in my life again.

"It was about cutting you off, and how you've been upset," Dad mentioned.

Once I came to understand the actions taken by Savio, my anger dissolved. It was a little annoying when he went overboard with the conversation. Nevertheless, I had to bear in mind that he came from a background of threats.

"I miss you both."

"You're our daughter, so tell us what's going on," Mom said.

"I saw—"

"McKayla," Savio cut me off and busted through the door.

"We'll have lunch and catch up soon," Mom said.

"I'd like that."

"Dinner's ready." Savio extended his hand, and I smiled in answer.

———

"Mr. and Mrs. Stanton, how long have you been married?" Adelina asked.

"Over twenty years," Mom replied.

"Elio and I have over thirty years. We're in for the long haul," Adelina commented.

"Adelina, your home is beautiful," Rena blurted out and cut into her steak.

"Do you see yourself getting married, Rena?"

"God, no. McKayla is the only one who can put up with a husband." Rena laughed.

I giggled at her statement, then tensed up when I felt Savio's hand on my exposed thigh.

"I wish all my boys would get married." Adelina pointed at her sons.

All of them groaned in annoyance.

"Leave my wife alone," Elio Sr. said.

"Control your wife," Renato quipped.

"Savio, you're the oldest, right?" Mom probed.

"He's my first baby boy." Adelina reached over the table and covered Savio's hand.

"Stubborn boy," Elio Sr. joked.

"McKayla is doing a story on your family, correct?" Dad asked.

"She's going to probably get a Pulitzer for the article," Rena implied.

I grunted, kicking her leg next to me.

"Fuck!" she blurted.

"Nothing fancy, Dad."

Savio's hand gripped my thigh.

"Well, I'm ready for grandbabies, so hopefully, my other boys will hurry up and get married."

"I'd love to see McKayla as a mom," Rena cheered and raised her glass.

"You've had enough drinks for the night." I grabbed the martini glass from her hand.

"Maybe I'll give a baby to Renato." Rena laughed.

Sante jumped up out of the chair and charged at Renato.

All hell broke loose, and dishes went flying across the table as Savio and Elio tried to break them up.

"Sante!" Adelina shouted, and Mr. Calabresi shook his head in disappointment, pulling his wife back.

———

The car was quiet as we drove home from his parents' house. Rena sat in the corner, texting angrily on her phone. The way she behaved tonight shocked me. Normally, she was goofy and funny, but tonight, she seemed to be all about antagonizing and overdrinking.

"Rena, is there something you need to talk about?"

"No. Why do you ask?"

"Just curious."

"I'm fine, McKayla. I just had too many drinks."

Savio scoffed.

"Savio."

"McKayla, you can pacify your friend all you want, but she disrespected my family," Savio argued.

"Can we discuss this later?"

"Look, I apologize. I just had too many drinks," Rena begged.

We made it to her apartment, the passenger side door opened, and she started to get out.

"Call me later."

"I will. Be safe."

"What did your parents say?"

"I was going to ask you the same thing."

He turned to me. "Explain."

"My father said you came to his office."

"I did my job, normally more or less."

"What's your job?"

"The less enemies I have the better."

"How long will I be an enemy of yours, Savio? I think I've proven how loyal I am."

"McKayla, I've had a long day and night."

"You're dismissing me again."

"No, I want a peaceful night without all the questioning."

"Is Rena sleeping with Sante or Renato?"

"Why would I know that?"

"You know everything, don't you?"

His eyes narrowed in lust, and he closed the distance between us and slammed his lips on mine. "The only thing I need to be concerned with is you."

CHAPTER 23

McKayla

THE WEEKEND WAS ALMOST HERE, and this was the last day I would try to meet with Rory and go over any notes. I thought it would be easier if I met him at the office rather than his home, so there would be less trouble with Savio. He put me in another bulletproof, black-tinted Range Rover with additional guards driving alongside and behind us. For the first time ever, I understood where he was coming from.

"Shit!" the guard said.

"What's wrong?" I looked out the back window.

I was praying it wasn't another shootout.

"Don't say anything."

"Call Enzo," I told him.

"I can handle this," Agosto said.

He was brought in as additional security from what Savio talked about.

"Maybe we should call Savio."

"Boss doesn't need to worry about this," Agosto explained.

The window rolled down, and a police officer held the flashlight through the window.

"Can you tell me why I was pulled over?" Agosto asked.

"Get out of the car," the officer said.

"You are making a big mistake."

"Either you get out, or I can drag you out."

"Don't say anything, Mrs. Calabresi." Agosto went to open the door, and the officer hit him on the head with the flashlight. "Arghhh!"

"Hey! What are you doing?" I screamed as I jumped out of the car, and he pushed me up against the side door.

"Shut the fuck up!" the officer shouted.

"Look, we don't want no trouble," Agosto said.

"My men are back there."

"They've already been locked up." The officer smirked.

My mouth opened and closed. "You can't do this."

"I will tell that to your husband." He put handcuffs around my wrists and yanked me off the door, along with Agosto, and put us in separate cars. My purse with my phone and notes were in the car.

"Don't talk, McKayla!" Agosto shouted.

The officer punched him in the jaw and stomach.

"Stop!" I yelled to bring attention, but no one stopped.

He pushed me in the back of the car. Tears welled in my eyes from the humiliation. As soon as I thought things were calming down, more drama came out.

———

The light flickered in the interrogation room. My mouth felt dry from repeating myself. I wanted to shout, beat, and kick this arrogant son of a bitch for thinking he could break me. From dealing with Savio Calabresi, the last thing I needed was another man trying to belittle me.

"Who are you running drugs for?" he asked.

"Officer Harris, I've said for the hundredth time, I don't run drugs."

"I don't believe you. You have a pretty face and body."

"I'm a reporter with a very important news organization."

"You're married to Savio Calabresi."

"That's none of your business."

"He's the don of the Calabresi family."

"He's a business owner," I half-lied.

"Do you know how many deaths he's ordered?"

"I think you're misplacing your anger onto me."

"I think I have the correct person."

"I want to talk to my lawyer."

"Do you know about the killing of Nevio from the Colombo family?"

"Like I said, I'm a reporter."

"I can keep you here all night."

"Where's my lawyer?"

"Bitch. You think you're smarter than me?" he barked.

"I know I am."

He slammed his hand on the desk. "Look at these photos outside of Sanctuary nightclub that your husband owns." He pushed them across the desk.

"I don't know anything about this place."

"Funny because this camera took a shot of you and another woman entering."

"So?" I pushed them back toward him.

"There's also a shot of Nevio and your husband entering that night."

"Then you should speak with him."

"How much is he paying you? Or did he threaten you?"

A flicker of doubt entered my brain that this was a test.

"That's it, he threatened you? We can protect you."

"I want my phone call."

"Too bad. A girl like you could have been some use to us."

The door burst open, and Rena walked in with my mom and another officer.

"McKayla, are you all right" Rena asked.

"I'm fine."

"She's free to go," the officer told Harris.

"She'll be back. Savio can never keep them." Harris chuckled, and I glared at him.

"Let's go, honey." Mom passed over my purse.

I saw over twenty missed texts. "How did you know I was here?"

"Enzo got a call from Agosto, and they told Savio," Rena explained.

"Is he here?"

"Outside. He didn't want to come in and cause a bigger issue."

"Are you hurt?" Mom inquired.

"No, they just kept asking me the same questions over and over again." I pushed the door open, blocked out the sun, and saw the black stretch limo parked out front. "I'm going home with you, Rena."

"McKayla, you know he'll go crazy and force you back to his place."

I sighed and paused before taking a step forward, and the door started to open. I knew he would freak out if I didn't come right to him. "You're right, Rena. Thanks, Mom. I'll call you later."

"Be safe, baby." Mom kissed me on the forehead.

Enzo stood at the car door and held it for me to slide in. I thanked him and fastened my seatbelt.

"Did they touch you?"

"No."

"I apologize for leaving you in there."

"They have photos."

"What photos?"

"Of me, Rena, and Nevio entering the club."

"They must have had help."

"Why are you hanging onto me, Savio, if you can't protect me?"

His eyes met mine. "Can't protect you? Is that what you think?"

"It's how I feel."

"You don't understand."

"Then help me to understand!"

"You're a pawn, McKayla! That's it. Maurizio set this up to show he can touch you."

"I don't care about your games!"

"Baby, we're long past that."

"I need a bath and food. Just take me home."

"I'll make this right."

"Something tells me this won't be the last time you have to make up for me getting hurt."

———

Once I got out of the shower, I blew dry my hair and curled up with a blanket in my room, watching TV. My head was still hurting from a migraine and then the argument with Savio, and I wasn't in the mood for any company.

It was late afternoon, and Marilyn had cooked spaghetti, roast beef, and salad to avoid me ordering out. Savio was up in his office somewhere, and we hadn't spoken since we got out of the car a few hours ago.

"Mrs. Calabresi." Marilyn knocked.

"Come in, Marilyn."

"I wanted to check on you before I go tonight."

"I'm fine, thank you."

"I have the food wrapped up if you get hungry."

"Thanks, but I'm still working off the first plate."

"If you need to talk, I'm here for you."

"I know, thank you."

"Sure. Mr. Calabresi is still in his office."

"Okay, thank you."

"Good night."

"Good night."

I picked up the remote, flicked through the channels, and heard the door shut. Already restless, I wasn't in the mood to finish working, and I never called Rory back. Joseph texted and wanted the list of what had happened, but I ignored his call as well.

I pushed the covers back, rose from the bed, and went to take my plate back to the kitchen. I was half full, and my stomach was stuffed. I came around the corner and almost tripped.

Arf!

"Oh my God! Where did you come from?" I put the plate down and picked up the cutest brown pup I'd ever seen. "How did you get in here?" I thought aloud and then looked up at the closed door of Savio's office.

I took the plate to the kitchen, held onto the dog, and went to find out what had made Savio buy me a dog.

"Yeah," he called out.

"Hey."

"I see you met a friend."

"What's his name?"

He shrugged.

"Where did you get him?"

"Rena picked him out."

"So, this a make up gift." I walked around his office, admiring his photos of when he was younger and pictures of his family.

"Call it what you want."

I jerked my head back. "Can you ever say you're sorry?"

"I don't."

"When I think we've made one step forward."

"Come here."

"Why?"

"I'm not about to yell across the room."

I sauntered over and stood in front of his desk.

"I'm sorry."

"Thank you."

"What would you like to call him?"

"Savi."

"No."

I giggled and kissed Savi on the head. "Yep, I like getting the chance to boss you around."

"My mother called and yelled at me about you."

"Really?" I took a seat on the edge of his desk, crossed my legs, and my shorts rose. I noticed he licked his lips and stared at my thigh.

"Eyes up here, big boy."

"She was pissed, and so was my father. I'm going to have a talk with Harris."

"Officer Harris?"

"Yep."

"No killing, Savio."

"I don't need to kill him to get my point across."

"What point is that?"

He stood from the chair and moved between my legs. "What belongs to me is not to be touched."

"What about Maurizio?"

"Him too."

"I don't like this."

His thumb skimmed down my cheek as he leaned over and kissed me.

"Did you apologize to Rena?" I backed away from the kiss and watched his expression.

"I promised her a shopping spree."

"Great, and I'll pick up some things for Savi."

"You are not calling him Savi."

"Yes, I am."

"I have work early tomorrow, so I'll be up for a while." He waved around his office.

"No problem. I'm sleeping in my bed tonight."

"I won't even answer that statement."

"We'll see."

I walked out of his office carefree. I was taking a little control back of the situation, and the breaking down of his walls was letting me see a side of Savio Calabresi that no one else was allowed to see.

CHAPTER 24
Savio

WHEN RENA SUGGESTED the dog to make things up with McKayla, I was against bringing any filthy animal in my condo, especially a pup that would shit at any moment. After hearing Adelina Calabresi basically say she would come and beat my ass, that let me know McKayla had gotten into her heart. She was too close for my comfort. I didn't want my family to like this girl; hell, they barely liked to deal with Viviana. I was past having feelings for her, and I couldn't fight them any longer. When I yelled about her being a pawn, it was a half-truth. She started as a pawn in a game, but she meant more to me now, and I was determined to make them all pay.

I got out of the car, waved my guards off, and met up with Vincenzo at the front entrance of the mall strip. "What do you think?"

"Looks like you're going to have a lot of work cut out for you."

Some of the windows were busted, and the paint was depleted.

"My team can handle all the demolition. This can be a moneymaker."

"You speak with Sante and Elio?"

"They've been here."

I checked the front door and wiped the dust off my hand. "How much are they asking?"

"We can negotiate them down from quarter of a million."

I sucked my teeth. "This is barely worth a hundred thousand."

"I was able to meet talk them down to one fifty."

"Plus, the property taxes, the neighbors." I looked up the strip at a few local stores.

"You were onboard the other day."

"I didn't see the place in person. I make money, Vincenzo, not set up to lose it."

"As president, I made a call."

"What if we need to dip in and out? All these neighbors, have you checked them out?"

"I have my team on standby."

"You should because—"

Pop! Pop!

The glass of the window busted, and I dropped to the ground, pulled my gun, and sent bullets flying. "Stay behind me!" I shouted to my little brother.

"Argh!" One of the construction workers was hit.

"Who the fuck is shooting in broad daylight!" Vincenzo blasted his gun. He was trained to shoot, but I hated putting my baby brother in situations when he was better in the legit world.

"Somebody who's ready for me to break their neck."

Pop! Pop!

"Let me call Renato."

"Tell him to hurry the fuck up."

"Yeah, Savio," Renato said.

"Mom's dress is ready. Mall strip twenty-fourth and third," I spoke in code and hung up.

Ring! Ring!

"McKayla," I mumbled.

Bark! Bark!

Renato's car sent shots back at the red Mustang, and it took off down the street. I stood up and saw two of my men on the ground.

———

"I want blood," I demanded, picked up the table, and tossed it across the room in the warehouse.

"How did they know you'd be there?" Sante asked.

"You don't think we have a snitch."

"I want Maurizio's area set on fire."

"Savio…" EJ started to say.

"Send the same message to Gennaro."

"You're taking it a little far," EJ said.

"Shit, I'll burn Gennaro if you want."

"Motherfuckers think I'm weak."

I paced back and forth. My hand was bandaged up from accidentally touching glass on the ground.

"Have you talked to the other bosses?"

"Fuck them."

"Savio, you need to calm down."

I jacked EJ up by the collar of his shirt. "Who the fuck are you telling to calm down!"

"Savio, stop. We don't put our hands on each other," Sante said.

I looked at him like he was stupid. "So why did you fight Renato at dinner the other night?"

"That was different."

"Over some pussy."

"Watch what the fuck you say." Sante stepped in my face.

Renato chortled on the left side of us.

"Or what? I'm the motherfucker who calls the shots!"

"Then act like it!" Sante shouted back and shoved me.

I clenched my fist.

"Hit me, let's see you lose your temper like always and have me clean it up."

"Look, we all need to relax and think about how we're being played," Renato told us.

"That's the first smart thing you've ever said," Vincenzo responded, and Renato punched him in the arm playfully.

"Loverboy needs to stay in a child's place," Renato teased.

"Loverboy had our bro's back," Vincenzo said.

"First and last time," I replied.

"Do we tell Pops?" EJ asked.

"The minute he gets involved, we're bringing him out of retirement," Sante remarked.

"I don't want him involved. I can handle everything."

I was the center of attention.

"So, you're ordering to burn down his area?" Sante clarified.

Taking a deep breath, I rubbed my head and sighed in frustration, covering my face. "Burn one or two small businesses. Make sure no one is there."

"I like when the beast comes out to play," Renato commented.

"Make sure no one is inside, Renato," I demanded.

"Understood."

"What else do we have to discuss?"

"Did you make that phone call to Joseph?" Sante said.

"Shit!"

"I will now."

I grabbed my phone out of my pocket and dialed his number while my brothers talked over the plan.

"Joseph Editor-in-Chief."

"Why did I hear you're still running this article?"

He cleared his throat. "Mr. Calabresi, I'd put the word out with McKayla to soften the story."

"What do you mean soften the story?"

"It's more of a fluff piece," Joseph explained.

"Joseph, I bought the newspaper, and I can have you replaced."

"I know—"

"Shut the fuck up when I'm speaking."

"Sorry."

"If anything, and I do mean anything, puts my family in a bad light, you won't make it home."

"Yes, sir."

"Long as we're clear."

I ended the call and shoved the phone in my pocket, closing my eyes in thought.

"She's changing you," Vincenzo commented.

"No one can change me."

"Where is she anyway?"

"Home."

"You probably have a camera inside your condo, watching her every move." Vincenzo chuckled, and I flipped him off, walking out.

CHAPTER 25
McKayla

I'D DIALED Savio's number to check up on Savi, and it went straight to voicemail for the third time. I was getting worried. He didn't seem like a pet type of guy, and if he sent my baby away, he'd feel a cold bed for the rest of the year.

"Oh, these would look so cute on him." Rena picked up some doggy jackets.

"Savi is not dressing up."

"You're no fun."

I held the phone to my chin in thought. "Sorry, what did you say?"

"Okay, why are you distracted?"

"Savio isn't answering his phone."

"Good, the more trouble we can get into."

"I've had enough trouble for a lifetime."

"Have you told him about taking a girls' trip?"

"I think I will wait on that conversation. Just going to the mall causes a big stir." I grabbed a few boxes of doggy treats and threw them in my basket. "What are we doing after this?"

"I want to go to Fashion Nova and check out a few things before lunch," Rena explained.

"I'd been meaning to ask you."

"Don't."

"Don't? I tell you everything," I said.

"I know what this is about."

"Well."

"I like causing trouble."

"You had two brothers fighting."

"That was nothing. Renato is actually funny when you get past the killer part."

I cocked my head to the side. "And Sante?"

"Jackass. Are you getting anything else?"

"No, let me pay for these." I went to the front counter, pushed my basket forward, and removed my credit card.

"Anything else for you today, Mrs. Calabresi?" the sales associate asked.

"No, thank you."

"Forty-two dollars and seventy cents," she said.

She bagged everything up and passed me the receipt. I thanked her again, walked out behind Rena, and accidentally bumped into someone.

"Ouch!" I said.

She shoved me back. "Finally, you can't run behind Savio," Viviana snapped.

"Bitch! Who do you think you are?" Rena yelled.

"Rena."

A guard stepped over and pushed Viviana back.

"She thinks we're scared of her bodyguards, Viviana," the same girl from the charity event growled. It was four of them to us three.

"We're in a public place," I tried to plead.

Viviana smirked. "So, you're scared."

"No, unlike you, I don't want innocent people getting hurt."

"Viviana, let's go," a guy with a scar over his eyer suggested.

"No, I want her to apologize for stealing my man and bumping into me," Viviana said.

"If you wanted Savio, you would have him," I remarked, turned to leave, and felt my hair being ripped out of my head. "Arghh!"

A fist hit the right side of my face and I heard screams and shouts all around me.

Pop! Pop!

Everything froze at the sound of a gun going off.

"Rena…" I whispered, slowly moving to get up.

"This isn't over," Viviana spat, then kicked me on the side of my waist.

"Savio's going to take care of her," Agosto said.

"That bitch is going to wish she was never born," Rena told me.

I limped after I got up and grabbed my bags. Rena helped to hold me up, wrapped my arm around her neck, and led me to the car.

"Take me home." I felt the tears form.

———

I locked the bathroom door of my bedroom, lit some candles, turned my phone off, and soaked in the tub with some Epsom salts. Joseph was waiting on the story, Savio was demanding I couldn't leave, and Viviana was constantly threatening me and getting in the middle of shootouts. This all started because I decided to try to be the one person to break down the world of the mafia from within.

Bang! Bang!

"Go away!"

"Mrs. Calabresi, it's Marilyn."

"I'm not hungry."

"Mr. Calabresi is calling."

"Tell him I've gone to bed."

"He's ordered that you call him ASAP."

I waved off her comment, leaned up, and grabbed the wine, and drank straight from the bottle. I blew out a breath, unplugged the water, and let it drain, while I decided to go out tonight and get over the chaos in my life.

I lifted the towel from the cabinet, wrapped it around my body, and came out of the bathroom to Savi standing at the door.

"Marilyn!" I called out and bent down to pick up Savi.

She popped her head back in my room.

"If he calls again, tell him I'm sleeping please."

"I think you should talk to him."

"I will. I'm not mad. I just need a little girls' night out."

"Is that wise after the day you've had?"

"I'll have a bodyguard, so it shouldn't be a problem."

"If you're hungry, I left some food in the microwave."

"Okay, thank you. Are you leaving for the night?"

"Yes, Savi was walked already, and the food stocked. Be good."

"Always."

I placed Savi on the floor, went to the closet to pick out the best dress I had, and paired it with the highest heels I could manage.

An hour later, I was dancing with Rena in a club outside the city that Agosto recommended, that was under Calabresi control. In case Savio had a problem with me going out, he'd at least be okay with me being surrounding by his people. The bass of the music thumped through my chest as we twisted and turned, tossed our hair around, danced with some random guys, and had a good time. The vibe was great, and I didn't feel like I was someone's wife, or the daughter of a doctor, or a journalist reporting on the bad stuff in the world. Just McKayla, twenty-three and free.

I laughed at Rena slow dancing with some guy. He whispered in her ear, and she ignored every word he said. It was going on midnight, and I had work to finish. We'd been gone most of the day. The club lights flashed from green to red for final calls for drinks.

I tapped Rena on the shoulder. "One more shot before we go!"

She nodded, telling the guy she was going to the bar. "My feet are killing me." Rena fanned herself.

"Me too. This was fun, though."

"Yes, it was. We needed this."

"What can I get you ladies?" the bartender asked.

"Two Patron shots," Rena said.

"We have work tomorrow." I giggled.

"I'll drink a double espresso in the morning." Rena shrugged.

"Here you go." He placed them on the counter, and I pulled a hundred-dollar bill out of my purse.

"To living life on our rules." Rena held the shot glass up in the air.

I clinked my glass with hers and took the shot straight back. "Yes!"

"One more dance for the road." Rena grabbed my hand and escorted me through the crowd. I pulled my hair up, swayed my hips to the beat of the music, and let my stress go away.

———

"Shit!" I tripped and almost fell over in laughter when I stepped in the condo. It was supposed to be one more dance, and it ended up being three more and more drinks.

"Do you know what time it is?"

"Savio? Is that you?" I giggled.

The lights in the living room came on. "Have you any idea what's going on?"

I pushed my dress down, swished over to him sitting on the chair, and stood between his legs.

"No, what's going on?" I chortled.

"You think I want my wife out in public drunk?"

"Please, it was just a few drinks." I removed my jacket and tossed it on the couch.

"Where did this dress come from?" He pulled at the bottom seam.

"I've had this for years." I went to remove the dress from my body and dropped it on the floor. I wore just a thong, no bra, and black heels.

"You're not allowed to wear that again." He slid his hand across my stomach down to my inner thigh.

"You don't boss me around."

"Why didn't you answer my call?" he probed.

"I was busy, something you know about very well."

"You think I'm playing games with you?"

"I think you have me mistaken with Viviana." I slid down to my knees, rubbing my hands on his legs up to his thick member.

"What did you say?"

"I know what this is about"

"You don't know anything."

"Where were you when I called you?" I stopped undoing his pants and peered at him.

"I had something to do."

"Like what?"

"I don't speak on my business."

"Did you know Viviana tried to jump me at the mall?"

"I heard, and I was in a shootout."

"What!" My mouth gaped open in shock.

"Come up here."

"No, tell me what happened."

"The threats are real, and I need you to follow my orders."

"I need to feel that she doesn't get to have a step ahead of me."

"She's not a thought in my mind." He caressed my cheek.

"Where's Savi?"

"Locked in your room."

"Why did you lock him up?" I tried to get up but stumbled and fell in his lap.

"Savi is not your concern right now."

"What is my priority?"

"Fucking your husband to make it up for ignoring his calls."

"Can you make another meeting with your father happen?"

"I don't want to talk about my father right now."

"I promise to suck your dick so good you'll forget about every other woman you've had sex with."

"Prove it." He rested his hands on the chair and dared me in a challenge.

CHAPTER 26

Savio

MCKAYLA SLID BACK DOWN to the floor and unzipped my pants, reached in my boxers, and pulled my member out, teasing it by running her hand up and down slowly.

"I don't like to be teased."

Her eyes lowered, and she concentrated on pleasing me. My head fell back on the chair, and my stomach sank in as her other hand went under my shirt and touched my chest.

"Shit!" She was the devil. "That's right, keep going."

McKayla rubbed up and down on my shaft, watching the darkening of my eyes. I was intimidating to everyone, massive even like a god. I watched as her full lips grazed the tip, and saliva dripped down to ease me going deeper.

"Suck it with your pretty mouth."

To hear her moans wanting me to fill her aching pussy up, my hips jerked, and she let me think I was in control. She then moved a hand up my thigh and took me further down her throat.

"Let me fill your mouth up."

McKayla's head bobbed up and down. The desire in her

eyes for me to fuck her right here dominated her body, and the need to give into her whim consumed me.

"Mmmmm." She teasingly popped my dick out of her mouth, lifting to slide her tongue across my balls.

"Fuck!"

"Good boy."

"Get up here." I reached to grab her, and she smacked my hands away. She shook her head, squeezed her breasts together, and wrapped her hands around my dick, rubbing her full titties around my dick.

"McKayla, Goddamn it. Come here now."

"Yes, Daddy."

My eyes darkened, and I froze. "Bring your sexy ass up here."

"Let's try something," McKayla suggested. She turned with her back to me and spread her legs, motioning for me to scoot lower in the chair. She did some type of acrobatics with her ass in my face and her mouth on my dick for a sixty-nine.

"Fuck me, Savio."

"You're pushing me over the edge." I spread her butt cheeks, swiped my tongue from the top of her asshole to her clit. With my thumb wet with her juices, I pushed in her tight hole and listened to her cries.

Her ass bucked toward my face, making me suck in my tongue. I held her around the waist with one arm, tucked my tongue in her pussy, and teased her when her juices gushed out on my shirt and down my face. This was the best meal I'd had all day.

"I missed you," I muttered. I smacked and squeezed her butt as I watched her take my dick to the back of her throat and groaned. "Enough."

She thrust her hips back, and I smacked her again, teasing her with a kiss on her ass. I helped her to sit up, grabbed her breast, and kissed the back of her neck. She shivered in my arms.

"Ohhhh… Savio." She eased down on my dick.

This was the best feeling in the world. I'd kill anyone who tried to take her away, or if she ever thought she could leave me. I pumped upward and pulled her back to my chest, speeding up my thrusts. Our skin slapping together grew louder around the room.

"Don't you ever ignore my calls," I demanded and pounded her so hard and fast.

"I won't! Yesss… Savio!" She squirted.

———

The next morning, I called Renato to bring one of his soldiers to me at the warehouse. Agosto was at two different incidents where McKayla was harmed, and I wondered about the people I had around me. The door opened, and Renato trailed behind Agosto and a few of my other men.

"Agosto, take a seat."

"What's this about, Boss?"

"Tell me why you thought it was a good idea to have my wife out at a club."

"Savio—"

I cut him off. "Mr. Calabresi or Boss."

"She asked to go out."

"You do everything a woman tells you?"

"I thought it would be fine. We were in our territory."

"My territory!"

He shifted in his seat. "I'm sorry."

"Why wasn't I notified immediately about the mall incident?"

I reached behind my back, removed my gun, and held it to the side of me. He started to sweat.

"Mr. Calabresi, I didn't know it would be a problem."

"I don't pay you to think, motherfucker!" I slammed the gun in the side of his face.

"Fuck! Savio," Agosto shouted.

I pounded it in his face two more times, and Renato pulled me back.

"Get him out of here," Renato said.

"Why the fuck didn't you have someone on Viviana?" I demanded to Renato.

"Viviana's not the only thing we have to deal with, Savio."

"Did you take care of what I asked?"

He lit a cigar and pushed it toward me. "It's all taken care of on my end."

"You brought him, take care of him."

"Sante and Elio might not like that."

"Since when do I give a shit?"

"Sante's pissed at me," Renato blurted out.

"For what?"

"He thinks I'm interested in Rena."

"Are you?"

"Hell no. She was fucking with him and using me."

"Leave me out of your mess."

"Besides, unlike you and Sante, I don't do commitment."

"Take care of the bullshit and leave Sante alone."

Renato raised his hands in the air. "I like to cause trouble."

We walked out of the warehouse together, and I jumped in the back of the car and checked my watch to see I had a few minutes before I needed to get to a meeting with some of my executives at Calabresi. I arrived twenty minutes late and stepped in the conference room while Vincenzo talked at the head of the table.

"Finally, he's joined us," Vincenzo said.

"The question should be is this worth my time."

"If you think bringing in ten million dollars on mall strip projects is small change, we can back out now."

"Keep talking."

"I locked in the construction costs and talked with inspectors."

"Neighbors."

"Won't be an issue."

"Who are you putting in charge of while you're here running as president?"

"I'm going to oversee both."

"That's a lot to juggle, Vincenzo." I narrowed my eyes at him. He knew what I was really talking about with using a mall strip to push our money and drugs.

"I can handle myself."

"Give us the room."

All eyes glanced at me.

"Yes, sir," everyone spoke at the same time and stood to leave.

"I can't save you if something goes wrong. If my product is screwed, I won't be kind."

"You act like I'm not a part of this family."

"This isn't a dick size contest."

"Either you stay out of my way or find someone else to handle Calabresi Holdings."

I smirked at my little brother.

"Who's been sucking on your balls for you to think you're grown?" I jested.

"Too many to count."

"All right, I can't force you to cut one out, but you better handle yourself accordingly."

"We have a deal?" He extended his hand.

"Deal."

"Would you like anything specific to drink, Mr. Calabresi?" Carolyn asked.

"Usual, please."

McKayla requested a night out for dinner, and I felt we needed to have some time alone outside the bedroom, since the past few days had kept us both caught up with work and fighting. She was glowing under the candlelight with her red lipstick on, full makeup, and hair up in a tight bun. She looked more of a don's wife than a girlfriend. I couldn't stand the first day I met her back when my father introduced us.

"Anything for you, Mrs. Calabresi?"

"I'll have what he's drinking," she replied.

"Coming right up."

Carolyn took the drink orders and walked off to the bar. I licked my lips and stared at McKayla as she blushed under my stare.

"Why are you staring at me?"

"Because you're my wife."

"I think everyone here knows that."

"Who cares what they think?"

"Here you two go, and I'll have your meals out in a few moments." Carolyn placed the glasses of scotch on the table.

"Thank you," McKayla responded and raised her glass in the air.

"You're drinking hardcore tonight."

"I've had a long night, hanging with Savi, plus work. I need a night off."

"Can you go a day without thinking about that dog?" I growled.

She giggled. "Are you jealous of my dog that you bought, Savio?"

"Yes."

"Tell me why."

"Because nothing should have your attention but me."

"Ah, poor baby. What can I do to make you feel better?"

"Suck my dick like you did the other night."

She choked on her drink. "Savio, why are you so mannish?"

"I like your pussy and need it at all times."

"Well, she's on a break for tonight."

"If she's sore, I can help her."

"You're talking about my vagina in third person." She shook her head.

"I take care of what's mine."

"Here's your meal, hot and ready. Let me know if you need anything else." Carolyn placed both plates of lasagna down with garlic bread.

"It smells delicious." McKayla picked up her fork and cut into her food.

"How are you coming along with your article?" I investigated to see if I could stir her along to change the story altogether.

CHAPTER 27

McKayla

I STUFFED my face with another bite of lasagna, moaned, tasting the full flavors in my mouth, and closed my eyes. This was heavenly and the only thing I'd wanted all day. "Very close to being finished. I need to type up a few notes, and I called your dad to see if we could meet soon."

"Has Joseph given you any more problems?"

"No, and I'm surprised."

"Keep me updated if he does."

"How are things with your business?"

"We're going into the third year of projections on pace."

"You love the legit business part or the mafia more?"

"I feel like you're fishing again."

"Just observation."

"For different reasons, I like them both."

"No judgement."

"How are things with you parents since the dinner?"

"We've gotten better, but it's still a slow process."

"I'm glad to hear that."

"Does Renato have a girlfriend?" I questioned.

"Why?"

"Not for me."

"What are you asking for?"

"I never see him with anyone."

"He's a private person."

"Any of your brothers?"

"We don't sit around and talk about our love lives."

"But you talk about who you're having sex with?"

"Actually, we don't."

"Seriously."

"McKayla, not all men talk about who sucked their dick to their brothers or friends."

"Well, Vincenzo is the youngest, so he has to have a girlfriend."

"We're not having this discussion."

"You're such a killjoy."

"Eat."

I stuck my tongue out. "Nope."

He smirked, slid his hand under the table, and caressed my leg. "Tell that to Savi the dog, not me."

———

I stretched my back, lifted my leg, and mimicked the poses on the TV screen. Rena wasn't paying attention, and I gave up on trying to force her into what I liked to do for fun. Last night at dinner, I talked with Savio about letting Rena come over to hang out while he was off doing God knows what. He had his men drive her to his place, and we ordered breakfast, talked, and now sitting through a yoga session before working.

"Are you going to the office today?"

"Yeah, Joseph gave me another story to work on."

"That's great."

"It's fine. I just need to remind myself to stick to my schedule."

"I forgot to tell you about the night of the club."

"What happened?"

"I came home super drunk and late, and Savio was pissed, sitting in the chair right there."

"Did he say anything?"

"He was his usual angry self."

"Did you tell him where you went?"

"He knew and asked why I ignored his calls."

"Married life is too much for me." Rena blew out a breath.

"I asked him about his brother Renato." I glanced up to see if she would make eye contact.

"What did he say?' She continued looking at her phone.

"Nothing, but that he and his brothers don't talk about the women they're dating."

"I think Savio's a jealous, possessive prick, but he's perfect for you."

"Leave my husband alone." I threw a pillow at her.

She chuckled and threw it back. "What about the fight with Viviana?"

"He told me not to worry about it as usual."

"She has it bad for you."

"Obsessed sounds more like it."

"Where's the cute bodyguard you had at the mall?"

"I didn't ask. Enzo was busy with Savio, so he brought a new guy with me."

"You're not paying attention at all."

"Hmmm."

"I need to set up some time with Mr. Calabresi."

"Have fun with that."

"His mom asked about us going over there for lunch one day."

"You should go and get to know them outside of Savio."

"I can't believe I actually like his parents."

"Even though you two came together under these circumstances, he loves you."

I jerked my head back. "Who loves me?"

"Savio."

I laughed at her comment. "He doesn't love me."

"You believe that?"

"He's never come out and said that he loves me."

"Sometimes it's in a man's actions."

"I'm done talking about him. Let me shower, and we can get started working."

———

Later in the afternoon, I finished research on Elio Calabresi and the Colombo and Greco families. Rena was still here; only this time, she was asleep from drinking the last bottle of wine.

"Rena." I touched her on the shoulder.

"Hmmm…"

"Wake up and look at this."

"What is it?"

"You remember that detective who arrested me?"

"Yeah."

"He's in a photo with Maurizio and Nevio." I turned my computer around and showed her.

"I mean we knew he was up to something."

"Yeah, but I might use this in a new article."

"Where are they?"

"Looks like outside some restaurant."

"I wonder if they were setting up Savio from the beginning."

"I remember yelling that night about stealing."

"We were pretty drunk though."

"I had a few drinks, nothing to put me over the edge."

"This is interesting."

"Are you going to tell Savio?"

"No, he already knows Officer Harris is dangerous."

"I still can't believe you were arrested."

"I can still feel his disgusting hands on me."

"Sorry you had to go through that."

"I've been through worse."

"I'm going to head out. I have a deadline to finish," Rena said and jumped up to pack her computer, shoes, and backpack.

"Be safe getting home and text me later." I walked her to the door.

"I promise."

I sighed and shut the door in thought. "Small world."

Arf!

"Savi, are you hungry?" I bent down to lift him in my arms.

The front door opened, and Savio came through holding flowers in his hands.

"Who are those for?" I walked toward him and kissed him on the lips.

"You."

"Say hi, Savi." I held his palm up to greet Savio.

"I saw Rena leaving," Savio said.

"We'd just finished working."

Savio followed me to the kitchen and placed the flowers down. I put Savi near his water bowl, washed my hands, and grabbed the flowers to smell.

"Was it productive?"

"Yes."

"Good."

"So, I have you all to myself tonight."

As Savino walked up to me, he put the flowers back on the counter, lifted my chin, and gave me a soft kiss. "That was lovely."

"I missed your voice all day."

"You could have called."

"I didn't want to disturb your workday."

"Well, we have the afternoon and night to ourselves."

"Did Marilyn cook?"

"Yes, but we mostly ordered out."

"I never asked. Can you cook?"

"Yes, but I never tried to impose on Marilyn."

"She wouldn't mind."

"She needs a vacation for putting up with you."

"Give it to her." He released his hold, went to the fridge, and grabbed leftovers from the casserole.

"She's your cook."

"You can handle some things as the woman around the house."

"Oh, you let me run the house."

"On certain things."

"Doubt that." I rolled my eyes as he pulled out a plate to heat up some food.

"I have some work to do in my office. I'll be pretty late coming to bed."

"Can't you put that off for one night and watch a movie with me?"

"It's a big deal we're trying to close."

"Just one night, and tomorrow you can handle the deal." I stood on my tippy toes and pecked his lips.

"Trying to distract me?"

"Is it working?" I wrapped my arms around his neck and pulled his bottom lip into my mouth.

"Yes."

CHAPTER 28

McKayla

A WEEK LATER.

I finished the last edits on my story for Joseph and asked Curtis to drive me over to my job so I could chat with Joseph. Enzo was with Savio out of town on business and wouldn't be back for a few hours.

I picked up my laptop, slid it in my backpack, reached for my smoothie, and followed Curtis to the car. Rena hadn't answered my calls since we went to lunch and shopping the other day. I hope she hadn't pissed off Sante to cause some type of conflict, I'd hate to kick my husband's brother in the balls like I did Savio.

I checked the time on my watch. It was just past nine a.m., so Joseph should be out of the morning meeting. I glanced down at my ring and still couldn't believe I was married and let alone happy. He was still the same jerk to people, but with me, I could see he had calmed down and let loose a little more.

I'd told him I was finished with the story and that I'd made a few changes to how it was a love story to Italy and his family's legacy. At first, before I even knew of the Calabresi family, I'd made it a point to get as much information as I could find, and what they'd built off the backs of the people they'd hurt. Speaking with Adelina, I knew that being the wife meant I had to be his peace away from the world of the mafia. When we were together, it was just Savio and McKayla watching old *Honeymooners* episodes and eating cold leftovers.

"We're here, Mrs. Calabresi," Curtis told me.

I gawked out the window and scanned my home away from home for the past few years. "No need to get out, Curtis. I can handle it from here." I held my palm up to stop him.

"My job is to keep an eye on you at all times," Curtis muttered, opened the door, and came around to assist me.

I thanked him, lifted my backpack, and walked in, waving at some of my coworkers. I noticed not much had changed since I was kidnapped. I pressed the button of the elevator. It dinged, and I stepped on. Curtis came in behind me. Someone else started to walk on, and he held a hand out to stop them.

"It's full," Curtis said.

"Curtis, they probably work here. I see a badge," I explained.

He stared at the guy's badge around his neck. A second later, he stepped on, and I moved to step back to give us space. Curtis moved his hand close to his gun, and I placed my hand over his.

"I think we're safe." I pointed to the back of his jacket that said security.

When the doors closed, I punched the twelfth floor and waited as the numbers moved upwards. I looked at the time again. I'd made plans to meet with my mom for lunch and have dinner ready for Savio when he got back.

When the elevator stopped on my floor, we got off, and the security guard pushed the button again, and it went back down. I didn't think anything of it and shook it off. I waved and hugged some of my co-workers.

"McKayla, is it true?" Gabby asked.

"Is what true?"

"You married the boss," she whispered.

I chuckled, not ignoring her comment of Savio being the boss. To me, he was just my husband and nothing more. "I married Savio Calabresi; he's not my boss."

"What about—"

"You're here to rub it in my face." Rory stomped over to me.

"I'm here to give Joseph my story."

"You mean the story that your deviant husband swindled from me."

I was unfamiliar with the attitude and the aggressiveness coming from Rory and wanted to ask him what he was talking about.

"I suggest you move away from Mrs. Calabresi." Curtis stepped between Rory and me. I tried to move around him, but he blocked me with his arm.

"You won't to get away with this," Rory growled and stormed off.

"What was that about?" I murmured to myself.

"McKayla, what are you doing here?" Joseph walked in from the breakroom.

I smiled and held up my backpack. "I have my story for you. I know we have less than an hour to get it to press."

"What story?"

"Elio Calabresi."

Joseph ran a hand down his face. "Did you talk to Savio?"

"Why do I need to talk to Savio?"

"We need to talk in my office." Joseph detoured to his office.

"Stay here, Curtis. I'll be a second."

"Keep the door open."

"Nothing's going to happen to me here."

"Doesn't matter. Mr. Calabresi has specific instructions."

I groaned and aimlessly went to his office, saying hi to other team members.

"Shut the door," Joseph spoke.

"What's this about, Joseph?" I closed the door but stood close by in case I needed to call for Curtis.

"I killed the story of Elio Calabresi."

"What did you say?" I followed the nervousness in his demeanor.

He rubbed a hand across his head. "The story is dead, McKayla. Just do something else."

"I worked months on getting this story, and you're just going to dead it!" I squinted as I staggered to his chair.

"Nothing personal."

"Nothing personal?"

"Talk to your husband."

"What does Savio have to do with this?"

"Again, talk to your husband."

"No! I want a straight answer now."

"He owns the paper and told me to kill the story."

I stumbled back, feeling flush. I put a hand on my stomach, feeling nauseous at the news of what Savio had done. "That's not true."

"It is, and he wanted Rory to be fired, but I convinced him to let me keep him on until I find a replacement."

I rubbed my forehead and flashed back to Rory's words. "He's a monster."

"I'm sorry, McKayla."

"No, you'll be sorry if you don't run this story."

"Did you not hear what I just told you?"

I strolled back over to his desk and pointed in his face. "Either you run my story, or I'll make sure you end up dead."

His eyes widened in shock. "You're threatening me?"

"I make promises, and I can handle Savio."

"McKayla."

I pointed to the phone.

"All right. I'll put your story to the press."

"No, I want another story to replace that."

"What story?"

"The killing of one of the Five Family's men."

"Do you know what this will cause?"

"It's business." I shrugged, sat in the chair, and wrote down everything I knew about that night on a piece of paper. Savio had lied to me for the very last time, and I hoped he paid dearly in jail.

"What if he asks who gave the account of the details?"

"I want my name on the front page with the article." I pushed the notes toward him.

"This won't end well, McKayla. Have you thought about where you'll go?"

"Just run the story. I'll handle everything else."

When I opened the door, Curtis held up his cell phone. My stomach churned at what was about to happen. I could wait for him to come home and confront him, but the only way to get away now with no detection was to distract Curtis and call my parents later.

"I have Mr. Calabresi on the line."

"He can't go one day without bugging me," I joked and took the phone from his hands.

"I hear you're at work turning in your story," Savio said.

I switched the phone to my left ear and walked behind Curtis, biting on my bottom lip and thinking over my plan. "Yes, and Joseph loved my concept."

"Really? Tell me what your concept was."

I examined all the eyes in the room as I hopped on the elevator. "I'll tell you when you get back, Mr. Calabresi."

"You sound different."

"Savio, you overthink everything."

"Did something happen?"

"No, now get back to your work. I'm heading home to take a nap." I yawned on the phone, stretching.

"If something's wrong, you'd tell me, right?"

"How's work going?" I asked, changing subjects.

"Changing the subject won't distract me, McKayla."

"It's worth a try." I giggled and threw my head back.

"My mom wants you to come to the house for breakfast."

"I'd love that."

"Good, I'll see you when I get back home."

"Okay."

"McKayla."

"Yeah?"

"If you're having doubts, just remember I have eyes everywhere."

I gazed over at Curtis. He winked, and I smiled. I ended the call and gave him his phone back right when the elevator doors opened.

"Curtis, do you mind driving me to the mall?"

"Mrs. Calabresi, my orders are to take you right back home."

"My husband doesn't need to know. Please, I promise I'll be in and out." I held out my pinky finger, and I swallowed the lump in my throat, stretching the tension out of my neck.

I released a long-held breath and got in the back of the car. He started the car and pulled into traffic. I took out my cell phone out, turned off the tracking device, and texted Rena.

Me: *Don't look for me, I'm fine.*

Rena: *McKayla, what's wrong?*

Me: *Savio lied and screwed me over for the last time.*

Rena: *Are you running?*

Me: *I'll be in touch soon. Tell my parents I love them.*

The second I made the decision to run, I knew he would go first to see them and then Rena. I had to be smart about this, or I'd never be free. We finally made it to the mall thirty minutes later when I got a text message from Adelina.

Adelina: *Hi hone., I look forward to breakfast tomorrow.*

Me: *Me too. Can you make those strawberry biscuits?*

Adelina: *Of course. Elio can't wait to see the article.*

I'd completely forgotten about the book and article as soon as Joseph told me Savio bought the company and forced him to kill my story. He took away my independence, and that was the one thing I told him I wanted to keep before we got married and went to Italy.

Me: *It's going to be a big surprise.*

I wiped my face, grabbed my backpack, and stepped out of the car.

"I can carry that," Curtis said.

"No thanks, I got it."

"You have an hour before the boss will be looking for you."

"Don't worry, Curtis. He's going to get a big surprise tonight." I grinned, sauntered through the door of Macy's, and picked through the first dress rack, looking over my shoulder at Curtis. "You can take a break, Curtis. I'm going to try these on." I held the two dresses up for him to see.

He stood back near the shoe section, and I went to the salesperson and showed her the dresses I wanted to try on.

"Hi. I need to try these on, but my boyfriend over there wants to know about the shoes." I pointed back at Curtis.

"Sure, I'll help him right now." She unlocked the dressing room door and strolled over to Curtis.

I went behind the wall of the dressing room and peeked out to the sales floor. She approached him and motioned at the shoes. He looked down at his shoes, and that was my cue to leave the dresses and run out. I went behind a mannequin, crawled to the escalator on the opposite side of the store, and mixed in with the crowd.

I checked the time on my phone, opened the door of the back entrance, and spotted a cab. "Can you take me to the airport?"

CHAPTER 29

McKayla

FORTY MINUTES LATER, I made it to the airport, and my phone was blowing up. I saw missed calls from Curtis, Rena, and my parents.

Not looking back, I passed the cab driver fifty dollars, thanked him, and shut the door. Going through the double doors, I dropped my cell in the trash can and continued toward the line for Paris Airlines. Savio wouldn't be able to manipulate his way out of this lie. If he thought I would be quiet, he would learn.

Once I purchased a ticket, I went behind a family and put my backpack through the scanner. The security agent motioned for me to walk forward to the metal detector. I grabbed my backpack and held my passport and ID in my hand with my ticket and headed to my flight.

A family of four came over and sat near me. I smiled at the little guy who waved at me.

"Sorry, he's overzealous," the wife explained.

"No problem, he's adorable."

"Jake, say hi to the nice lady."

"Hi!" Jake said.

"Nice to meet you, Jake." We shook hands, and the airline called for our flight to board.

"Are you going to Paris for pleasure or business?" she asked.

"Pleasure."

"I'm so rude. My name's Jessica." She held out her hand, and I grabbed Jake's hand while her husband picked up their bags.

"Ruby. It's nice to meet you."

"This is my husband, John, and Jacob, our baby." She passed her tickets to the flight attendant.

"Your boys are gorgeous."

"Thank you. No kids for you?"

"No, I'm not ready for that step."

"But you're married, right? I see that huge ring on your finger." Jessica pointed at my left hand, reminding me that I forgot to remove my wedding band.

"Still in the honeymoon stage."

"He's not going with you to Paris?" she interrogated.

"He's a workaholic, so I suggested I take a solo trip."

We found our seats and loaded our bags in the storage units. I buckled my seat near the window and sighed, resting my head on the back of the seat and closing my eyes.

"Ruby."

I turned my head and saw Jake smiling at me, holding his Superman doll at me.

"He wants to play you, sorry," Jessica said.

"It's okay. He can sit next to me."

Jessica helped Jake sit in the seat next to me, and we played Superman and watched movies together for the rest of the flight.

My memories of Paris were during a break between high school and college. I took a few months off to travel, and Paris was the goal to see the museum, theaters, food, and culture.

When I got to the hotel, I turned the water off in the tub, pinned my hair up, and stepped in. I laid my head back and let the warm water soak up the long flight.

"This ring was a lie." I twisted the ring on my finger.

———

The next morning, I walked out of the bathroom and heard the doorbell ring. I sauntered to answer it to get my morning started.

"Room service." The young woman pushed the cart in my room.

"Thank you." I picked up the strawberry from the table and groaned in satisfaction.

"Where would you like everything?"

"The patio would be great."

I reached in my bag and grabbed money for a tip. I turned around and dropped my smile when I saw a gun being held on me.

"No need for a tip."

"Who are you?"

She reached in her pocket and held out a phone. "Take it."

All my time as a journalist never compared to the amount of chaos and drama I'd sustained since meeting Savio Calabresi. I grabbed the phone and hesitantly answered. "He...lllo"

"Mrs. Calabresi," a raspy voice answered.

"I think you have the wrong room. My name is Ruby."

He laughed at my comment. "No need to lie, McKayla. I don't want to hurt you."

"Sorry if I can't feel good about that when a gun is pointed at me."

"I do apologize about that, but your husband has made things difficult for me."

"Who are you?"

"Where are my manners? I'm Gennaro Greco."

"Viviana's father."

"Yes, and I understand you've left your husband."

"Again, what do you want?"

"Smart."

"I might be young, but I've learned about men in your world."

"Your husband tried to kill my daughter and vote my family out."

I gasped in shock, raised my hand to cover my mouth, and sat in the chair near the desk.

"For repayment, I unfortunately will have you accompany my assistant."

My eyes glazed over to the woman wearing the hotel uniform. "He doesn't love me. I doubt you'll get anything out of this."

"Let me worry about what I get out of this deal."

"We're no longer together."

"So, you ran, and you don't think Savio Calabresi is looking for you."

"I doubt me leaving would cause him to get out of bed."

He chuckled again. "A man like Savio doesn't like to lose."

"Mr. Greco, I can pay you."

"I don't want your money. My family and daughter have been insulted."

"All right, so you don't want money."

"Oh, I do, just not from you. I want Savio to step aside as the don."

"Like I said, Savio and I aren't speaking."

"You will be. Get dressed and have breakfast, and my assistant will help you travel."

"Where?"

"I'm a man of my word. You won't be harmed, but do not question me." He ended the call, and I dropped the phone.

"Go get dressed." She motioned for the bathroom.

I looked around the room, thinking of a way to get out, but as fast as I got to the door, she might shoot me. She was about my same height, maybe an inch or two taller, with red hair and a mole on her upper lip.

I walked over to the bag to grab my clothes.

"Don't make me shoot you!" she shouted.

I raised my hands to show I was getting clothes out of my bag. "It's just a shirt."

"Hurry up," she snapped.

After fifteen minutes, I came out of the bathroom and saw she was standing next to my bag, holding my wallet. "Grab your things."

"Where am I going?"

"Mr. Greco wants to visit with you."

"Am I coming back here?"

"He will decide that."

She threw my jacket at me, and I stuck my feet in my shoes and picked up my things. She pushed me to walk forward out of the room and toward the elevator.

"Try to run, and I will kill you." She pushed the down button, and the doors opened. I stepped in, and she stood beside me with the gun in her pocket, still aimed at me.

"What's your name?

"None of your business."

"You know my name and threatened me. I felt maybe knowing your name would make it easy."

"Keep quiet, and you'll survive."

Five seconds later, we got off the elevator, and I tried to walk over to the front desk, but she gripped my arm and pulled me toward the doors to leave.

"Don't be stupid." She pushed me, and I almost tripped, but she caught me by the arm.

"Okay, I'm not trying to run."

The door of a black SUV was open, and she nudged me in. I scooted over, and she went to the passenger side upfront.

"Mrs. Calabresi, thank you for not making this difficult." A man puffed on a cigar, then blew the smoke in the air.

"Mr. Greco."

He nodded. "Would you like a drink?"

"No. Can you tell me where you're taking me?"

"A little drive."

"I have nothing to do with Savio's business."

"That may be true, but my business has everything to do with you."

Even if I were ready to walk out on Savio and his family, I would never betray him and tell his enemies any of his business. We had our problems, but I'd rather die than talk. His dark cobalt eyes, gray hair and beard showed a distinguished handsome older man, but beneath those features, I could see someone who thrived on killing and hurting people.

Mr. Greco reached down, picked up his phone, and dialed a number as he continued smoking his cigar. "I have something you've been missing."

I heard yelling and shouting coming from the other line.

"I suggest you calm down and speak to me with respect."

From Mr. Greco's smile, I took it that Savio relaxed and calmed down. "You can speak with her, but I want payment and your agreement to step down."

"I'm not his wife!" I shouted.

"Silenzio!" Greco spat in Italian.

"Let me out of this car!"

"One more word from you," the girl spoke from the front seat.

"Here, speak with your husband." Greco held the phone out for me to take.

"No."

"Yes!"

"I'm not going back."

I heard heavy breathing on the line. "McKayla, did he touch you?" Savio asked.

CHAPTER 30
Savio

A DAY BEFORE.

I walked into the dimly lit room of Tommaso Gallo's headquarters in Miami with Sante and my guards a few steps behind. Tommaso normally didn't let anyone enter with guns, but as the head mob boss, I never followed the rules.

Tommaso sat at the head table, and I sat on the other end of the five-chair table. Everyone waited for me to sit, and I adjusted my jacket to get comfortable before I blew everyone's world up.

"Thank you for coming, Savio. I know you've recently married. Congrats," Tommaso said in his thick Italian accent and held up a shot glass.

I never drank in front of them, nor did Sante. Unless you were my brother or father, I never trusted a soul. Friends made the worst enemies in my world, and Tommaso could try anything.

"I didn't think you called me here to congratulate me."

"My apologies. We understand things have gotten a little out of hand with Nevio and Greco." Tommaso crossed his hands in front of him and scooted forward at the table to wait for an answer.

He liked me, and he was starving to be in my place, but respected me and the Calabresi family. I hoped he never tried to cross me. I'd hate to break an arm or worse, send flowers to his mother on her loss.

"I've ratified the situation with Greco, but he's still adamant about me marrying Viviana, which as you know will never happen."

"Why not have Viviana as your mistress?" Alize asked.

"I barely wanted to marry the one I have, and you think I want a second woman to juggle?" I joked, never giving away any feelings that I'd come to fall in love with McKayla. She'd become more than a transaction for me.

Sante cleared his throat, and Alize held his hands up in surrender.

"Problem is that this is bringing more problems to our territories." Tommaso tapped his finger on the table.

Sante sat up, removed his gun, and put it on the table.

"No one is thinking of that, Sante. Right, Tommaso?" I asked, letting him know we could damn sure end this one way. I could promise it wouldn't be me or my brother.

"Forgive me."

"What do you propose we do, Savio? My men have their load getting ripped off," Alize argued.

"I say we officially vote Greco out."

"He's a made boss, Savio," Tommaso commented.

"I know what he is, but he seems to think he's above what I say goes."

"And Maurizio?"

"Maurizio won't be a problem."

"How can we be so sure?"

"Sante."

Sante pulled out his phone, scrolled through to photos

of Maurizio, and shoved the photo over to Alize. "That's Maurizio in a photo with the police."

"Nevio's case?"

"That along with him trying to kill me and my girl."

"So, why does our territory have police running through it?"

"You have to ask Carmine or Maurizio," I replied, bringing up his underboss.

"A setup?" Tommaso's eyes dipped low, and he rubbed his chin in thought.

"I wouldn't put it past Carmine to try something underhanded to make it look like it's my family."

Sante's phone vibrated, and he scanned whatever the message was when his eyes rose in shock.

"I still think you and Gennaro need to talk. We have too much money on the line for a war," Tommaso said.

Sante leaned over and whispered in my ear, "You need to stay calm and step over to the corner to talk to me."

I held up my hand for a moment and pushed the chair back. I rose and followed Sante to the nearest exit. He unlocked his phone and passed it to me.

"What's this?"

"McKayla ran away from Curtis."

"How long?" My jaw clenched, and I tried to stay calm, but my heart dropped at the message from Curtis.

Curtis: *911 McKayla ran.*

"He can't determine how long because the saleslady distracted him."

"Saleslady." I gripped the phone tight, to the point of wanting to throw it across the room.

"Is there a problem, Savio?" Tommaso asked.

"We can't let them know you're preoccupied. It will show weakness," Sante explained.

"What if."

She could be hurt somewhere.

"You can't think like that."

I put on a brave face, even though my heart pounded out of my chest. "I have to get back home to Chicago, a family emergency."

"Something we can do?" Alize stood, extending his hand.

"No. I'll have Sante contact you to finish the conversation."

My men cleared the walkway and escorted me back to the black SUV and headed back to the private airport to fly home. I dialed from my phone to get in contact with McKayla.

"You've reached McKayla Stanton. Please leave a message," the voicemail recording said.

"McKayla, I'm not mad. Just let me know you're okay." My stomach churned at the thought of her leaving me.

"Savio, look at this." Sante brought me out of my thoughts and shoved his phone in my face.

"Savio Calabresi killed Nevio Colombo," the news headline reported.

"I told him to kill this story."

"Obviously, she must have gotten to him." Sante continued to text on his phone.

"What has Curtis said?"

"He went by your condo and your parents. McKayla never showed."

"Get us to the airport now!" I shouted to my men and removed my tie.

"On it, Boss." Mario sped up and cut through traffic. Cars honked as he sped down the ninety-five freeway.

Buzz! Buzz!

I grabbed my cell and lifted it up when I saw my mother calling. "I can't talk to her now."

"You need to say something, so she doesn't worry."

"Yes, Mother."

"I haven't heard from McKayla. She usually calls me back," Adelina said.

"She's probably working." I squeezed my eyes shut.

"Well, let her know I want to meet for breakfast."

"Of course, Mother."

"Something wrong, Savio? I can hear it in your voice."

The SUV swerved into the private airstrip, and I hopped out, not waiting for Sante, and ran toward the jet stairs.

"I'm boarding a flight. Let me call you back." I hurriedly got her off the phone and hung up.

Sante sat across from me and buckled his seatbelt as the plane prepared to take off.

———

The next day, I was running on empty, and my entire condo was full of my men and my brothers as I paced back and forth, still wearing the same clothes as yesterday. I never went to sleep, tracing McKayla's phone. It was turned off with the last location being the airport.

"What was she like the last time you saw her?" EJ interrogated.

There was no question that McKayla was hurt somewhere and unable to call me. Even though she would run, I would still be able to have eyes on her in my city, so she had to have flown out of state. Maybe even out of the country.

"Everything was fine, until... that fucking article." I punched my fist through the wall.

"Are you sure we should have killed him?" Sante remarked.

I waved him off, thinking about last night when I had Joseph taken out for disobeying my orders. They rigged his car, and he went over a ditch.

"Fuck that!" I shouted and pushed over the glasses on top of the bar.

"Savio, we're going to find her, but you need to calm down," EJ said.

Ring! Ring!

"That's your phone," Sante said.

I quickly grabbed it off the coffee table and answered without looking. "McKayla? McKayla!"

"Savio, I take it you're missing something," Gennaro's raspy voice came through the phone.

"Where is she?" I gripped the phone tight, my breathing heightened. If Gennaro had McKayla, and if he touched her, I would burn his entire bloodline for going against me. "Put her on the phone."

"You owe me."

"If you want to have your next breath, you better not touch her."

"He… lllo," McKayla stuttered.

"McKayla, did he touch you?"

Carlos raised his thumb.

"I'm coming for you, baby." I heard the dial tone and groaned in frustration. Gennaro had made me his enemy.

"I got a trace," Carlos said.

"Where is he?"

"Paris." Carlos turned his computer around and showed an address in Paris.

"Get the plane ready."

———

A few days later.

Renato sent me a screenshot of Viviana at some club, partying without a care in the world when her father put a death wish on her back. Tommaso and Alize texted back and forth about Greco kidnapping McKayla and offering to help me in any way they could, on the condition I didn't do any more damage than I'd already done.

I had two of Greco's blocks burned down and robbed his gun and drug shipments. Now I had Renato watching his daughter and waiting for the perfect time to snatch her up and show him what it meant when you betrayed me.

McKayla was sleeping in her bed at her old apartment, and I sat in the corner chair, watching her. I hadn't let her out of my sight, and she ignored me when I tried to apologize for getting her in this situation. The last few days had been chaotic, and the beast came out that I never wanted her to see.

Flashback Greco.

Pop! Pop!

I kicked in the door and blasted the first person I saw. Gennaro thought he was protected, but we paid some of his men off to get his schedule and whereabouts. He'd just come back from some meeting, and we caught him slipping. I flew straight here from the States and had eyes on the house to make it easy when we landed. The house wasn't isolated like I thought it would be, so we needed to be discreet and come in early in the morning before someone called the police. A few of my men shot his as I climbed the stairs and went to Gennaro's room, but he wasn't there.

"Boss, he's trying to run!" He pointed out the window of a side door.

"Get him! Did you find McKayla!"

"I got her, Boss," Carlo said.

Present day back in her apartment.

"I want some space," McKayla mumbled and turned over in bed.

"McKayla, I don't do space." I started to stand.

She held her hand up to stop me from coming forward. "Please, Savio. If you have any type of feelings for me, I need some space."

"If I didn't have any feelings for you, I wouldn't have agreed to let you keep this bullshit apartment!" I raised my voice.

She covered her face and cried. "Leave me alone!"

"McKayla."

"No, just leave." She jumped out of the bed and ran to the bathroom.

I wanted to go to her and hold her in my arms, but I knew I couldn't make things worse and force her back into my life. She would learn our life was bonded, and it would never end, but I'd let her have some time to come to grips with seeing me in that way.

I walked out of the room, with Renato waiting on me.

"You good?"

"What's going on with the Greco family situation?"

"We have it under control, and they've surrendered."

"Viviana?"

"She's isolated."

"Keep it that way."

"Don't worry, her time will come." He opened the front door.

I grabbed my coat off the chair and looked back at McKayla's bedroom, closed my eyes, and prayed she would come around soon.

CHAPTER 31

Savio

I LOOKED out the window of my family's estate and watched as a herd of reporters posted out front filmed and talked about the Calabresi being a diabolical crime family. I'd stayed at my parents' home for the past few days because the news followed me to my condo. I'd thought about selling, but I loved my home and couldn't fathom letting someone run me out.

The flashes of the cameras went off again as they noticed me in the window.

"Savio, step back from the window," Mom remarked.

"Have you gotten any sleep?" I inquired and hugged her. Putting her hand on my chest, I covered it with my own.

"No. When something is happening with my children, I never sleep."

"Mother, I'll be fine."

"You don't look as though you've slept."

"Not until McKayla comes home."

"Give it time."

"*Savio Calabresi brought in for questioning,*" the reporters repeated non-stop for the past few hours on the news cycles.

"Savio, turn that off," Father said.

"Mr. Calabresi, we need you to be calm when you go in and answer questions," Leonardo stated, holding some files in his hands.

"He's not being arrested right?" Adelina asked.

"No, ma'am, but we need to make sure Savio doesn't lose his temper," Leonardo pressed.

"How does it look that the highest profile mob boss is being blasted on all the news channels?" Vincenzo barked.

"Vin, stop it!" Adelina shouted.

"I agree with your mother. We don't need any more Calabresi in the news." Leonardo stood at the entrance of the office door. "Have you spoken to McKayla?"

"No." I sighed, rubbing a hand down my face.

"She's still avoiding your calls?"

I grabbed the pen in my hand tight, then threw it across the room. "Fuck!"

"Savio, honey," Adelina spoke softly and rubbed my back. "I'll be fine."

"He's not to say anything that would imply that he was at the scene," Father demanded.

"Sir, I'll do my best."

"Your best shouldn't have my son being called down to the police station in the first place, let alone in the news!" Father spat.

"Officer Harris," Renato blurted out, rubbing his hands together.

"No, Renato." Adelina pointed her finger in his face.

"I need some air."

"We need to get going, Savio."

"My son better be home within an hour, Leonardo."

"We're riding with you," Vincenzo demanded, and I

didn't fight them, even though the only person I wanted next to me was avoiding me altogether.

"I'm going to try to call McKayla." Adelina reached in her purse.

I placed my hand on top of her. "No, she wants space, and I'm giving her that."

"But Savio, you need your wife."

"I know where she is. I don't plan on her being gone forever," I vowed to myself.

As we piled into the limos, everyone was dressed in their best suits and coats, ready to face what the day would bring our way. The evidence was fabricated, and I knew Officer Harris was lying and using Maurizio to help him. As Leonardo explained, I shouldn't answer any questions; he should do all the talking. I nodded in agreement.

The iron gates parted, and a swarm of people bombarded the limos, banging at the windows and doors. Flashes of light went off repeatedly as I kept my head down.

———

"Mr. Calabresi. Can't say I wouldn't see you so soon," Officer Harris taunted.

"Speak to me and not my client," Leonardo responded.

"Your clients have been very busy."

"He's a billionaire, along with his brothers and father," Leonardo teased.

Harris clenched his jaw. "His money can't get him out of this."

"We'll see," I said.

"What was that?" Officer Harris leaned over the table and stared at me.

"He didn't say anything," Leonardo replied, and I smirked.

"Where were you the night of Nevio's death?"

"Fucking your wife," I joked.

He glared. "You think this is funny?" He pointed to the file on Nevio.

"I think you're obsessed, along with your other friends." I waved at the mirror.

Harris sat back in his chair. "How's Mrs. McKayla?"

The smirk I had on my face disappeared.

"Silence," Officer Harris teased.

"Officer Harris, stick to why we were here," Leonardo told him.

"I mean, someone as beautiful as her, sexy full lips, big tits and nice—"

I jumped over the desk and punched him in the face repeatedly for talking about McKayla. The doors opened, and more cops came in to help pull me off him.

He chuckled, wiping the blood off his lip. "You're arrested for assaulting a police officer."

"That's bullshit! We'll have those charges dropped immediately, and I'm filing a suit against you, Harris," Leonardo shouted.

The cops handcuffed me and took me out of the interrogation room. My mind went blank when he brought up McKayla, and all I could think about was him putting his hands on her.

———

"Savio, you need to learn to control your temper," Father complained, shuffling behind me after getting the charges dropped a few hours later.

Our contact on the force looked at the footage and listened to Harris act like an ass, so he could pull some strings to get me out. I was ready to find him and make his life a living hell.

"Where's Renato?"

"No, you're going to the house and sitting down."

"I have to handle some business."

"If anything happens to that policeman, you're the first person they'll come for."

"All of this is your fault," I murmured.

"As a man, I expect you to speak to my face."

The car drove into traffic, and I fastened the seatbelt. "I think you know what I said."

"No, I want to hear the words."

"Take me to my condo."

"Leonardo thinks you should be at the house behind gates. News reporters are everywhere."

"Fucking reporters." I laughed and clapped my hands together.

"Maybe a trip out of the country would be good for you."

"I'll go to the house, but I'm not leaving the country."

The car angled back home, and the premises was cleared of any reporters. Finally parked, we stepped out and went inside to peace. I stalked to the bar. My hand was a little swollen from the punches I threw at Harris, but I didn't regret what he had coming. Spending any time in jail for McKayla was something I'd never have to question.

"That was foolish, Son." Mom sat on the couch. Father followed and reached for a glass of whiskey.

"I don't regret doing it." I tossed the drink down and went to pour another one.

"Can this hurt his case, Elio?" she interrogated my father.

"Adelina, go make sure the chef is preparing dinner."

She watched for a few seconds, then stood and kissed me on the cheek and left the room. Renato and Vincenzo came in, and they looked like something else had happened.

"What?"

"The news outlets have been sniffing around the Calabresi office."

"Shit."

"You shouldn't go there. Try to work from home."

"I won't let them run me out of my business," I fussed.

"Savio, think smarter." Father's brow lifted.

"A bunch of piranhas," Renato commented.

"McKayla."

"She's fine," Renato replied.

"Keep it that way."

"We understand."

"Vincenzo, I'm not stepping away from the company."

"At least try to be discreet." Vincenzo picked up the shot glass and poured some scotch.

"Never was a habit of mine."

CHAPTER 32

McKayla

I SIPPED ON MY SMOOTHIE, removed the key to my car, and headed out of the gym. I hadn't been in such a long time. It was foreign to me, and I remembered why I stayed away, preferring the comfort of my home, and watched videos.

"McKayla Calabresi! Do you know where your husband is?" An unexpected flash of light appeared in my eyes.

"Leave me alone!" I shouted.

A microphone was pointed in my face.

"We understand you're a witness to a murder." A reporter shoved a video camera in my face.

"I don't know what you're talking about."

I tried to push through the crowd.

"Come on, McKayla. We know you kept your husband's secrets."

I slid the key in the door and slammed it shut, starting the car. No one would move until I pressed on the gas.

"Get out of the way!" My heart pounded. I backed out of the parking lot and accelerated. The Bluetooth connected to Rena's phone.

"Hey, did you work out?"

"No, because reporters are hounding me."

"At the gym?"

"Yes, there were at least six or seven of them."

"Where are you now?"

"Going home."

"You sound like you need a girls' sleepover. Come to my place."

"I don't want to impose on you."

"You're not. You're my best friend."

"Are you sure?"

"Yes, more than likely, reporters are camped out at your place right now."

"I can think back on doing the same thing to other people." I felt my stomach twist in knots.

"You're nothing like those vultures. Come here, and we'll pig out on food and wine."

"Thanks, Rena."

"No thanks is needed."

I made a U-turn at the light and went in the opposite direction to Rena's apartment.

Two weeks later.

"Hello, how can I help you, ma'am?"

"I need to see Savio Calabresi."

"Mrs. Calabresi, he's in a meeting right now."

"I understand, but this is an emergency."

"Let me check." The secretary picked up the landline and dialed his office number.

I waited with my stomach in knots. I hadn't seen him in two weeks, but I'd felt his presence everywhere. I was tired of him trying to send his brothers to check on me.

"Mr. Calabresi said you can come right in."

"Thanks."

Before I opened his office door, I pushed my hair behind my ear and released a long-held breath. Letting my guard down around Savio was not on the agenda today.

"I need you to call off your men." I slammed the door to his office.

"Why?"

"Because I'm no longer in need of your protection."

"Says who?" He stood from his chair, slowly trailed around the desk, and leaned against the edge.

"Says me."

"You look beautiful."

"I'll give back Savi and whatever else I cost you."

"I gave you that dog as a gift."

"I just want this to be over."

"That will never happen."

"Run your own life, not mine."

"Come back home."

"I have a home."

"Next to me is your home; that's a temporary vacation."

"This isn't getting us anywhere."

"I know where I stand."

"I'm leaving."

I reached for the door handle.

"Remember you still have my last name."

"Not if I find someone else."

"You can try to watch how they end up missing."

I stormed out of his office and down the hall to the elevator in a huff. I punched the elevator button and waited for the doors to open when the biggest culprit stepped off.

"Stay out of my life, Renato!"

"Doing my job." Renato grinned.

"You're an asshole like your brother."

"That's a good trait to have."

A few minutes after getting out of the building, I

jumped in my car, locked the doors, and closed my eyes to control my breathing. "Put him in the back of your mind."

Ring! Ring!

I reached in my coat and grabbed my ringing phone. "What?"

"Drive safe."

"Ugh!"

I looked around the street, over to the entrance of the building, and noticed Savio and Renato staring back at me. I flipped him off, started my car, and drove off, headed to pick up some groceries for my apartment.

Ten minutes later, I arrived at the local market down the street from my apartment and I parked, grabbed my reusable bags, and scrolled through my list of groceries.

"Salad mix," I mumbled to myself, grabbed the cart, and pushed down the aisle. I checked through the fruit and veggie section to get the freshest before bagging them up.

"McKayla?" I heard a familiar voice and looked up to see Adelina Calabresi.

"Hi, Mrs. Calabresi." I tossed the tomatoes in my cart.

"I didn't know you shopped here."

"I live near here."

"That's wonderful."

"What are you doing here? This seems far from your area."

"I was grabbing some things for Savio, to cook him dinner at his condo."

"Oh."

"Have you seen him?"

"Today."

"I know he misses you."

"I'd rather not talk about him."

"Completely understand."

"What are you making for dinner?"

"I'll probably end up ordering, even though I'm grabbing groceries."

"It happens."

"I don't want us to be strangers."

"Savio and I need to cut ties."

"He's my son. But I'm a woman first."

"Then you know what I'm doing is for the best."

"What I believe is that you two need to work on your relationship."

"He's repeatedly lied."

"But you could have left him in the beginning."

"He threatened to kill my family."

"I never agreed with the threat to your family."

"Can you tell him to stop having them follow me around?"

"Who's following you?" She scanned the grocery store.

"His guards and Renato."

"Renato is protective of his brothers and the people they love."

"This will never end, will it?"

"Love never ends; it just slows down for you to catch up."

"Well, I need to get home and feed Savi."

"Don't be a stranger." Adelina hugged me and kissed me on the cheek.

"I won't."

———

"I love this part!" Rena swooned and scooped more ice cream in her bowl. I invited her over to watch a few romantic comedy movies to keep me distracted. Savi sat at the foot of the couch, biting on his toy as I typed on the computer.

"Matthew and Kate Hudson are the best duo together."

"He or the one with Sandra Bullock and Benjamin Bratt?"

"That's more action and comedy."

"Still good."

Ding!

"I got it!" Rena hopped up and ran to the door.

"What is it?" I called out.

"Thank you. A bouquet of red roses along with a note."

"Who are they from?" I asked.

"Your husband."

"Throw them away."

Rena placed them on the table. "You can't say he's not persistent."

"Toss them."

"Let me read the card."

"I don't care what he says."

"He's not the only one stubborn."

I sucked my teeth.

"*I'm sorry for not living up to my pledge,*" she read aloud.

"Whatever."

"Savi, you see the flowers from your daddy?' She pointed up to the vase. Savi looked like a deer in headlights.

"That's not his father."

"Somebody needs to be fucked," she mumbled.

"Watch the movie or go home."

"Testy."

She sat back down and picked up her bowl of ice cream.

"My focus is work and nothing else going forward."

"Okay."

"I'm serious."

"I didn't say you weren't."

"Just support me."

"I will always support you."

"All right, now throw the flowers away."

"No, take them home."
"Why?"
"To make somebody jealous."
"Who?"
"None of your business."

CHAPTER 33

McKayla

A MONTH LATER.

Gabby and I were going over notes for a story on the latest scandal with a bank skimming customers out of overdraft fees. My body was still adjusting from the train wreck of Greco trying to pawn me in front of Savio, and he ended up getting killed. Viviana was nowhere to be heard from after news of her father getting killed.

"This could be a great lead graphic," Gabby mentioned, holding up a Post-It note.

"*Money scam. The old trick,*" I rambled off.

"I like it."

"So, have you heard anything about Joseph getting killed in a car accident?"

"No."

"I heard it had something to do with the Calabresi family."

"You shouldn't believe everything you hear, Gabby."

"Normally I don't, but it was so fast."

"What other notes do you have?" I queried, trying to change the subject.

"Here, have you met the new editor?" She opened her folder and pointed to line items highlighted.

"Not yet."

"She's pretty cool. Seems open to ideas."

"That's great."

"You seem distracted. Am I boring you?" She chuckled.

I smiled and shook my head. "You're fine. I just want to get this done so I can head home."

"Oh, what are your plans?"

"Food and bed." I laughed.

"Aren't you still married?"

"Gabby."

"Sorry, force of habit." She held her hands up in surrender.

"Let's just focus on the story."

"Gotcha."

"Thanks."

"One thing."

"Ugh… What is it?"

"There's a man standing behind you with flowers."

I swung my head around, and there was a delivery guy with flowers in his hands. I closed the book and stood. I already knew who sent them.

"McKayla Stanton." He lifted his clipboard.

"That's me."

"Sign here."

I took the clipboard and signed my name.

"Have a nice day."

"Thanks, let me grab you a tip."

I turned to put the flowers down.

He stopped me. "No need, I was given a tip already."

"Oh, thank you."

"They look expensive." Gabby leaned over and smelled the flowers.

"You like them?"

She nodded. "They're beautiful."

"You can have them."

"What? You're kidding."

"I'm serious. Take them."

"McKayla, no."

"Please, you should take them."

"Are you sure?"

"Yep. Enjoy." I placed them near her and picked up my backpack and keys.

"Are you leaving?"

"I'm exhausted and need a break. I'll email you my notes."

"All right, have a good day and thanks again."

———

I dropped my work bag at my apartment door, removed my ponytail, scratched my scalp, and headed to the kitchen when the doorbell rang. It was going on seven at night, but I was pretty wiped out since I came back home. Having guests was the last thing I needed when I could barely keep my head up.

"Ugh, not in the mood." I groaned, marched to the door, and yanked it open to see Rena about to knock again. My work schedule had been nonstop, cramming myself back into getting my work up again.

"I have wine."

"Good, because it's the only reason you're invited in tonight."

"Well, good thing I came with gifts." She held a bag of takeout in her right hand.

"That's why you're my friend."

"Yes, and you should shower and change while I set this up."

"Wait, how did you get away from Sante?"

"Sante doesn't own me."

"Rena."

"Tonight is about you relaxing… no men."

"Rena Clark doesn't care to talk about men?"

I reached up and touched her forehead.

"I'm not man crazy."

"Today you're not."

She stuck her tongue out, and I laughed and went to the bedroom to shower and change. Savio liked me to sleep naked. Some nights I did miss him, but it was hard to find the balance between my heart and my head.

Thirty minutes after washing the day away, I came up to the living room with the TV on to *Goodfellas,* and I couldn't help but laugh at her little dig.

"Rena, you pick the oddest things to watch." I plopped down on the couch next to her and picked up the glass of wine.

"I thought this would help clear your mind." She grinned.

"You're an ass."

"Sante tells me that all the time."

"What's going on with you two?"

She lifted the glass to her lips. "Nothing."

"You can tell me if you like him."

"I don't."

"So why are you squirming in your seat?"

"Tonight, I'm here to help you. My life isn't complicated."

"Yet."

"Yet, what?"

"Your life isn't complicated yet."

"He's not my type."

"A sexy, tall man with broad shoulders and kissable lips?"

"Nope."

"Did I mention a billionaire?"

"Someone told me once, there are more things in life than a billionaire."

"Mhmm…I wonder who that was." I chortled.

"Anyway, we have a little work gathering tomorrow at the bar. You're coming."

"No."

I grabbed the plate and fork off the table to feed my grumbling stomach.

"Yes."

"No, Rena."

"McKayla, you've been cooped up here or in the office since you've been back."

"I like my quiet and structure."

"You're becoming a hermit."

"I feel guilty."

"For what?"

"Everything."

"You fell in love."

"With a crazy, arrogant, possessive man."

"Don't forget sexy."

I pushed her in the shoulder, and she fell over laughing.

"Seriously, I want you to be happy with or without Savio."

"Thanks."

"Don't rush anything. Until then, we're going out."

"If I go, which I didn't agree to, I won't be staying long."

I scooped some rice in my mouth and took a sip of my drink.

"At least stay an hour."

"The things I do for you."

"Did I tell you Sante tried to crash one of my dates?"

"What? No. When did this happen?"

"A few weeks ago."

"You like him?"

"No."

"I can see you turning red. I'll leave it alone for now."

"This is my favorite part with Ray Liotta." She grabbed the remote and turned up the volume, ignoring my last statement.

———

The next night, as promised, Rena and I came out to the bar to hang with a few coworkers who I'd been ignoring for a while. I could see the looks on their faces; they wanted to ask about my marriage. I hadn't started the process of even filing for divorce. Savio stopped calling and texting, so I guessed he got the hint that I didn't want to talk. I promised I would start the process once I cleared my head and thought clearly.

"You look like you don't want to be here." Nick came over, sipping on his beer, and sat beside me in the booth.

"Is that obvious?"

"Rena said you needed a little conversation."

I glanced over at her dancing with some guy in the corner. "I'm a big girl. I don't need a babysitter, Nick."

"I can see that."

"Aren't you and Gabby dating?"

"No."

"Interesting."

"Is that the gossip going around the office?"

"That, and the new editor is cool."

"She's all right," he responded.

I reached for my martini and took a sip. "From what I gather, she has a crush on you."

"Why do you say that?"

"She hasn't taken her eyes off you since you came to sit."

He scanned the bar and noticed her turn her back to us. "She's a friend."

"Nothing wrong with that."

"You look like you could use a friend."

"I—"

"She has a husband. No need for friends." Renato stood in front of the booth.

I almost choked on my drink when I noticed Elio next to him. "Renato."

"Who is he?" Nick asked.

"The guy who's going to make you disappear." Renato's cold, dead eyes glared at Nick.

"I suggest you get up and leave," Elio warned and held Renato back.

Nick peered at me, and I felt sorry for how they were acting. As an only child, I'd always wanted siblings, but to get four crazy brothers who would threaten someone off an innocent conversation was over the top.

Nick walked off, and I jumped up and pointed a finger in his face. "Are you two crazy!"

"You've had enough fun. Time to go home to your husband."

I chuckled and threw my hands in the air. "I don't have a husband."

"McKayla, we can do this easy or hard."

"Renato, if you threaten me, I promise to call your parents."

"I don't take kindly to threats."

"Tell your brother to go to hell."

"You tell him yourself."

"He's here?"

"Outside in the car waiting."

"I'm not going."

"McKayla, for our safety, it's best you walk out now."

"I'm not scared of him."

"It's not about your safety; it's about everyone else's," Elio explained.

CHAPTER 34

Savio

A FEW HOURS BEFORE.

I sat in my office, looking over pictures of McKayla going to work and spending time with her parents and friends. My men were assigned to keep track of her whereabouts. Even if she hated me and claimed to want a divorce, I wouldn't let it happen. In the beginning, it was a benefit to get her to marry me, but we'd grown closer, and I could admit the love I had for her caused me to think irrationally.

I'd started drinking more and stopped taking calls from anyone. The only person I wanted to hear from was McKayla. Marilyn hadn't been by to cook or clean, but I still paid her since she'd been with me for so long. McKayla still looked the same, even more beautiful than before. My mom was mad at me and told me to not even come around until I made things right.

"I told you, he's here looking like a wimp."

"You owe me fifty dollars." Sante held his hand out to Renato.

All my brothers standing at the door of my office in my

penthouse was the usual routine whenever one of us went underground and didn't want to be disturbed.

"How long have you been stuck in here?" Sante came to sit in the chair.

"Not today, Sante, and no smartass remarks, Renato.

"I should feel hurt, but you look like you need a friend."

"She still hasn't called?" EJ queried.

"No."

"Maybe that's a sign for you to move on from her," Vincenzo said.

I growled and tried to leap over my desk. Sante pushed me back down.

"Enough! You're ready to fight your brother over your lying," Sante shouted.

I waved him off.

"This is all your fault, Savio. You made the choices."

"I don't need a lecture, Sante."

"No, you need some pussy," Renato mumbled.

All of us burst into laughter.

"Fuck all of you."

"Time you got out of this funk."

"I'm busy."

"Doing what?"

"Working."

"Now that Greco is no longer a threat, you should focus on adding more real estate."

"Handle that for me," I replied to Vincenzo.

"Well, there's something else you should probably handle," Renato said.

"Renato," Sante grumbled.

They both had a look in their eye of something going on that I wasn't privy to.

"What?"

"Nothing."

"Sante, he needs to know."

"What is it?"

"No, because all you're going to do is get him riled up," Sante explained.

"Now you have me curious."

"Your woman is on a date," Renato blurted out.

I cracked the pencil in my hand and jumped out of my seat. "Who the fuck dares to go on a date with my woman?"

Sante and Renato jumped in front of me.

"Savio, calm down."

"Get out of the way, Sante." I narrowed my eyes and pushed him in the shoulder.

"Don't get your ass beat," Sante responded and shoved me back.

"Renato, where is she?" I ignored Sante's glare.

"At some bar with Rena."

Sante's head swiveled toward him.

"All this is going to do is upset her even more."

"My wife is on a date, and you think I'm worried about her being upset?"

"All I'm saying is you need to proceed with a little common sense."

"If Rena was on date, would you proceed with common sense?"

"That's different. She's not my wife, and I don't like her."

"Renato, take me to this bar." I reached my desk, grabbed my pistol, and slid it in a holster, walking out of the office with them arguing for me to calm down.

"If you go in there now, she's going to hate you."

"I don't care."

"Savio," Sante called my name, and I stopped at the door. "I'm riding with you, but if you want her to come home, think about what you're going to say."

"Or he could kidnap her again," Renato suggested.

"This was why he was my enforcer."

————

Present time in the car.

I watched from outside the bar when Renato and Elio escorted McKayla outside. Rena was right behind, trying to fight Renato.

I shook my head at the crowd taking photos and videos of them. I didn't want a scene, but the second I heard my wife was on a date, I was ready to blow the entire place up.

Sante jogged over and grabbed Rena in his arms, and Renato pointed to the limo. McKayla rolled her eyes. I smirked at her feistiness and hated it at the same time. Enzo opened the door, and McKayla slid in and crossed her legs, showing off her thick thighs in a short skirt. I wanted to go in and find the guy she was on a date with and smash his head in.

"Do you want me to go kill everyone in there?"

She ignored my comment.

"Baby, I suggest you answer me or suffer the consequences."

She still ignored me and stared ahead.

"Okay." I extended my head to the open door and stepped out. I reached behind my back and pulled my gun out.

"Are you nuts!" McKayla tried to jump out of the car.

I pushed her back inside, passing Enzo my gun, and shut the door. "Yes!"

1McKayla tried to fight me, and I pinned her down by her wrists between her legs.

"Get off me."

"One thing I don't do is joke about you."

"You can't go around killing innocent people."

"I do whatever I want."

"Get off me."

"Who is he?"

"Who?"

"Don't play dumb, sweetheart."

"It wasn't a date. I was hanging out with coworkers."

"My brothers said you were on a date."

"Are you spying on me?" She tilted her head to the side.

"Yes."

McKayla's eyes widened in shock. "You're crazy."

"We've established that already. I need you to tell me which guy I need to kill."

"Savio, I wasn't on a date. Rena thought it would be nice to get me out of the house."

"What's wrong?"

"Not sure if you've noticed, but my husband is insane."

I smiled at her reference to husband. "So, I'm still your husband." I pressed a kiss to her palm.

"I can't answer that question."

"So, you want to leave me." I trailed kisses up her chest, to her neck and chin.

"This won't work… Mhmmm."

Knock! Knock!

"Savio, open this door," Rena yelled.

"Rena, get back here. Savio won't hurt her," Sante replied, and I heard scuffling.

"Go away!" I snapped.

"Savio."

McKayla tried to get up, and I grabbed her around the waist and helped her to sit in my lap. I rubbed a hand up and down her back.

"I don't like these clothes."

"Not your choice."

"I'll burn it when we get home."

"Who says I'm going home with you?"

"McKayla, we've been apart for too long. Time to forgive."

"You're so selfish."

"I want my wife back."

"You should have thought of that before you lied and betrayed me."

"I'm sorry." I held her chin, keeping eye contact, and showed I was wrong.

"Did you kill Joseph?"

"You don't want the answer to that question."

"This is crazy."

"I never apologize, McKayla, but you need to know what I will do when something comes between us."

"Death isn't the answer."

"In my world, it is."

"What about Viviana?"

"She wasn't touched."

"No more killing, Savio."

"When you took those vows, you knew my life."

"Savio, I wasn't exactly married in a traditional way."

"We can get married again."

"With our family?"

"Yes, anything that makes you happy." I gripped the back of her neck, tightening a hand in her hair. "Never walk away from me again, McKayla Calabresi. Do you understand?" I bit her bottom lip, then licked across her lips with my tongue to ease the sting.

"Yes."

"I need to hear you."

"I understand."

"Good. Let's go home. Our bed misses you."

"Can I talk to McKayla, please?" Rena knocked again.

I dropped my hand from around her hair and waist.

"She won't leave until I tell her we're good."

"Fine." McKayla lifted her leg to move, and I stopped her. "You stay right here."

"Savio."

"Baby, my dick is hard, and I won't make it home. I need to be with you now."

She kissed me on the lips and pressed the button for the window to come down. "Rena, I'm fine."

Rena glared at me. "Are you sure? If he's holding you hostage…"

"I promise I'm okay."

"Well, I'll let you go then and call you tomorrow."

"She won't be available."

"Savio." McKayla smacked me on the arm.

"We're going out of town, McKayla."

"Did you talk to Nick?" Rena asked.

I smacked her on the ass. "Who the fuck is Nick?"

"Savio!"

Rena burst into laughter, and I picked my gun up, causing McKayla to chuckle.

"I love you, Savio Calabresi."

"I love you too, McKayla, but I hate your friend."

"Let's go home and make up."

"Good. I've missed your sexy ass."

"Have you spoken with your parents?"

"My mom banned me from the house until you come back."

"I love your mom."

"What about your parents?"

"They'll come around."

"Maybe I can buy them a new house."

"You can't throw money at everything, Savio, and expect it to go away."

The limo started, and Sante leaned down in the window next to speak. "Call me tomorrow."

"Arrange the plane for us to go to Fiji," I said.

"Why?"

"We're getting married."

"Aren't you already married?" Sante's voice heightened to a level I wasn't expecting.

We stared into each other's eyes, and McKayla held out her hand to mine. "For real this time," she replied, pecking my lips.

"Savio, handle your shit from now on," Sante grunted, leaving to get in the car with Rena.

"Do you think they're dating?" McKayla probed.

"I don't care to know."

Using my fingertips, I touched her thigh and then moved up to her breasts, lightly biting her nipple through her shirt.

"Savio… I want to wait." She threw her head back and moaned.

"No." I shook my head.

"Please, we can go one night until our wedding night."

"McKayla."

"Do this for me. One more night, and I promise to make you feel good." McKayla ran a hand across my dick.

"You're torturing me for payback."

Before I could calm myself down, I smashed my lips on hers and dry humped her for a few minutes.

"I did learn a few things from you," McKayla pulled away, whispered in my ear.

CHAPTER 35

Savio

THE NEXT AFTERNOON.

Our private plane landed in Fiji, at Laucala Island, and we brought my brothers and parents along with hers. Rena and Sante seemed standoffish, and I didn't know why, but McKayla was trying her best to keep her mood up.

I wanted to just be buried deep in her walls and say fuck this wedding. I should have demanded we forgo this wedding and do something simple at our place or my parents' and take a trip away just the two of us alone. Her parents seemed to be fine with me, but I couldn't tell when they stuck around my parents more than talking to me.

The sun was out and windy on the beach of Fiji. I'd rented a villa with everyone having their own villas away from us. I planned on having her naked everyday walking around. This time I wouldn't stop until I'd completely drained every ounce of energy, and my dick broke off.

"Savio, you made a wise choice." My father put his hand on my shoulder, and I kept my eyes on McKayla.

"She's everything to me."

"So, you finally understand what love can do for you."

McKayla laughed at something Rena said, and that made me smile.

"I think I'm getting there."

"Word got out that the Greco family has left Viviana unprotected."

"Her father is to blame."

"You don't want to leave things alone." He lit his cigar.

"I wouldn't be Savio Calabresi if I left my enemies to come back."

"I've done some things in the past. Your mother would never look at me the same if she knew."

"She's not going anywhere."

"Live life as though she will."

He headed to my mother and Vincenzo, who was still bringing in luggage. I walked over to Renato and Elio talking.

"The package arrived safely." Renato handed a cigar to us.

"You're going to kill her?" EJ asked.

My jaw clenched, and my fists tightened. That bitch caused more drama with my wife based on something her father set in motion, and I would never have agreed even if McKayla didn't show up.

I smiled at McKayla kicking her feet in the water with Rena, and that calmed me down. She liked me when I was less crazy and less possessive, and I promised I would try to relax more, keeping the beast locked up. Waking up every day to her smile, her smell, her comfort, brought me peace no one would ever take away from me.

Viviana had meet with her father for the crimes she attempted against the Calabresi family. I hadn't decided who would take over for Gennaro's position, but right now, keeping it to four families came with less chance of defiance.

"Elio, when it comes to McKayla, I will do anything."

"What if it backfires on you? Your name has appeared."

"It won't. Get it done."

`The last thing I wanted to do was think about Viviana on this trip where I was about to renew my vows and spend time reconnecting with my wife.

"Savio! Come here," McKayla called out.

"No, you come here, so we can go find our room."

"After the wedding, Savio." McKayla splashed some water.

I strolled toward McKayla in the water and held my hands out. "Can I get a kiss?"

"Nope, you took too long."

"McKayla, I don't like to be denied."

"Then punish me."

"My dick grew hard at that." I closed the space between us and wrapped an arm around her waist.

"Are you hungry?" she asked.

"Not for food." I ran a hand down to her ass cheeks and squeezed.

"Rena's looking at us," she whispered.

"Then let's give her something to stare at."

"Stop, you're going to have to wait like you promised."

"Ugh... I don't care about this anymore."

She giggled. I turned, and she jumped on my back.

"I love you," McKayla said.

A flood of emotions came at me, but all I could do was show her how much I would treasure and protect her going forward.

CHAPTER 36
Savio

TWO DAYS LATER.

We'd been nonstop swimming, eating, snorkeling, and visiting locals. McKayla created an entire plan of things we could do for our trip. Now we were back on the beach with chairs lined up, and our family and friends held up their cameras, taking pictures. I wore white pants and a shirt, with my father standing as my best man. McKayla had Rena standing next to her, and I smirked as she wiped the tears away as the pastor went through our vows.

"Do you McKayla Calabresi take Savio Calabresi as your husband?" he asked.

"I do." She smiled, and I gripped her palm and lifted her wrist.

She looked beautiful in a lacey white, spaghetti strap, flowy dress that I wanted to rip off her before we even came out of the room.

"Do you Savio Calabresi take McKayla Calabresi to be your wife?"

"Yes." I went to pull her into my chest to kiss her.

"Wait, Savio!" She laughed, and the pastor chuckled at us.

"I have declared you Mr. and Mrs. Calabresi."

"Come here." I lifted her by her legs, wrapped them around my waist, and walked off, leaving everybody to laugh at me.

It had been too long since we'd been that way, and I craved her more and more since we got down here. I pulled back from the kiss and walked us off back to our room and pushed the door open, then shut and locked the door.

"What about the reception?"

"No."

"You said we'd have a traditional wedding."

"We're about to have our own party." I opened the bedroom door and placed her on her feet, and she gasped in astonishment.

"When did you do this?"

"I had your mother and Rena fix this for us."

The bed had pink rose petals formed in a circle on it. Candles were lit on the table with our food and champagne. I made sure to have the presidential villa with a balcony on the side, a king-size bed that was raised off the floor, with photos of us from Italy plastered around.

"You really paid attention."

"I want to make sure you're happy."

"Be honest and trust me."

"I do."

"Come and take this off me." McKayla turned her back to me.

I raised my shirt over my head and dropped my pants. I ran a hand across her back, and she shivered under my touch. I pressed a kiss to the back of her neck.

"You're so beautiful."

"Show me how much you love me." Her hand reached up and rubbed the back of my head as I slipped her dress off her body.

Wearing a thong and no bra, I held her breasts in my

hands and squeezed, listening to her moans. "Fucking gorgeous."

"Make love to me."

"Your smooth, sweet skin melts under my touch."

I rubbed down her arms, shifted her to face me, and captured her lips. I stepped back, stared at her, and moved around her to pick up the glasses of champagne. "Let's toast."

"To what?"

"To you, for walking into my world and changing it for the better."

"Mr. Calabresi, are you smiling?"

I gulped the champagne down and took the glass out of her hands. "I'm going to love wiping that smile off your face."

"Promise?"

I growled, dropped down to my knees in front of her, and raised her left leg over my shoulder to smell her essence.

"Mmmmm…"

"You smell so good, baby."

"Fuck me, baby."

I grabbed the back of her legs and sucked on her sweet sex, savoring her cries as I tweaked her nipples and smacked her ass.

"Ahhhhh… Savio." Her moans bounced off the walls.

She held the back of my head and moved her hips. I bit the inside of her thighs gently, then kissed the sting away and moved up her stomach to trail kisses and suck on her breasts, twisting her right nipple. Her heavy mounds were ready to be devoured. I teased her long enough and raised her up, lining her up with my dick, and eased inside as she reached around to hold onto my shoulder.

"Shit!" I grunted and pumped slowly.

"Fuck… Yes, baby." Her eyes clamped shut.

I kissed along her chin, cheek, and forehead. "I'm going to fuck you so hard you won't be leaving this room for days."

We went to the bed, and I laid her down on her front, still connected, and slowed my pumps, teasing her lovingly as we looked at each other. She ran a hand up my chest and pulled me forward to hover over her body for a kiss. Leaving kisses down her back, then both butt cheeks, I kneaded and spread her ass wide. I stuck my tongue into her ass.

"Ah! God!" She tried to reach behind her and push me away.

"Stop moving, or I'll stop," I growled, grasping her arms with one hand, and went back to feasting on her ass and swiping my tongue across her pussy.

"You like this, baby?"

McKayla tried to hump my face.

"Let me hear you."

I spat in her pussy, slammed back in her, and picked up my pace, punishing her for leaving me.

"Yesss... Oh, God!"

"Damn... McKayla." I leaned over her back and placed both hands on the side of her body.

She looked over her shoulder and reached to kiss me. The smacking of our skin picked up throughout the room.

I removed my lips and stuck my finger in her mouth. "Get it wet." As she sucked on my finger, I groaned as if she were sucking on my dick. "Stop."

McKayla grinned, and I finished sucking on her bottom lip and slid the finger she sucked on into her tight hole.

"Ooohhh... Mmmmm..." she moaned.

I slowly moved my finger in and out as her juices covered the sheets.

"I'm about to come," she cried out, gripping the sheets.

Her body convulsed, and I pulled my finger out and let her release.

"Yeah, baby, wet these sheets up." I pounded into her uncontrollably when I released.

"Come in your wife!"

The words charged me up, and I released all my seed. Removing myself from her, I lay next to her and lifted her to lie on my chest. We both let our breathing calm down, and I rolled her onto her back, and she welcomed me between her legs.

"We're married."

I nuzzled my face in her neck. "We've been married, baby."

She chortled. "This is for real though."

"It was real for me when we went to the courthouse."

McKayla puckered her lips and kissed me on the cheek, and we fell into a long, deep sleep together, never leaving the bedroom until it was time to come out for the family dinner.

———

Two days later, we were at a family dinner, gathered around drinking and eating on our last day. McKayla was dressed in a floor-length silver gown, with her hair up in a ponytail and wearing the sexiest red lipstick and dark eyes. She made me look at her differently.

"Sei bellissima." I called her beautiful in Italian. "Hai delle labbra così deliziose… Baciami." I told her she had delicious lips and to kiss me. I bent down, reached my hand around her neck, and sucked on her bottom lip, then sucked her tongue into my mouth.

"Can you two breathe for a minute? You're messing my stomach up." Rena pouted, picked up her margarita, and gulped it down.

"Rena, your love life will improve if you stop being so grouchy," McKayla said.

Rena rolled her eyes and picked up her fork to continue eating.

Everything was decorated under a canopy with a long table, and my father sat at the head, with my mother next to him. I sat at the foot of the table with McKayla next to me. They had the table full of food that my mother made sure to incorporate our favorites from Italy from pasta to seafood.

I covered McKayla's hand on top of the table and kissed the back of her palm.

"All right, I want to give a speech," Renato said.

"Oh, God." McKayla tried to cover her face.

"Savio knows I'm not the best at doing this type of thing. But I wanted to let you know, good looking on having in-house pussy."

McKayla choked on her drink, and I glared at Renato and tried to jump up.

"Savio, calm down."

"Renato, shut up." Adelina slapped on the arm.

"I'm congratulating him."

"You're embarrassing McKayla," Adelina explained as McKayla's parents shook their heads.

"He's your brother," McKayla said.

"And your brother-in-law."

"Okay, it's my turn." Rena clinked her knife against the glass of champagne.

"You've had enough to drink." Sante tried to pull Rena to sit down.

"Anyway, I want to say congrats to my best friend and her husband on a wonderful wedding and this fabulous vacation," Rena explained.

"Congrats!" everybody said at the same time, and we drank and ate for the rest of the night.

I watched McKayla dance with her father and then mine

as the music played. I stood back and admired the smile on her face as she looked carefree and relaxed with my family.

"I have something for you to see." Sante stood next to me and held out his phone.

"Is it done?" I glanced at his phone.

"Take a look." He punched around on his phone and passed it to me.

I saw a video of Viviana in a room, tied to a chair with her mouth gagged, as she screamed. A man wearing a mask came into frame, holding a knife in his hands.

"This is for the Calabresi Family."

He walked behind her, grabbed her wrists, and slit them. He then moved around to the front of her body and cut across her knees as she screamed out in pain.

"End it," a voice that sounded a lot like Elio came through.

"With pleasure." He gripped her by the neck, pulled it back, and slid the knife across.

I clicked off the video and thought of how this could have been avoided if she and her father had stayed away and not try to harm my McKayla. People knew me as the beast when I was only focused on taking care of my family's safety.

CHAPTER 37

McKayla

IT HAD BEEN a week since we'd been back from our vacation and vow renewal. The trip was much needed. I got to see Savio a little carefree, and the sex was beyond gratifying to where every time I thought about it, it made my thighs tremble. I needed to help the ache when I was alone by using the vibrator I had stored in my bedroom drawer.

Tonight, he'd agreed to come to a work event that the paper put on every year for upcoming journalists. He didn't give me too much pushback, and I gladly showed him what I was wearing beforehand. The asshole came out when he threatened to cut it up after I came back from wearing it at this event.

Rena and Gabby were talking in a corner, watching all the single men come in and out. I waved to get their attention, and they came toward us.

"How much longer is this again?" Savio challenged.

"Babe, you're the owner of the newspaper. You should know this."

"I have someone to handle these things for me."

I repeated the same statement he always gave me whenever it came up about something with the paper. I still didn't like that he went behind my back to purchase the company, to keep me under his thumb, but I couldn't fight him about that anymore. I just accepted my fate as his wife.

"I love you in this tux."

"Great job on the guest list, Savio." Rena twiddled her fingers together in excitement.

"How many phone numbers have you gotten?"

Gabby laughed at my question. "She's gotten about three numbers already."

"That's supposed to stay between us, Gabby," Rena fussed.

"Does Sante know you're here?" Savio asked.

"Why would I need his permission?"

"My brother may come off calm and nice, but he's a ticking time bomb."

"Sante seems so reasonable though, compared to you," I blurted out.

Savio gripped me around the waist, pulled me into his chest, and smashed his lips on mine. "There's a reason I made him underboss."

"What about your brother, Renato?" Gabby inquired, and Savio's brow furrowed.

"You don't want to know," Savio, Rena, and I all said at the same time.

"There's a big turnout tonight, I think we'll have a lot of interns coming in this year," I said.

"What about getting together for lunch?" Rena asked.

"Not this week, but we're having a family get together at Savio's parents' house."

"I don't know about that," Rena responded and blew out a breath.

"Why not? You like his parents."

"His parents, not the rest of the clan."

"I should be offended, but I know you've had a lot to drink," Savio told her.

"You've kidnapped me already and sent your crazy brother out to get me," Rena spat.

"As long as you know it can be done again." Savio's eyes darkened.

"All right you two. Rena, you're more than welcome to come to the house."

"We don't allow outside people in our family's home," Savio explained.

"This one time can't you make an exception?" I batted my eyes and bit my bottom lip.

Savio sighed heavily and leaned over to whisper in my ear, "You're sucking my dick for this favor."

"I'll do that anyway."

`He growled at my response, kissing me on the neck.

"They're starting the announcements," Gabby said.

The jazz music stopped playing, and the large screen showed the newspaper's name and interns who were coming in for the new year. When Savio said the event would be held at the Calabresi Hotel, a division of the family's business, I was blown away at the huge twenty-story building and landscape. The place was massive and expensive. We had the largest ballroom rented out to hold up to five hundred people, and he wanted to get us a room for the night, but I wanted my own bed.

The presenter finished running down the names, and we clapped. Food was then served, and we took our seats and enjoyed ourselves. Everyone wanted to meet Savio and came up to our table to shake hands with him.

———

The next morning, I had a meeting with the editor about the next steps with my ideas since the article and book were doing well on the charts. I came in extra early, even though we made it home late. Savio stuck to his word, ripping my dress apart and making love to me all night long.

"McKayla, thank you for coming in today." Samira extended his hand out to me.

"Thank you so much."

"Have a seat."

"Thanks."

"So, you know why I wanted you to come in, right?"

"Yes, hopefully I do." I chuckled, and he laughed.

"Well, your piece on the Calabresi struck the book."

"It caused a lot of emotions and controversy."

"I understand, and I want you to know that it's up to you if you agree to my proposal."

"What proposal is that?"

"If you'd like to oversee the organized crime unit news."

I swallowed the lump in my throat.

"I know you'll need to talk it over with your husband, and this could be a little dangerous."

"What would it entail exactly?"

"A lot of late nights if something breaks. Meeting with the police and talking with some people who aren't the friendliest to reporters and media."

"I'm not sure."

"I understand. This is a huge job, but I must tell you… Your husband wouldn't be a factor in the decision of me having you oversee the work."

"When you came onboard, what made him hire you?"

"Let's just say I have some familiar ties with the Calabresi family."

"Wait, your family's in the mafia?"

"A few on my mom's side."

"They're not mad about your job?"

"We clash on occasion."

"I thought I had it bad."

"Don't stress about your answer right now. Keep me updated. You have a few weeks before I make an announcement." She stood up and reached for my hand again.

I promised to give her an update soon after thinking everything over and left to head back to my desk and finish working. I sat and made some notes on the piece Gabby and I finished together. I glanced across my desk and saw my phone vibrating with my mom's name across.

Mom*: Hi baby, are you up for lunch today?*

Me: *Sure, where do you want to meet?*

Mom: *We can do a place close to your job.*

Me: *Panshce?*

Mom: *Great and see if Rena is free.*

Me: *I will.*

I looked up from my cubicle and saw Rena walk in with papers in her hand and her hair pulled up in a tight bun and bags under her eyes. That wasn't like her to be so off when it came to her looks.

I marched over to her desk and leaned against as she sat. "What are your plans for lunch?"

"I'm not really hungry."

Rena stretched her arms and yawned.

"You seem off today. What's wrong?"

"Nothing. I had a long night with one of my friends."

"My mom wants to go to lunch. Can you free up an hour?"

"I wouldn't be much company."

"You have bags under your eyes, and your hair seems unkempt. Are you sure you're telling me everything?"

"Yes, why would I lie to you?"

"Good, so you're coming to lunch. Grab your purse."

"McKayla," Rena hissed when I grasped her wrist, picked up her purse and jacket, and headed to my desk to grab my things.

Twenty minutes later, we were laughing and drinking

with my mom at Pansche, and Rena's entire mood had shifted.

"Savio doesn't know about the work opportunity?" Mom asked.

I shook my head.

"No, but I'll ask him later."

"Be careful, honey."

"I think it's brave of you to take on a big role like that," Rena told me.

"I haven't agreed yet."

"But I can see the light in your eyes," Mom said.

The waitress refilled our drinks of mimosas, and I asked for a to-go bag for my salad and shrimp. Pansche wasn't crowded, and we sat outside for the cool breeze.

"The money would be good."

"What do you need money for? Your husband's a billionaire," Rena quipped.

"That's his money. Who knows what can happen in five years."

"I've always taught you to be independent."

"I know, Mommy."

"I need me a billionaire." Rena gulped her drink.

"You're not dating, Rena?" Mom questioned.

"No, too many men for me to settle," Rena replied and ate more of her calamari.

"The days when I was single." Mom shook her head.

"Are you ready to head back to the office, Rena?"

"Yeah, I still need to type my article."

"Thank you for having lunch with me girls. It's on me."

"I can't let you do that, Mom."

The waitress approached and placed the to-go box down. I pulled out my card to pay, and she blocked me.

"No need to pay. The bill is already taken care of, Mrs. Calabresi."

"Huh? How? I just got the final cost."

"Your husband."

"Wait, is he here?"

"No, an associate of your husband informed us that he is paying for your meals." She thanked us and strolled back inside.

"That's why I want a billionaire," Rena said.

"Savio has you watched?"

"It's a long story, Mommy."

"I thought you've worked through the trust issues."

"We have, but he's never going to stop being overprotective and having his men around." I scanned the street and saw one black Lincoln town car parked up a block with tinted windows. I more than can assume it's one of Savio's men.

"We need to get back to work. Thank for inviting us to lunch." I leaned over and hugged my mother and left the restaurant with Rena teasing me about Savio.

Later in the evening, Savio came into the bathroom while I was soaking in the tub with music playing. He loosened his tie and sat on the edge of the tub, dipping his hand in the water to caress my thigh.

"How was work today?"

"Long," he answered.

"Thank you for lunch."

"You're welcome."

"How was your lunch?"

"Boring if it's not you." He smirked, then pecked me on the lips.

"I wanted to talk to you about something."

"Go ahead." He dipped one finger in my sex, and I felt the intense feeling of wanting it to be his dick.

"The editor…"

"What about the editor?" he teased me, stroking me slowly with a second finger.

"She asked me about taking over a new division of the

paper."

"That's good news, correct?"

"Yesss—"

"I love when your voice becomes shallow, and you wither underneath my fingers."

"Baby… I can't concentrate."

Savio chuckled, removed his fingers, and stuck them in his mouth. "Sweet, like always."

I cleared my throat. "What I wanted to say is that it would be overseeing the organized crime section."

"This is what you want?"

"I don't know, but it could become something big for me."

"I like when you're happy."

"I'm happy with you."

"Glad to know I can put that smile on your face."

"Let's have dinner and talk more about this later."

"Let me wash you up."

"No."

"Why not?" He grinned and reached for the soap and towel.

"You love to taunt me."

"That lovely red flush that comes across your face when you're coming gives me pleasure."

"You're so bad."

"Better to be bad than good."

"Why?" I picked up the end of his tie, twirled it around between my fingers.

"You know what you're getting when I'm bad. I make no apologies, McKayla. You're my weakness, strength, and heart. The second you crumble, then I do."

"Let's make sure it never happens."

CHAPTER 38
McKayla

TWO DAYS LATER.

Savio laughs at Sante and Rena arguing back and forth near the pool. I rubbed through his hair, and he ran a hand up my leg near my inner thigh. A tingly feeling of our night together sprang to mind and if we were not at his parents' home, I would take him in the bathroom and remove the thong bikini I wore today for the family gathering.

Elio wanted all his sons to come over with their significant others for lunch. We'd talked about this while away and finally got around to making it happen. Marilyn was here to make sure the food was made to their liking, and I basked in the family atmosphere.

Everything was set to Adelina's specific directions with large canopies to block out the sun. A buffet of food was lined up near a DJ booth, and some people from the Five Families showed up with their wives. I was surprised to see them be so normal compared to what you hear in the media. Maurizio Colombo either was happy to see me on his own or threatened to be nice to me because he'd had to come to deal with the fallout of Nevio dying and still working with Calabresi.

"You hungry?" Savio called out.

"No, not yet."

"I'm going to talk to the guys." Savio leaned up, turned, and pressed a kiss to my lips.

"Okay, have fun."

"Behave."

"Never," I sassed and winked at him.

Savio smirked, flexed his muscles, and left to talk with the boys. I gawked at Sante, Renato, Savio, and how they all looked similar in height and facial looks. Vincenzo came out of the house and had two girls under his arms, and everything was hanging out. Vincenzo released his arms from around the girls, pointed at each one, and they waved hello. A few seconds roamed by, and Adelina sat at the chair next to me and handed me a strawberry martini.

"Savio is happier," Adelina said.

"What was he before?"

"Content. They all think I'm some innocent woman who doesn't know the lifestyle."

"He's told me how your husband keeps things from you. For safety reasons."

"One thing about my marriage is that I know Elio's heart and the decisions he makes."

"Have you two ever broken up?"

"One time. Savio doesn't remember. He was about seven, Sante was five, and Renato two."

"They were young."

"Ah!" We both turned our heads at the sound of someone screaming and saw Rena swimming to the other end of the pool.

"I have a feeling she's next in line."

"Who? Rena?"

Adelina pressed her lips to the drink and sipped. "Elio wasn't always a sweet man. Over time, he became gentler."

"I guess the mafia hardens a lot of people."

"McKayla, I swear to God! I'm going to kill him," Rena fussed, plopped down, and picked up the towel to dry off.

"Kill who?"

"I'm sorry, Mrs. Calabresi, but I hate your son," Rena told her.

Adelina and I chortled.

"Sante causing problems?"

"He's an ass," Rena mumbled.

"You said you weren't coming. Obviously, something changed your mind."

"Free food," Rena responded, snatched the drink out of my hand, and tossed her hair back.

"I'll let you two girls talk. My husband is looking around, which means he's missing me." Adelina stood and hugged me, then Rena, and sauntered away.

"Spill it."

"Spill what?"

"Rena, I've known you for a long time, and you've been very secretive."

"There's nothing going on."

"You wouldn't lie to me, right?"

"I'm starving. Let's get some food." Rena jumped up and reached to pull me with her.

I pointed. "Who is Maurizio talking to?" I noticed a young woman of no more than thirty, with jet black hair, shaped in a tiny bikini, and long nails standing next to him and Savio. I hadn't seen her before, and my jealousy was tingly.

"Probably his wife or mistress," Rena replied, and I laughed.

"Let me run to the restroom, and I'll come back to grab a plate."

"Okay, you want me to start one for you?"

"No, I can get it."

"Hurry back."

I jogged back into the house and through the kitchen. Marilyn was still prepping food when I bumped into someone.

"Sorry."

"No problem.

"You're McKayla, right?"

"Yes, do I know you?" I placed a hand on my hip. If she was one of Savio's old flings, I was ready to fight.

"No need to fight. I'm Marilyn's daughter, Cora." She held her hand out.

I reached out to shake. "Nice to meet you, Cora."

"My mom talks about you all the time."

"She's become like a second mom to me."

"I appreciate your kindness toward her," Cora said.

"Anytime, what do you do?"

"Nothing fancy like a journalist, but I'm a vet."

"Completely out of the mafia life."

"Yes, normal."

"You've known the family for a long time?"

"I kind of grew up around them. A second family, but some of them treat me well." She had a far-off look and glared at Elio walking by with his brothers.

"Cora, are you all right?" I asked and caught her attention.

"Oh, yes, sorry. I spaced out for a second."

"I have to use the restroom. Are you going to be here a little longer?"

Cora looked down and touched her watch. "About another ten minutes, then I need to leave."

"Okay, I won't be long. I'd love to talk with you more."

Cora smiled and went back through the kitchen, as I opened the bathroom.

Five seconds later, I flushed, washed my hands, and checked my makeup when someone pounded at the door. "Occupied."

Bang! Bang!

"I said—" I opened the door and shook my head when Savio shoved me back in and locked the door.

"What are you doing?"

"Spending time with my wife." He lifted me up on the counter.

"Not in your parents' home, Savio!" I slapped his hands away and felt a shove.

"This is the perfect time."

Savio pushed his shorts down, and his dick sprang out before I said another word. His hands squeezed and groped my breasts, and he pushed my thong to the side and plunged into me.

"Uggghhhh!"

"Fuck!"

"Savio…" I hissed and bit his shoulder.

"You're walking around here in a thong?" He wrapped his hand around my throat.

"Oh, baby."

"Say my name."

"Savio."

His pumps got faster and faster.

"I'm about to come!"

"Come for me, baby."

"Love you so much," I panted and clenched my teeth as I came over his stomach and shorts.

Savio released himself in me and gently made love to my tongue. We hugged up together against the mirror when he pulled back and turned my head to look at us attached.

"Come on. Get down so I can wash you."

"Your mother's going to kill me."

"She's probably done the same thing with her in-laws at one point."

"That's not something I want to think about, Savio."

"Kiss me."

I turned the water off, passed him the towel, and pecked him on the lips. "I just met Cora."

"Marilyn told me she was coming."

"Is there something going on between her and Elio?"

"No, Cora's like a sister to us."

"Okay." I checked my hair in the mirror.

"I see a look in your eyes, and I don't want to be a part of anything."

"No look."

"That journalist look is coming out."

"Babe, you worry too much." I wiped my lipstick off his lips.

"No snooping, McKayla."

"Of course I wouldn't do that."

Savio pursed his lips.

"Let's go. The food is getting cold."

He grasped my hand and opened the door for me to walk ahead and smacked me on the ass.

"Savio, behave."

"I can say the same for you, Mrs. Calabresi."

———

After the weekend, I asked Cora to meet with Rena and me for lunch, so we could get to know her a little better. She was off from work and just moved into her new place. She had gotten broken into, and her mother didn't want her to continue paying rent for an area that wasn't safe.

"Cora, how old are you?" Rena questioned.

"Twenty-seven."

"How long have you been a veterinarian?"

"About five years now. After college, I took a little time traveling, but I've always loved animals," Cora explained.

"Me too. I went to Paris."

"I'd love to go there one day."

"Maybe a girls' trip," Rena proposed.

"That's if Savio doesn't freak out."

"I heard he kidnapped you, and then Sante kidnapped you, right?"

"It's a long story."

"I have plenty of time. My life is very boring."

"No boyfriend?"

"No, unless I sneak around and date."

"Why is that?"

"Calabresi men aren't the friendliest bunch when it comes to outside men."

"That's true."

"Savio said you're like a sister to them."

"Savio has a hard exterior, but he's loyal and gives the best advice."

"What about Elio?" I asked to gather a little information.

Cora's eyes danced around the room for a few minutes, then she took the rest of the drink down. "Same. I appreciate all the guys."

"I can just imagine growing up with a headache like Sante," Rena responded, then tapped on her glass with the fork to get the waiter's attention.

"The Calabresi family is different."

"The Calabresi mafia family is different."

Epilogue

SAVIO

SIX MONTHS LATER.

My eyes fluttered open. I scanned around the room, extended my hand, and felt around the bed. My eyes zoned in on the empty spot next to me.

I reached over to the chair in the corner, snatched up my robe and boxers, and stalked to the bathroom. McKayla loved to sneak out in the middle of the night or in the early morning and work, but she'd promised to leave work at home.

I finished in the bathroom, stepped back in the room, and slid my feet into my house shoes. I opened the double doors of our home and smelled the most delicious morning coffee and bacon. I tightened my robe around my waist so as not to frighten the staff, since they lived on the estate while we were away. I made the promise to bring us back to Italy, just the two of us, and finally we'd been able to get away once I put Sante in charge of everything.

I rubbed my stomach, went into the kitchen, and saw McKayla talking with our housekeeper Amelia. I shook my head and came up behind her to kiss her cheek.

She turned, wrapped her arms around my neck, and stood on her tippy toes. "How did you sleep?"

"Good, would have been better if you stayed with me."

"I didn't want to disturb you."

"You know I like to roll over and feel you underneath me."

"Savio, not in front of Amelia."

"It's okay, Mrs. Calabresi. I'm used to Savio being overly explicit." She chuckled.

I shrugged and took the coffee out of McKayla's hand. She passed the newspaper, and I went to sit down at the table.

"Amelia made so much food, honey, we won't be able to finish."

She was right. Amelia outdid herself with the croissants, muesli, ricotta pancakes, fruit and yogurt, cappuccino and more.

"I have ideas on how we can work it off." I wiggled my brows.

"Not today, cowboy. I'm still sore from last night."

"Are you denying me the pleasure of your body with my tongue?"

"Only for a few hours, and if you play nice."

"Anything."

"You don't even know what it is that I want to do." McKayla giggled and sat in my lap.

I held my hand on the back of her neck. "Anything you wish, I will grant."

"I'd love to explore some more. Maybe a museum, some more of the places you grew up at when you visited."

"That is your wish?"

"It is." She slid her hand through my robe, rubbing up and down my chest.

"Your wish will be granted. Have you eaten?"

"Yes, so you go ahead, and I'll talk about the places I want to visit."

"What time did you get up?"

She started to answer.

Ring! Ring!

Amelia answered the phone.

"I got up about an hour or two ago."

"Mr. Calabresi," Amelia said.

McKayla's eyes dropped in sadness as I picked up the napkin to wipe my mouth and stood to grab the phone in my office. "I'll take it in my office."

"Yes, sir," Amelia said.

McKayla jumped up to grab the plates of food and took them to the kitchen. "This better be life or death."

"Maurizio is dead," Sante said.

I sighed, rubbed my temples, and sat on the edge of the desk. "When?"

"A few hours ago. There was a car bomb."

"Do we know who?"

"No one is taking responsibility."

"I go away for a few days, and this shit happens!" I pushed the photos and pencils off my desk.

"I called for a meeting."

"Get it figured out, Sante."

"I will."

"This is a warning shot."

"We have everyone covered."

"You better. and don't retaliate."

"We don't operate like that, Savio."

"I know how the fuck we operate. I need to know the why and who before anything is done. We've already had heat from Viviana and Greco."

"I understand."

"Good."

"Are you enjoying your time away?"

"It's a trip. Speak with our brothers and keep everyone safe."

"I will and Savio?"

"Yeah."

"Two families down. That only leaves three left."

"Just make sure we're the last family standing," I said, ending the call, and looked at the damage I did in my office.

McKayla wouldn't like that we had to fly back home and cut our trip to Italy short when we made a pact to be honest and compromise in our marriage. I stood, rubbed a hand down my face, and gathered my thoughts before going back to the dining room.

Our family home was just as lavish as Highland Park with acres of land and pool, with a tennis court and golf course. It was over fifty thousand square feet with our own private landing strip in the back for us to fly private whenever we wanted. The walls held pictures of my parents, grandparents, and ancestors with colors of gold and black stitched throughout.

"Where's McKayla?" I asked Amelia.

"She went to the bedroom, sir."

"Thank you."

I groaned, jogged back up the stairs toward our bedroom, and pushed the door open. I saw McKayla packing our bags.

"What are you doing?"

"Packing."

"Why?" I smiled and stood in the middle of the room.

"I know what that phone call means."

"You do?"

"Yes, something happened, and they need you back."

I chuckled, walked in the room, and reached out to stop her from pacing. I pulled her to my chest and kissed her on the forehead. "Thank you."

"For what?"

"Being you, but we're not leaving."

"Huh?"

"I planned on spending time with my wife, and that's what's going to happen."

"But what about that phone call?"

"Sante is handling it. When it's time for me to get involved, I will do it from here."

"Really, Savio? We get to stay?"

"All my decisions include you, beautiful, and I promised to make you happy."

"Then you have." She pressed a kiss on my lips.

"I knew the moment you walked through my father's door, you'd be trouble."

"I hope it was good trouble."

"The best trouble I could find."

———

I hope you enjoyed Savio and McKayla's story. Please also check out the sneak peek of Sante's story here.

In my capacity as underboss of the Calabresi family, I was respected and held in the same high esteem as my brother Savio, the don of the family. The decision he made caused a chain reaction, and I made the decision to clean it all up. Unfortunately, it came with six-inch heels, red lipstick, and a mouth that liked to push all my buttons.

CHAPTER 39

Sante

SAVIO SAT with his back to us in the conference room of the Calabresi office, where he normally wouldn't have us discuss mafia business. After retaliation for Maurizio's murder on a few of our spots, we needed to discuss what the next move would be. To see my brother married and happy with a wife and baby soon was shocking for the entire family, but my mother hadn't stopped crying since the news was broken at a family dinner.

"How many warehouses did they hit?" He turned in his chair and looked my way.

As the underboss, it was my job to keep things running without causing him any distress. Lately, things had gotten out of control. Carmine also was now in position as the head boss for Colombo family. "At least three."

"Three, Sante," he growled

"We need to strike back, or they'll think we're weak," Renato complained while he removed his gun from his holster.

"Put that gun away," I demanded.

"Nobody's in here."

"Renato, this is a palace of business." Savio pointed his

finger to the table.

"I agree with Renato on this one," EJ said.

"Usually, you're the one who wants less death," Savio replied.

"We can't be seen as weak. Already have Greco's team," Elio responded.

"You have to wait!" a loud voice called out.

The conference room door flew open, and Satan's spawn in six-inch heels narrowed her eyes on me. I didn't move, only gave the same menacing look right back.

"You bastard!" Rena stalked around the table, and Renato blocked her pathway.

"Rena, this is a private meeting." Savio looked at her, then me.

All I could do was shrug. Her problems had nothing to do with me.

"No, let me go, Renato. Your brother is going to die today," Rena shouted and shoved Renato, but he wrapped his arm around her waist and held her back.

I didn't like their closeness, so I motioned for him to let her go. "Give me the room," I told them.

Everybody looked at me like I was crazy, and maybe I was, but she wouldn't try to spin this around on me. Savio rose, and the rest followed. Renato whispered something to her, and she nodded, released his hold, and walked out.

"Speak."

"You got me fired."

"I didn't get you fired."

"Then tell me why I was told to clear out my desk." Rena's bottom lip poked out. She crossed her arms over her chest and glared at me.

"I had nothing to do with you getting fired. Excuse me, I have business to handle." I walked around her.

She grabbed my arm, and my eyes scanned down at her grip. "I know you got me fired."

"I don't have time to play childish games, little girl."

Suddenly, her bottom lip trembled, and tears gathered into her eyes as Savio and the rest of my brothers stared at each of us hard.

"We need to finish discussing business, Sante," Savio remarked.

I sat down. They stepped in the conference room, and Rena paused, shook her head, and walked back out. I released a harsh breath and rubbed my temples to relax. I hated to get angry. Like Savio, I tried to suppress the beast inside me unless it was necessary.

"What was that about?"

"She thought I got her fired." I loosened my jacket.

"Did you?"

"Rena Clark is not important enough for me to get fired."

"But you tried to fight me when you thought she wanted to sleep with me," Renato recalled.

"That was different. I know your track record with women," I explained.

"You're just as bad, Sante," EJ blurted out.

"Fuck you, and let's get back to business."

"Do we know where Carmine's head is?" Savio probed.

"I think we need to keep an eye on him. Right now, they can't pinpoint we made the hit, but we had the most beef with the Colombos." I leaned forward and explained.

"Keep me updated, but no more meetings here." Savio stood, shook hands with Renato, and hugged us both.

"Sante, hold up." The moment I arrived at the door, Savio called me by name.

"Yeah?"

"Is there anything going on with you and Rena?" Savio slid his hands in his pockets, standing tall.

"No."

"What happened when you had her held up in your

apartment for those weeks?"

My teeth chattered as I recalled those first few weeks when he requested that I kidnap McKayla's best friend.

"Let's just say I'm looking into better security." I walked out of his office, catching up with Renato and EJ as they got on the elevator.

———

I closed my eyes, recalled her on a date, and I was a kidnapping, angry mobster.

Upcoming Releases: 2022/2023
Sante
Renato
Elio
Vincenzo
Playlist:

1.
  2.
  3.
  4.
  5.
  6.
  7.
  8.
  9.
  10.

Thank you so much for reading. If you enjoyed the crazy ride and decide to leave a review, we'd appreciate the support.

Calabresi Mafia Series

Savio: Book 1
   https://books2read.com/u/mlEAW7
   Sante: Book 2
   Renato: Book 3
   Elio : Book 4
   Vincenzo: Book 5
   Thank you so much for reading. If you enjoyed the crazy ride and decide to leave a review, we'd appreciate the support.

About the Author

L.K. Ryan is an author of Romantic Suspense, Dark Romance, and Contemporary Novels. Join my newsletter and sign up for the latest news and updates on my books and releases:

www.ingramcontent.com/pod-product-compliance
Lightning Source LLC
Chambersburg PA
CBHW071730190726
48292CB00003B/684